Cyprian the Fair

Book Nine

Salvaggio's Light

An Epic Contemporary Romance Serial

By C. L. Cattano

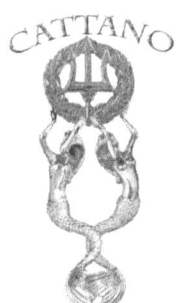

VAGARY PUBLISHING

Cyprian the Fair
Book Nine
Salvaggio's Light

A Vagary Publishing Book
Copyright © 2018 by C. L. Cattano
Cover Art, Title Page Art and Typesetting Copyright © 2018 by Chynsia Hinesley

Published by:

VAGARY PUBLISHING

www.vagarypublishing.com
inquiry@vagarypublishing.com

Rogena Mitchell-Jones, Independent Literary Editor
RMJ Manuscript Services LLC *www.rogenamitchell.com*

ISBN: 978-1-947852-09-9

First Edition

WARNING

It is suggested readers of this story be adults over the age of eighteen.

This dramatic romance series has many scenes describing sex as well as intense emotional scenes and acts of violence.

This is a serial story with themes flowing from one book into another with lots of twists and turns. Reading this series from the beginning is highly suggested, or the reader may not be able to follow all the storylines.

Go to the Salvaggio's Light Facebook page to join other readers who are talking about the series.
www.facebook.com/SalvaggiosLight/

Join the C L Cattano mailing list and check out my website at www.clcattano.com

Acknowledgments

THANK YOU TO those readers who are spreading the word about the Salvaggio's Light serial. We all wear many different hats in life, but to an independent author, the most important hat you wear is that of a reader. You leave reviews, spread the word, and show support to those of us who toil away in the night not knowing if our creations will ever see the light of day. Keep reading...

Dedication

For Marie — who fans the delicate flame.

Salvaggio's Light

An Epic Contemporary Romance Serial

Shattered Paradise
Blue Inferno
Secrets & Rivalry
Wildling's Claim
Sowers of Discord
Fire of Wrath
Confronting Darkness
Traditorè
Cyprian the Fair
Frenzied Love*

Coming Soon

I fled from the world, while still a girl, to follow her.
— Dante Alighieri, *The Divine Comedy*

1

Seconds later...

EDEN KINGSLEY STOOD frozen with the folded piece of paper Chiara had forced into her hand, and she watched as the front door closed. Her mind wouldn't accept the reality of what was happening. Eden scanned the paper then looked up, eyes wide with a terrifying understanding. Rafe had made Gabri her power of attorney. Suddenly, the world sped up, and she lunged for the door.

"What the hell!" Letty cried out still holding on to Bronte.

"No!" Eden sobbed as she flung the door open with the paper grasped tightly in her hand. She burst outside with Letty and Julia close behind her. "Please, Gabri! Don't do this," she begged, but Gabri already had Rafe in the car.

Standing at the back of the car, Chiara turned to Eden and held her hands out to stop her. "Mr. De Angelis is now informing you Rafaella has left all matters to him at his discretion," announced Chiara. "He will be honoring her wishes to retrieve her father and the sentimental items of his and of her mother. He does not feel you know how to take care of her best, even if you are calling yourselves family and friends," she said gravely. "He will take her home so she might get better, in the place she will get the most help."

Chiara quickly walked around the car, slid into the front seat and closed the door.

Eden could see Gabri pulling Rafe up and holding her close as the driver closed the back passenger door. Eden turned toward Julia, unable to wrap her mind around the fact her worst nightmare was actually happening. Rafe was leaving and might never come back. Eden could feel her body tremble and couldn't catch her breath. Her heart beat so hard in her chest it hurt, and then the world swirled in her head making it hard to stand.

Julia caught up to Eden and took hold of her. "Hold it together," she said firmly seeing Eden was losing her battle with her fear and anxiety as tears welled from Eden's eyes. "Look at me," she said and took Eden's face in her hands. "What was the woman talking about when she said they had to get Rafe's father?"

"I. . . I don't know!" she cried as she shook and heard the car engine start. She pulled away from Julia, ran to the Town Car, and pounded on the window. "Rafe!" she screamed at the dark tinted windows. "Rafe, don't do this! Don't leave! Rafe!" She sobbed mournfully as the car eased away from her, and she fell to her knees in anguish.

Julia went after Eden and pulled her up. "Eden, we have to figure out where they're going. They can't leave tonight because they have to make travel arrangements. Think," she said and shook Eden to try to snap her out of her anxiety attack and to get her attention. "What did she mean about Rafe's father?" She took Eden by the arm and dragged her to the car and put her inside. "Letty, we'll be back later. Hopefully, we'll have Rafe with us."

"Okay, please, bring her back," said Letty distraught as she held on to Bronte. She watched Julia get in her car with Eden and then drive away after Gabri's car.

Julia looked over at Eden who was trying to control her anxiety and terror about what was happening. "Does she have storage anywhere?" Julia asked as she tried to see if she could catch up with the Town Car carrying Rafe away. "Is she storing some of her father's and mother's things here?"

"I don't know," Eden insisted through her tears as the pain of her anxiety thrummed through her. "I only know about her car storage."

"Car storage? No." She shook her head. "Where did you store your things from your apartment?"

Eden looked up at Julia with wide eyes as she remembered what she saw in the trunk of the Maserati. "I think it's her car storage," she insisted. "I saw she had some things in the trunk when we got out our prizes from the arcade. She also has his hat in the glove box."

"Where does she store the car?" she demanded.

"Rick's Auto Detail and Storage," she said. "It's close to your offices."

"Okay," she said and turned the corner at the light. "I hope you're right. Do you know the number? Call and see if they'll stall them," she said and handed Eden her phone.

"Okay." Eden wiped her tears and looked up the number for Rick's on Julia's phone. She called but only got voice mail.

When Julia pulled into Rick's, they saw the Town Car in front of the office facing the exit. Julia parked quickly then they got out, rushing to the office. They found it empty.

Eden looked over at the Town Car and ran to it. "Rafe!" she called and tried to open the door, but it was locked. She pounded on the window. "Rafe, please, open the door. Please," she sobbed.

Julia heard voices and started toward them. "Eden, they're up here," she said then ran to the second level with Eden close behind where they found Gabri, Chiara, and Rick standing next to the Maserati.

"Rick!" Eden called out and rushed up to him. "Where's Rafe?"

Rick screwed up his face in confusion. "I don't know," he said. "I got a call from her telling me to let them get things out of the car," he said indicating Gabri and Chiara. "Plus, they have a letter saying they have the right to take care of Ms. Salvaggio's business." He put the key in the trunk lock, opened the trunk, and then stepped back.

"Mr. De Angelis says you should not be here," said Chiara a bit nervously. All the confrontation she had to do on her employer's behalf was unpleasant. "He says there is nothing more for you to do for Rafaella now."

Gabri reached into the trunk and took out a brown cardboard box that held the urn with the ashes of Rafe's father, and a wooden case with a handle and extendable legs, clearly the portable easel and paint supply case belonging to Rafe's mother. He handed the wooden box to Chiara then went around to the passenger side of the car. He got in then opened the glove box pulling out the cap Rafe had been wearing the last time Eden was with her in the car.

Rick was about to close the trunk but looked up at Gabri. "There's a small bag in here too," Rick said and picked up the canvas bag. The bag was made of a brown waterproof canvas with buckles to keep it closed and shoulder strap so it could be hung on one shoulder or across the body.

Eden saw Gabri going back around to get the bag, and she ran up and snatched it from Rick then backed away. "I need to talk to Rafe," she said desperately as she clung to the bag. "Let me take this to her and talk to her. Please, Gabri. I love her, and I don't want to lose her. I don't want you to take her away!"

Gabri was in shock at what Eden had done as he listened to Chiara translate her words. He spoke angrily emphasizing his words with hand gestures and Chiara translated. "Rafaella told me about you and what you are doing to her. You will not speak with her." Chiara paused to listen then spoke again. "Rafaella said nothing about needing an old school bag. She will tell me if she wants it. Then you will give it to her, or we will take legal action." Chiara turned to Rick. "He says you are our witness. If she does not hand over the bag and does not return it when Rafaella requests it, then she is the thief. We will be requesting surveillance tapes of tonight."

"I don't want any trouble," said Rick as he held up his hands. "I'll help Ms. Salvaggio in any way I can."

Gabri walked away carrying the box and the cap, and Chiara followed with the wooden case as they walked back to the Town Car where the driver already had the trunk open for them. They placed the items in the trunk, and Gabri said something to Chiara then got in the back seat of the car. Chiara went to the passenger door and looked back at the two women. "Mr. De Angelis says he will be in contact with

Rafaella's lawyer and with you as soon as is possible." She got into the car, and Eden watched helplessly as Rafe was taken away again.

"Call Katheryn now!" Eden demanded frantically. "We'll go to her house right now if we have to. We can't let him take her!"

They went to Julia's car as she tried to contact Katheryn again. "He can't take her anywhere if he doesn't have her identification. Did you see if he had it?"

"No," said Eden with frustration. "I was too busy worrying about the fact he carried Rafe out of the freaking house!"

"Okay," said Julia and took a breath. "Just calm down. Katheryn hasn't answered or picked up her messages so she must be out or something. Let's go back to the house and see if her driver's license and passport are still there. If they are, then we know he can't take her on a plane."

They drove back to the house where Letty was watching over Bronte. Eden rushed into the house and past Letty to get to Rafe's room.

"What's going on?" Letty asked. "Is Rafe coming back?"

"We don't know yet," said Julia and followed Eden into Rafe's room.

Eden was in the room, desperately going through Rafe's things. She looked in Rafe's jeans for her small wallet. It wasn't there, so Eden looked on the dresser and in the drawers without result. She flung open the closet door and saw the small safe had been opened and was empty. Eden sat down on the closet floor and burst into tears.

"He has everything." She continued to sob. "He probably got it all when he was in here with her alone."

Julia sighed and ran her hand through her silver hair. "Fuck, Rafe." She groaned. "I can't believe this is happening." It had to be Eden's choice to walk away from Rafe, now Eden's choice had been taken away. She wasn't sure if this was actually best for Eden or if this would just make things worse.

2

AFTER BEING ON the phone until late in the evening, and again early this morning, Katheryn Hardam pulled her car into the driveway of Rafe Salvaggio's house. A white moving van parked on the street behind her. She knew this was going to be a difficult meeting, but there was no way she could think of to make it any easier. She got out of her car and motioned for the driver of the van to stay and wait for her to call him and his crew. Taking her briefcase from the passenger seat of her car, she walked up the steps to the front door and rang the doorbell.

The door opened and Julia looked out at her. "Katheryn, we've been trying to call you all last night and this morning," she said as she opened the door further and motioned her inside.

"Is Eden here?" Katheryn inquired, doing her utmost to keep it professional.

"Yes, I made her call in for a personal day because she's in no shape to do anything right now," Julia told her. "She'll be relieved you're here." Julia had spent the night trying to console Eden. She wasn't successful, but Eden did finally fall asleep for a while. When Eden woke this morning, the tears started again, and Julia still hadn't been able to get her to eat.

Katheryn shook her head. "We'll see," she said with a sigh. "Let's meet in Rafe's office." She made her way to Rafe's office and sat down at Rafe's partner desk, then took some paperwork out of her briefcase while she waited for Eden and Julia to join her.

"Katheryn," said Eden desperately as soon as she walked into the room. She immediately put the piece of paper Gabri gave her on the desk in front of the lawyer. "What does this mean? I need you to help me get Rafe back."

Katheryn picked up the paper and smoothed it out. "Sit down," she said and nodded to the chair. She waited for Eden to sit down across from her in the other partner chair and for Julia to pull up a chair beside Eden. "This paper," she said as she held it up, "is a summary of the legal paperwork granting Gabrielli Braulio De Angelis, or Gabri as you call him, full power of attorney over Rafe's personal, business, medical and any other matter of importance anywhere Rafe has holdings."

Eden's eyes widened from shock. "No," she said softly with dread.

Julia stiffened in indignation. "This is why she wanted all her financial information," she said, clenching her jaw angrily. Julia didn't understand why Rafe wouldn't choose her father over *that man*, Gabri, to hold her power of attorney. Her father thought of Rafe as a daughter, and this was how she treated him and how she treated them all? She worked to calm herself for Eden's sake, but the sympathy she held for Rafe was waning.

Katheryn held Julia's gaze for a brief moment in answer and could see she was angry. But Rafe's choices were her own, and it was not their place to question them. She turned her attention back to Eden. "I got a call from Mr. De Angelis and his translator yesterday, wanting to confirm the meaning of the paperwork, and we discussed Rafe's situation," she told them calmly. "He was concerned about some emails he had received and the fact she was not returning calls or emails as she normally did. I was directed by him not to discuss anything about Rafe with anyone until he could assess the matter further. I was obligated to do as he asked because of the covenants and instructions Rafe put in the legal paperwork allowing him to direct me, even if he only thought it might be necessary. She's given him permission to act upon his own initiative regardless of what I or anyone else thinks."

"So he can just. . ." Eden sobbed, "just take her?"

"He can, and he has," said Katheryn firmly. "They're already on their way to New York, and from there, they'll be going on to Italy."

"No!" Eden cried and put her face in her hands. "This can't be happening," she moaned.

"Why did they go to New York?" Julia asked as she tried to comfort Eden. "They could have got a flight to London then Italy from here."

"Apparently, Mr. De Angelis felt there was some business they needed to take care of, but I was not privy to what it might be," she said as she looked down at the papers in front of her. "Rafe was not physically present in our meeting. She talked to me over the phone. I think she was at his hotel, and she didn't sound well."

Julia watched as Eden just sat rocking with her hands clasped together and eyes closed tightly. She could tell Eden was trying to control the anxiety she had been dealing with throughout the night. Already this morning, it was once again, devastating her emotionally and physically. "Why are you here now then?" asked Julia. "Did Gabri or Rafe leave a message or anything for Eden?"

"Not exactly," Katheryn said with a sigh. "I am here to collect personal and business paperwork from this office and arrange for it to be taken care of by either my office or other appropriate entities." She focused her attention on Eden again. "I'm also here to tell you the cohabitation agreement is still in force. Gabri assured me the agreement was one Rafe would want to keep, and he agreed to honor it as long as you wish to live in the house." She pushed a piece of paper in front of Eden. "This paper gives you the right to use the entire house, including Rafe's room, until her return, if she decides to come back. All current contents of the house, so long as things are cared for, and nothing is removed or sold without permission, can also remain. She requests a few things be stored elsewhere or shipped to her in Italy. I have a moving company here to get the items today."

"No!" said Eden mournfully. "I can't bear this," she said as she leaned into Julia's shoulder.

"What things?" Julia asked softly as she held Eden.

Katheryn cleared her throat and glanced down at the list. "She made this list when Eden left her and moved in with Jake. It lists what was hers before Eden moved into the house." She looked directly at Eden. "I had Rafe make it in case you were going to file a separation and support petition with the court. Most of the things she has requested are from this list along with a few other things. There are several paintings, other art, photos, personal items from her room, her computer and some items from her office. My job is to make sure everything she's asked for is taken from the house and dealt with appropriately."

Eden looked up at Julia sadly. "She's not coming back," she said weakly. "She's not," she said and broke down in tears again.

Katheryn picked up an envelope and placed it in front of Eden and Julia. "This—" She cleared her throat to get their attention. "This is Bronte's passport and a letter signed by Rafe giving parental permission for Bronte to travel. There are also copies of all the paperwork we filed and had processed for her dual citizenship. I've been directed to take care of anything concerning this to keep it current and enforced, if necessary."

"Did they say anything about taking Bronte to Italy?" Julia asked knowing Eden was worried about it.

"No," said Katheryn softly. "They said the passport and papers were to be given to Eden so if she allowed Bronte to visit Rafe, she could, or if, in the future, she and Bronte ever wanted to travel." She paused then looked across at Eden. "Rafe said she held on to it because you never asked about it, but she knew you had to have it in your possession now since she was not going to be here."

Eden stared at the envelope and could hear Jake in her ears demanding that she get the passport from Rafe. Now it was in front of her, and she finally understood why she had never asked Rafe for it. If she had, then it would mean Rafe wouldn't be with them and would not be part of their lives. Rafe having the passport was a way of tying them together, and now, even this small thing was undone. Eden looked over at Julia and shook her head sorrowfully. "She's really gone," she said and broke down again in sorrow.

"I suggest," Katheryn said, directing her words to Julia, "you take Eden to her room and let us get things moved. This way it won't be so upsetting for her. I'll do my best to get everything done quickly."

Julia stood up and helped Eden to her feet. "Come on," she said gently and led Eden out of the office.

She took Eden to her room and sat her on the bed where she laid down and cried. Julia went over and sat on the Chaise lounge Rafe had restored for Eden and put her head in her hands. She took a breath and looked over at Eden. "What did he talk to you about?" she asked. "Do you know why they went to New York? Maybe I can call my father, and he can intercept them."

Eden wiped the tears from her face in misery. "I don't know." She sniffed. "The only thing we talked about having anything to do with New York was—" She stopped, looking up at Julia with wide eyes.

"What?" Julia asked.

"The affair," she said softly.

"The affair?" Julia repeated with confusion. "What about it?"

Eden sat up on the bed then leaned her head back and took a breath. She knew that telling Julia what happened in therapy was breaking the trust with Rafe, but she felt like she didn't have a choice.

She let the breath out and looked up at Julia again. "I asked Rafe about it again in therapy. Actually, Dr. Cathcart asked her." She looked down at her hands. "It's what she was talking about when he realized she had an emotional blackout in New York." She looked up at Julia. "She couldn't remember part of what happened. She remembered a lot of details but none about actually, you know, sleeping with her. She said she just remembered waking up and crying."

Julia furrowed her brow in confusion. "So, what does the affair have to do with them going to New York?"

"He, Gabri..." She sighed. "He thinks she may not have had an affair, and she's making things up to help herself fill in the blanks."

"Holy shit, Eden!" said Julia as she stood up and paced. "If she— Holy shit!"

"I know!" said Eden distraught. "He asked if I ever confirmed things." She shook her head. "Why would I? Rafe said she did it."

"So you think he might be going to New York to confirm things?" Julia asked astounded.

"I think so," Eden said softly and lay back down, emotionally and physically exhausted, but the tears wouldn't stop.

3

EDEN KINGSLEY HAD been sleeping off and on over the last few hours. Now she was staring out the window from the bed. There was a soft tap on the door, and Julia got up to answer it knowing it was Katheryn. She opened the door and looked into the attorney's concerned face.

"Hi," Julia said softly and opened the door wider so Katheryn could come into the bedroom.

Katheryn remained outside the door. "We're all finished," she said solemnly. "I'll be in touch if they need to contact either of you through me. I have Rafe's car keys and will take them to Rick who will be here sometime today to pick the car up for storage." She looked over at Eden, who sat up and looked back at her with red-rimmed eyes. "I'm sorry things turned out this way. I was rooting for you and Rafe. She was always doing things to your benefit, even when I recommended against it. I thought she was working very hard to show you how much she loved you, and it was heartwarming, even though it usually went against my lawyer logic." She paused, regarding Julia then Eden with sympathy again. "Well, goodbye," she said softly then turned and walked away. She left the house to continue taking care of the things her client had requested.

Julia looked back at Eden. "Do you want me to go see what they took then come back and tell you?"

"No," said Eden sadly as she got out of bed. "I'll come."

They walked out of the bedroom and went down the hall. Immediately, they saw the bare places where art had been removed. Inside Rafe's office, everything still looked neat but the computer was gone. As Eden opened drawers, she saw almost all the files and paperwork were gone too. The things left were household things like instruction manuals, maintenance schedules, lists of service companies and warranties. Photos from the desk were gone along with several from the wall. Pictures of Rafe's parents and the paintings her mother had done were gone too.

They walked into the dining room and saw immediately the large painting Greer had done was gone. Eden couldn't help her tears. "You would think I wouldn't care about that one," she sniffed. "But it's not the painting—it's the thought she wanted it with her."

"You don't know it went with her," said Julia. "She may have had them take it to storage so you wouldn't have to have it in the house." Eden just looked over sadly at her then continued to walk through the house.

Several other paintings were gone from the dining room along with some sculptures and glassware from the built-in cabinets. In the living room, more art was gone from the walls and tables leaving gaping holes where the things used to be. Eden looked up over the fireplace, and the painting Rafe had done of her was still there. She sat down heavily in one of the chairs and began to cry. "I guess she didn't want anything to remind her of me," she said sadly.

Julia tried to comfort her by rubbing her back gently. "She said the same thing after you left when you didn't take the painting."

"She did?" Eden asked as she rubbed the tears from her eyes. "I didn't take it because Jake said I should destroy it and throw it away. He said it was sacrilegious. But I couldn't bear the thought of doing anything to ruin the painting, or to hurt Rafe more. So I thought it would be best to leave it with her."

"Jake really was an ass," said Julia irritably.

"I know," said Eden softly. She looked up at Julia and steeled herself. "Well, I guess just her room is left."

"You don't have to do this today, you know," she said sympathetically.

"I just have to get it over with," she said and made her way to Rafe's room. She opened the door and saw more art and photos were gone. She went to her closet. It was empty, and Eden's heart crashed at the sight. "Julia," she said softly. "Everything's gone."

She went to the dresser and saw the drawers were empty, but the small jewelry box was still there. She pushed open the lid and saw all the jewelry Rafe let Bronte play with was inside and in the ring section were the mood ring, the mother's ring and two gold rings side by side tied together with a small piece of white silk ribbon. Eden picked up the gold rings and sat down on the floor and wept again for the devastating loss she was feeling.

"Why?" she asked over and over again. "Why is this happening? Why did he take her like this? Why did she let him?" she cried in despair. "I love her," she said beseechingly to Julia. "I love her."

"I know," said Julia and helped Eden stand back up. "Let's go back to your room for a while." She took Eden, who was still holding the rings, back to her room. "You need to get some rest now. Bronte will be back soon, and you need to pull yourself together for her if you can. I'll stay as long as you need me." She pulled Eden into a hug. "I'll be here for whatever you need."

Eden pulled away and went to her dresser and opened the bottom drawer. She took out the canvas school bag she had taken out of Rafe's car and held it close to her.

"These are all I have left of her," she said indicating the bag and the rings. "The things she left were bought or given to us after we met," she gave a small manic laugh. "Even these rings were bought after we met, so I guess all I have of hers is this school bag." She began to cry again, and Julia took her arm then led her to the bed where Eden held onto the bag and the rings as she cried.

As Julia closed the bedroom door and made her way to the kitchen, she heard the front door open and then heard Abby call out, "Anybody here?"

"In here," called Julia as she made herself a stiff drink.

Abby made her way into the kitchen followed by Jude, Flynn, and Stacey. "So, who was here?" asked Abby trying to be nonchalant.

"Rafe's lawyer, Katheryn," Julia informed them. "She brought a moving company and removed all of Rafe's personal things."

"Holy fuck," said Abby distraught. "I thought she was going to help Eden like she did before."

"She's Rafe's lawyer and had to do what Rafe and Gabri told her to do," she said and took a drink.

"So," Jude asked hesitantly, "does this mean she isn't coming back?"

"Of course, it does," said Stacey exasperated. "Why else would she take all of her stuff?"

"Well, she didn't take everything," said Flynn. "I didn't see them go to the workshop, and they didn't go into the art studio."

"No," said Julia sadly, "she didn't take everything." She sighed and took another drink because even though Rafe did not take everything, it was clear she was gone.

"Hey," said Stacey suspiciously, "is she still paying the rent on the studio? I need to know if I have to come up with more rent money."

"I don't know," said Julia indifferently. "You can call Katheryn and find out." She turned to Jude. "You might want to call about your deal with Rafe too."

"I'm more worried about what's happening with her than if she is going to honor the deal," said Jude sullenly. "I'd quit if it meant she'd come back and was well."

"You can't quit now," said Flynn. "You have all those school projects you've worked on out there. I don't think Rafe would go back on her deal."

"Guys!" squealed Abby and started crying. "Who cares about all your crap? Rafe is gone!" she retorted. "How could she do this? How could she just let a stranger take her away like this?"

"He's not a stranger to her," said Julia. "He's known her practically all her life. She put him in charge of everything for now." Julia couldn't hide the fact she was angry and hurt at what Rafe had done, and she didn't know if she could stop being mad at her. Adding to her anger was the fact she was supposed to be Rafe's best friend, and Rafe chose *that man* over her or her father.

"I need a drink," said Abby and made herself a Captain and Coke then took a soothing swig of the spiced rum from the bottle. "I can't believe this."

"I know how you feel," said Julia as she took another sip of her drink. "Eden says nothing is left in the house brought in before she moved in. The only thing of Rafe's left is an old school bag Eden took from the trunk of Rafe's car. But they'll probably be demanding it from her some time too."

Stacey let out a laugh then snorted, and Abby glared at her annoyed. "What's so funny?" Abby asked with irritation.

"Nothing," said Stacey trying to hold in her laughter. "It's just," she snickered, "Eden was actually left holding the bag!" She broke out into hysterical laughter while the others didn't see the humor. "Oh, come on! You don't see it?"

"What I see is you're a fucking idiot, and you really don't care about Rafe and this whole situation at all!" said Abby angrily. "Maybe you should go back to your hole!"

"Hey, I care about Rafe," Stacey declared. "I told you Eden was fucking with her, and she'd be better off if she dropped her, and it looks like I'm right. She probably should have done it sooner. From what I've seen and heard, Rafe is lucky to have someone who's actually helping her instead of fucking with her!" She turned on her heal and walked out of the kitchen toward the door.

"You don't know what the fuck you're talking about!" Abby yelled after her. "Eden loves Rafe and would never do anything to fuck with her!"

"Calm down," said Jude and put her hand on Abby's shoulder as the front door slammed.

"How can you stand to live with such a-a bitch," she spat angrily.

"She doesn't know Rafe and Eden like we do," said Jude calmly. "Rafe was really nice to her, so she's just taking the side of the person she knows best."

"What makes me even angrier is, she's not all wrong," said Abby sullenly. "Eden took so long to figure things out, and with everything else happening, it's just turned into this big fucked up mess." To stop herself from crying, she took a large swallow of her strong drink.

"It was hard for Eden too," Flynn interjected. "All she thought about was how to help Rafe and keep her from getting hurt. She didn't know all the stuff Jake was doing."

"I know." Abby sighed and took another sip of her drink. "So what now? Is Rafe just gone? Is she ever coming back? Will she ever want to see us again?"

"I guess all we can do is wait," Julia said with a shrug and took another sip of her drink. "If you want to contact her, you can probably go through Katheryn."

"She'll probably have email," said Flynn. "Does she have an email account other than the school?"

"She had one from her old company, and I'm sure she has a personal one," said Julia, "but I've never used it. You can still call her or text. She has an international phone because of all her travel."

"I don't think she'll be answering our calls right now," said Abby as she wiped away her angry tears.

Eden walked out of her room and found everyone in the kitchen. "Hi," she said softly.

Abby went up to her and hugged her tightly. "I'm so sorry all of this is happening," she said sadly.

"Me too," was all Eden could bring herself to say. She didn't want to cry again tonight because she felt like she might not stop.

"We're all here for you, Eden," said Jude softly. "We know Rafe would want us to help you."

"Thank you," said Eden. She was glad she had all of these friends here. Eden was thankful they still cared about her after everything they had gone through. Having them was like having a little bit of Rafe around because she knew how much Rafe cared about them and how they felt about Rafe. If she didn't have them, she felt like she genuinely would be alone in the world.

Julia could see Eden was about to start crying again and hugged her. "We'll sort things out," she said softly. "We'll all help you stay strong."

Julia watched as the others gathered around and hugged Eden to show her they were there for her and shared her pain. She knew, even though it wasn't how she thought things would happen, now was the time she needed to step up for Eden. Julia would show Eden that she had other choices besides Rafe and do her best to show her they could have a happy life together. She knew it would take time, but it looked like they would have plenty.

4

AFTER SPENDING ALMOST a month in a fog, Eden Kingsley was once again sitting in front of Dr. Cathcart. She had been to see him every week, but until now, everything had been a blur of emotions. Every day, she woke up feeling the pain of being without Rafe, and it seemed nothing had been able to help her gain a foothold on her emotions except time.

Her friends, and especially Julia, were doing everything they could for her and helping with Bronte. But having Rafe back home was the only thing Eden felt would help either of them. She had heard nothing from Rafe, and when Eden called Katheryn, she could not tell her anything either. All Eden knew right now was Rafe had left and she may never come home.

"I don't know what to do," said Eden in misery. "I don't know, maybe she's better off without me in her life."

"You didn't know what was happening," Cathcart reminded her. "You reacted based on what you knew and what she told you."

"I keep going over everything she told me in my mind," she said, frustration with herself evident. "I should have known she was getting sicker by the things she was saying. Instead, I just blindly trusted she was taking care of herself and getting the help she needed. I didn't even think maybe she really needed me to do more for her and take care of her the way she took care of me."

"Yes," said Cathcart as he thought about the things Eden was saying and the things Rafe had revealed. "It seems like you and your friends didn't notice what was happening with Rafe then and ignored a lot of signals that something was wrong up until the moment she was carried out of the house by her friend."

"I just never imagined—" She couldn't continue because the pain of her own inaction flooded over her.

Cathcart gave Eden time to calm herself but knew he couldn't let too much time go by, or she would spiral until she shut down. He could tell by her drained look and the dark circles under her eyes that she wasn't sleeping and it took everything in her just to go through the motions of the day.

He decided to change the subject from the present situation in the hope that when Rafe eventually came home, Eden would be able to talk with her about all the issues left unresolved.

"Let's begin talking about some of the issues Rafe brought up. Maybe by working through them, you'll be able to help her understand where you were, and you'll be able to better talk to her and help her."

"I don't think I'll ever be able to tell her what was happening with me, or if she would believe it or even care to know," she said. *I wouldn't blame her*, she thought, looking down at her hands.

"She cares," Cathcart assured her. "She asked you to go with her to Italy, and she stayed even though she knew she was spiraling. She stayed for you and Bronte, and she only left when her friend took the decision from her." He let his words sink in for her. "Let's talk about things from the beginning. Rafe is still trying to work through things from when she had the affair, so maybe we should revisit those things too. Let's think back. What was happening?" he asked calmly.

"I remember I was angry at Rafe back then," she paused and looked up at Cathcart, "even before I thought she had an affair."

"Why were you angry?" he asked.

Eden sighed and rubbed her face. "I don't know anymore," she said sadly. "It just seemed like everything she did would make me angry. Then she would just block me, and it made me angrier."

"She blocked you?" he repeated.

"Yes," Eden nodded. "We would be in an argument, and suddenly, she would just stop talking or leave then I would just get angrier." She remembered it left her feeling as if Rafe didn't care about what she was talking about or even think it was important. It reminded Eden of how her father had treated her, and it had made her angry.

"What kind of things would you argue about?" he prodded.

"Everything, anything," she said sadly. She remembered complaining a lot about everything from the money Rafe was spending to her leaving clothes on the floor.

"What would you do when she left the argument?"

"You know," said Eden. "You've read the file. I went online and complained about her."

"I have," he said calmly. "Based on what you've told me, and what I read, I think you were suffering from your chronic anxiety. The stress of all the insemination failures and your own expectations along with your desire to please Rafe built up and enhanced your anxiety, and you weren't able to manage it like you had in the past."

Cathcart paused to give her time to think about his words then continued. "I think Rafe may have known, even if it was subconsciously, and she was walking away from a situation there was no way to win without both of you getting hurt. It might not have been the right thing for her to do but maybe the only way she knew to handle things. She left you to let you work through it on your own but would still be there for support when you would accept it. In the online conversations, you were saying some very irrational things. The people online were fanning the flame, as it were, by encouraging you and making suggestions while on the surface seemed innocent, but if they knew you were suffering from anxiety problems, and we know they did, what they were doing was not innocent."

Eden closed her eyes and thought about what Cathcart was saying, thinking again about what was happening back then. "Rafe's father was sick, and she was worried about him," she said softly. "It seemed like she suddenly needed to be with him in New York, or needed to be at work more or maybe she just wanted to be there more."

"Why do you think she would have wanted to be at work more?" Cathcart asked softly.

"I don't know. To avoid me, maybe," Eden said anxiously.

She remembered Rafe asking about how it was going with the things she had started taking care of for the house.

She remembered getting angry at Rafe for asking about it all the time. It felt like she didn't trust her to write a check or make a phone call, and it made her so angry sometimes she just ignored doing any of it, and then it would lead to another argument.

She remembered lying to Rafe about ovulating because she was angry. "Do you want to know why I lied about ovulating? Remember, it was something she was angry about?"

Cathcart held her gaze expectantly.

"It was after the second insemination failed, and she was being so sweet," she said as she thought back to when they were working so hard to have a family. "She made me tea every night and held me, and when I was ready, she made love to me," she stopped and wiped away a tear. "Then she suggested we stop the inseminations and go on a vacation. It just made me so angry," she confessed. "We got into a fight, and I accused Rafe of wanting to give up. She denied it. She said she just thought we should put things off and give my body a longer break. All I heard was that I was failing, and it made me angry."

"Then, when she found out you lied, she accused you of not wanting to have a family," Cathcart recalled.

Eden sighed. "Yes," she acknowledged softly. "I think she thought I was projecting when I accused her, and she said I was the one who really wanted to give up." She flushed guiltily under Cathcart's scrutiny. "She wasn't wrong. I was having second thoughts."

"But we know now it was because of the influence of the Stewards," said Cathcart.

"I guess," said Eden sadly. "It was after when I had—" She paused. "I had been talking online," she said regretfully. "I was feeling lonely and pressured, and I had the online affair." Eden leaned forward and put her head in her hands then groaned knowing it was the truth. "I've fucked everything up so bad." She sobbed. "I've lost everything, everything that matters. Rafe and everyone else is right. I should just leave her alone."

"I don't think 'Rafe or everyone else' knows all the facts, and if they did, they might understand your situation better," said Cathcart wanting to keep her from spiraling into negativity. "You suffer from chronic anxiety, and Rafe knows this about you. You were under stress, and at the same time, you were being influenced by the Stewards."

"Maybe," said Eden. "But Rafe doesn't think I should blame the Stewards for my choices."

"I agree you can't put everything on them," said Cathcart as he nodded. "You know you have anxiety, and there are times when you're under stress, it needs to be managed more than others. You know the signs, but for some reason, you ignored them. Maybe you were worried about taking medication while trying to get pregnant, which is a valid concern, or some other worry was keeping you from seeking help for your anxiety. Whatever the reason, it gave the Stewards a tool to use to manipulate you."

"I'm such a fool," Eden said softly. "You're right I should've gotten help. I should have talked to Rafe. Instead, I just blindly followed all the feelings I was having and hurt everyone including myself."

"Because your anxiety was making it difficult for you to communicate with Rafe, and it was being manipulated by the Stewards, things escalated," Cathcart reminded her. "If the Stewards weren't involved, I doubt things would have turned out the same. While not all the blame can be affixed to the Stewards, it's also true not all the blame can be affixed to you. There has to be room in both your minds to accept the blame and fault for what happened, and it can't be placed on a single person, group, or event."

Eden remembered Julia telling her that she thought Rafe had been acting differently back then and wondered if it was when Rafe started to get sick again. "I couldn't even see something was happening with Rafe. I left her in New York to deal with everything alone just like she said, and when she came back, I was punishing her for the affair. I stopped though." She looked up at Cathcart, "I really did. I did forgive her. I was just so messed up, I guess."

Cathcart watched as Eden took a breath. "Eden, we both know your anxiety issues are not an excuse for bad or wrong behavior. You know your anxiety doesn't give you the right to ignore others or expect them to let you always get away with the things you do. This is why we're working on things and why I pointed things out to you in previous sessions that I thought might have been Rafe's point of view."

"I know, I know you're right," she said in misery. "But I really couldn't see what I was doing because everything just seemed to be in chaos."

"I think Rafe knew you were suffering too," he said sympathetically, "and she walked away from arguments because she loved you and didn't want to argue when she knew there wasn't really an argument."

He knew it was difficult for Eden to hear all her mistakes laid out in the open, but knowing her mistakes would help her not to repeat them in the future.

"Should Rafe have been more receptive to your request for therapy?" he continued. "Maybe. But you weren't telling her the truth about why you thought you needed therapy, so it may not have mattered. Considering at least one of the therapists was recommended by the Stewards, it was probably a good thing Rafe refused to go back after the first sessions and wasn't enthusiastic about the workshops. Should she have suggested you see me or someone else? Probably. But her suggesting you see someone may have made you more irrational and argumentative at the time. It may have been hard for her to know what to do to take care of you, especially when she was going through the hardship of dealing with her father's illness and then losing him. Plus, after her father's death, we now know she was trying to take care of her own resurfacing issues."

"I should have asked or come to you," Eden said as she shook her head, "but I was so tied up in my emotional rollercoaster. I was focused on the inseminations and finding a solution to fit what I thought the solution should look like. I couldn't see any other options or how what I was doing made thing worse." She closed her eyes for a moment as the memory played through her mind.

"Tell me what you saw happening with Rafe during the insemination process," he said as tried to gently nudge her to talk and not dwell too long and shut down.

"Rafe wanted everything for me to go perfectly," she said and wiped tears from her face, "and it didn't. Maybe it's the real reason she was angry back then. Things weren't going perfectly for me, and she wasn't here to help as much as she wanted. She was angrier about the sperm not performing than about me. She never said she was angry at me, but she called and reamed the people at the sperm bank after the last insemination failed."

"It was after the failure and troubles with the sperm bank she introduced Gabri to you," he said referring to his notes. "You didn't want to use him as the donor at first."

"No," said Eden softy. "I think my hesitation about Gabri's sperm was because it didn't fit what I saw as the solution." She took a breath and shook her head at her own mistake. "We were supposed to go look through the donor catalogs again, but Rafe was angry with the place. I'm sure it's why she asked Gabri. She probably saw it as a solution to a lot of things, including she wouldn't have to deal with anything except the cryobank for storage."

"How did you feel when she brought him to meet you?"

"I don't know. I was surprised and maybe a little scared."

"Why?"

"I just wasn't sure, and I didn't know Gabri. I knew nothing about him. I told her this and why I changed my mind. Maybe that's why she won't tell me the reason the affair happened because she doesn't want to tell me she felt cut off because I was saying no to her solution. Maybe it's what I did to her. I just don't know."

She thought about the argument they had in New York and feeling so out of place and alone even with all the people around. It was hard to deal with people she did not know while being thrust into unfamiliar social boundaries. Her shyness and aversion to touching and hugging unknown people kept her off balance. Thinking about the donor being someone she knew nothing about at the same time heightened her anxieties. At least, with the catalogs, she had some information about the donor, and she didn't have to meet them in person.

"Maybe I shouldn't have left New York like I did," she said regretfully. "I know it had to be hard for her, but we were fighting over whether or not to use Gabri's sperm. We were both very far away from each other. It's possible the main reason for the distance was because I was going online and being influenced by who I thought were my friends. I really hate to use it as an excuse, but it really was happening." Eden wiped her eyes with a tissue and sat silently feeling the pain of Rafe's absence deeply.

"Then you found out about the affair," Cathcart stated, trying to keep her talking and engaged.

"What did I know, really," Eden asked sadly as she thought about Gabri's words. "She had received flowers. That was it."

"What made you realize the flowers were evidence of an affair?" Cathcart prodded.

"I don't know! I don't know!" Eden sobbed. "Maybe she didn't even have an affair."

Cathcart contemplated her, wondering why Eden would now have doubts that Rafe had had an affair. "What makes you think she may not have had an affair?"

She looked up at Cathcart in misery. "Her friend Gabri said he didn't think she had an affair. He asked me if I confirmed it," she said shakily. "I just believed the worst."

"You believed Rafe's confession," he reminded her. "Rafe told you and has maintained she had an affair."

"But what if he's right?" she asked softly as more tears ran down her face. "He said she might be making things up to fill in what she can't remember. Then he said, even if she did have an affair, at the time, she was innocent because if her mind wasn't there, then her heart wasn't either."

"If she did have the affair, even if her mind and heart weren't in it, it doesn't mean your feelings and pain were any less valid. You shouldn't feel guilty for feeling hurt because the person you love had an affair," he assured her.

"And if she didn't? How am I supposed to feel then?" she asked miserably.

Cathcart thought about Rafe's inability to remember what happened in New York and realized it could be possible Rafe had not had an affair. "Let's look at things from this new point of view," he suggested. Cathcart looked through his notes for a moment examining the problem from this new angle. Finally, a pattern appeared he felt may fit the scenario. "Have you considered, since you had an online affair, the guilt you were feeling had built up, and it led you to project a similar transgression onto Rafe when the flowers came, and you read the card?"

Eden looked up, cut by the possible truth of his words. "I was so blinded by my own guilt," she took a shaky breath, "and I did it to myself!"

Cathcart tapped his notebook as he thought about the session with Rafe. "It is possible she could have been trying to reconcile her lack of memory with the things she was being told had happened. Then she used the information to fill her mind with things to help her make sense as to what really happened. She remembered a lot of small details surrounding the event but not the details of the actual affair."

Eden felt sick again and couldn't speak for a while. So many things ran through her mind that it made her head hurt. She focused and thought about what the doctor had said to her and remembered what Katheryn told her about Gabri.

"I think Gabri took her to New York to confirm things," she said softly.

"Did he say if he would contact you about what he found out?" He paused and could see Eden's misery as she shook her head. "Maybe it would be good for you to do as he suggested then. See if you can confirm for yourself what Rafe told you and your suspicions."

Eden lifted her chin. "Or confirm she was sick and confused, and I pressured her into confessing something untrue because of my own guilt," she said racked with misery and pain because it seemed even more fault may rest at her feet.

5

INSIDE THE YELLOW New York taxi, Julia Hawthorn and Eden Kingsley were on their way to Strawberry Fields in Central Park. Julia made an appointment with Lauren Street, the realtor listed as the agent who sold Ettore Salvaggio's apartment. She told Ms. Street's assistant they wanted to discuss Mr. Salvaggio and his daughter.

Ms. Street's assistant said the realtor only had a short time between showings. Ms. Street liked to relax and have her lunch in Central Park on clear days, so the assistant arranged for them to meet her there. They were to look for her on the bench in front of the Imagine Medallion. Ms. Street would be wearing her gray pantsuit with an off-white blouse with a black cashmere full-length winter coat and would be watching for them.

The taxi pulled over close to the West 72nd Street park entrance. The park was covered with snow not entirely white anymore. The footprints of people and animals as they went off the paths to play occasionally broke up the snow. As Eden got out of the cab, Julia paid the driver. Eden looked around anxiously for the striking black woman Rafe had described.

"All right," said Julia after she finished with the taxi. "We'll have to walk in a bit to get to the medallion."

"Okay," said Eden nervously. She was worried about meeting and talking with the woman Rafe had an affair with, and it showed.

"Come on," said Julia as she took her arm gently and led her into the park.

Julia had been working very hard to help Eden through everything and be there for her. One thing she knew not to do was say anything bad or negative about Rafe right now. She had told Eden a lot of stories about Rafe since she left. Julia wasn't sure at the moment if the stories were helping Eden get over Rafe or making her stay connected to Rafe. She knew it made Eden want to have her over to visit a lot, and she would take it for now.

"Rafe and I used to come here," she said trying to be cheerful and calming for Eden. "Rafe was friends with a dance troupe. They all went to the performing arts school and came to the park to dance for money. I came with her one time, and it was a lot of fun," she said, remembering the last day she saw Rafe before she left for school in Italy. "I think they let her join them because of her sexy dance moves, the ones that got her expelled." She laughed hoping to put Eden at ease. "She probably joined them out of spite for being kicked out of school."

Eden didn't respond, and Julia knew it was because she was trying to control her anxiety. They walked along the snow-cleared path in silence, and in a short time, they saw the medallion in front of them. Soon, they could see the word *Imagine*, and they looked around at the people sitting on the benches reading, eating, visiting or just sitting quietly. There were a few performers out braving the cold further down the path and many people walking through the park. It was cold out but surprisingly mild for a New York December day.

"I don't see her," said Eden looking around for the woman Rafe had described.

Inspecting the line of benches, Julia saw several people with gray suits and long coats, but only one was wearing an off-white blouse. She gently put her hand on Eden's arm. "I'm going over to ask around. You stay here." She left Eden standing on the side of the path and approached the woman in the off-white blouse. "Pardon me," she said politely. "I'm sorry to bother you, but I'm looking for a Lauren Street. Would you be her?"

The woman looked up at Julia and smiled. "Why, yes, darling. Are you my lunch appointment?"

Julia stood stunned. Lauren Street was not what she had expected. Lauren was in her late sixties and obviously *not* a stunning black woman. She looked more like a Jewish grandmother—a beautiful one, but still not what she had expected from what Eden had told her. "Uhm," Julia said as she regained her composure, "are you the Lauren Street who helped with Mr. Salvaggio's apartment?"

"I am," said the lovely woman as she smiled up at Julia. "A pleasure," she said and offered her hand for a short but firm shake.

"Julia," she answered as Ms. Street released her hand.

"My assistant said you needed to speak with me about his daughter. You know her friend was here over a month ago, don't you? We had a fascinating conversation, to say the least," she said gracefully and laughed softly.

"Yes, I know," said Julia still a bit thrown, "or at least I suspected." She looked over her shoulder at Eden then back again. "Listen, let me get my friend and let her know I've found you. Then I'll be right back."

"Of course, darling," said Ms. Street and wrapped up her lunch.

Julia made her way over to Eden and stood close to her. "This is crazy," Julia said nervously. "That woman is not what you described at all. Are you sure about the description Rafe gave you?"

"I'm sure," said Eden as she looked over at the smartly dressed elderly woman in misery because it was looking like Gabri was right about what had happened. "Let's just go ask what happened. Maybe Rafe was talking about her assistant or someone else named Lauren in the company."

They made their way back over to Ms. Street and sat down on the bench. "This is Eden Kingsley," said Julia, "and I'm Julia Hawthorn."

"Hawthorn?" Ms. Street repeated. "Are you part of Hawthorn Financial?"

"It's my fathers' company," Julia confirmed. "I work in the California office."

"I remember Mr. Salvaggio talking about the company. He recommended it to several clients."

"He did?" Julia asked surprised. She wondered if her father knew.

"Oh, yes," she confirmed. "The firm is still on our approved recommendation list. People are always asking us about all kinds of local businesses."

Eden touched Julia on the arm. "Can we ask about Rafe?" she asked softly.

"Oh, yes," said Julia noting Eden was getting anxious and impatient. "Our friend Rafe, Ms. Salvaggio, is sick, and she's getting help, but something happened here when she was in her father's apartment, and we were wondering if you remember and if you can tell us what happened to her."

"I do remember," she said with a firm nod. "I told Ms. Salvaggio's friend what happened. The translator said Ms. Salvaggio couldn't remember."

She took a sip of her warm drink and looked up at the two women who were looking back in anticipation, so she began recounting what she recalled.

"I was helping select the things to be left for staging. Ms. Salvaggio seemed to need the help. There was so much to do, and everything was a bit overwhelming. I walked into the bedroom to ask her a question, and she was on the floor weeping in grief for her father. I tried to comfort her and contact the number in her phone saved as I.C.E., in case of emergency, but got no reply." She watched as the blond woman's face flushed red.

"So," Lauren continued, "I helped her to the guest room to lie down. I went back to marking things throughout the house. I was in the dining room when I smelled something burning. I made my way through the apartment to the kitchen and then to the living room. It was there I found her surrounded by black smoke burning a painting in the gas fireplace," she said, looking at them scandalized. "Well, I couldn't let her burn anything and possibly ruin the fireplace. Not to mention, creating an off-putting odor that might discourage buyers! I grabbed the tongs, even though they were decorative, and got the painting out of the fire and ran it to the kitchen where I doused it with water."

Lauren took another sip of her drink to wet her throat. "When I went back into the living room, she was distraught and said she had to burn the painting. I told her that she couldn't do it there and would have to do it somewhere more appropriate. She just got a funny look on her face and hugged me and told me I was right. She then started crying again."

She frowned at the memory. "I took her to the kitchen to wash the black soot from the ash and smoke off her hands and arms, and then I took her back to her room and told her to rest. When I finished with everything in the house, I went to let her know and check on her. When I woke her up, she just started crying and was inconsolable, so I tried the number in her phone again with no luck. I was afraid to leave her, so I stayed and comforted her for a time and talked to her about her father. Then, when she was calmed, I asked her to join me for an early dinner to forget about everything for a while."

Lauren smiled and put her hand to her mouth to cover her lips. She saw the two women were serious, but the memory was a happy one for her. "We went out and had a wonderful evening. She was such a darling, and everyone loved her wherever we went. We had a wonderful Italian dinner where the chef came out and spoke with her in Italian and brought us special things to the table. Then, since it was still early, we went to a performance in the park. I just love it here in the park," she said and looked around.

She brought herself back to the subject and continued. "Ms. Salvaggio apparently knew several of the dancers, and they invited us for drinks. After leaving the dancers, I shared a cab with her and dropped her off at the apartment and made sure she made it inside. Then I went home exhausted." Ms. Street chuckled at the memory.

"The next morning, she was fine. I brought some Bar Keepers Friend and other cleaning supplies over, and she helped me get the black soot off the marble and decorative copper on the fireplace mantle. Ms. Salvaggio mentioned she needed to go to the funeral home and take care of things there. I remember she was very anxious to get back home. She was upset she had to stay in New York longer because of all her father's business. Before I left, we got through the rest of the arrangements and paperwork we needed to finalize to get the apartment on the market."

Ms. Street smiled at the women and then took another sip of her warm tea. "That's all really until she came back a short time later. I wasn't able to see her when she got into town, but we did speak on the phone. She seemed on edge still and upset. I thought it was being in the apartment again and suggested she get out and have some fun with a friend. She refused and said she couldn't do it again but didn't explain why. Of course, I couldn't stay out to all hours with her. I can only take so many late nights at my age and once was enough for me! I'm spry, but I still need my sleep!" she said with a chuckle. "So, other than seeing her at the apartment the day after the funeral, I don't know what she did. All our transactions were done through Ms. Salvaggio's lawyer."

Eden frowned at the woman. It was hard to imagine Rafe crying inconsolably. It wasn't something she ever remembered Rafe doing. "So, your assistant wasn't there?"

"No," she said, "she only works from the office. I need someone to take calls, set appointments, and prepare paperwork while I'm with clients. If I need help at a listing, I call my decorator or a cleaning crew. Sometimes I am the cleaning crew," she joked. "But I usually have contract workers at listings when the client isn't there. It's easier on everyone. Sometimes clients get in the way of my system. They all know what will happen before they list with me, though. They know I'm very good at what I do. Buy or sell a house on any street with Lauren Street—that's my byline," she said with a chuckle. My late husband's was worse," she revealed with a smile, "and it wouldn't go over with the political correctness of today."

Julia saw Eden was upset then turned her attention to Ms. Street again. "Did you see Ms. Salvaggio with, as she described her, a stunning black woman who had coppery colored lipstick and was very well dressed?"

Ms. Street wrinkled her brow thoughtfully for a moment. "Not that I can recall. I have an excellent memory for faces, and I'm sure I would remember someone with copper-colored lipstick."

"Can you tell us the names of the dancers she met with?" Julia asked. "Maybe one of them can tell us something."

"Oh, yes!" said Ms. Street. "They were all such darlings. One was Hannah, and another was Miguel, and the other was, oh, let's see," she thought, "Geisel, yes, that was it. She didn't speak much at first. I think she was from France and when Hannah told Ms. Salvaggio why she seemed so shy, well, the three girls apparently had a very nice conversation. I was very well taken care of by Miguel." She smiled. "Such a sweet boy. I think he was gay and had considered introducing him to my grandson."

"Do you remember where they were performing?" Julia asked hopefully. She remembered Rafe had dated Hannah before she went to Italy, and she had seen her in France a few times. Also, she fits the description of a striking black woman Rafe gave Eden. It was just strange Rafe would confuse Hannah with Lauren. Unless Rafe was lying about who she had the affair with all this time. Julia took in Eden's desolate demeanor and made the decision to keep what she knew about Hannah to herself for now. No sense upsetting Eden more until she knew something for certain.

"Oh, yes, it was Winter Theater," she said with a nod, "but their troupe left for France the next day. They were talking about how lucky it was Ms. Salvaggio was in New York for their final night. We parted ways because they had to finish packing and be accounted for by the troupe manager."

Eden rubbed her temples in frustration caused by the fact this was the only person they could talk with, and she didn't know who Rafe was talking about. She had an image in her head now of the woman Rafe described and could not wipe it from her mind. But after listening to this woman, Eden thought maybe Gabri was right and that Rafe did create the whole scenario and the woman to fill the gap in her memory. She remembered getting the flowers and using them as proof of the affair and didn't understand why Rafe would admit having an affair with Lauren when it was clear she had not. Maybe Rafe had an affair and just let her think it was Lauren for some reason. She bit her lower lip. "I don't know what to do now," she said softly.

"Is there anyone else who may have information about Ms. Salvaggio back then?" asked Julia.

"If you think someone visited her, you can ask to look at the guest log at the manager's desk," Ms. Street suggested. "All visitors must check in before they're allowed in the elevators unless they have an elevator card. Usually, just the apartment owners or tenants have those. They list their full name and apartment they're visiting. Then the desk calls to announce them and sends them up to the appropriate floor. It's a building with rigorous privacy and security procedures. It's the reason the apartment sold so fast. The amenities are everything people want. Ms. Salvaggio made quite a profit on the sale. It went well above listing because of the bidding war."

"Thank you," said Julia. "I'll call and see if they'll give us the information. Thank you so much for your time."

"You're very welcome, darling," Ms. Street said sweetly. "Mr. Salvaggio was one of the best brokers I ever worked with since my husband died. They were similar in many of the same ways. He talked about his daughter a lot, and I was honored when she chose me to help her sell the apartment."

Julia stood and shook Ms. Street's hand then Eden offered her hand, too. "The flowers you sent Rafe were beautiful," Eden said softly.

"I'm glad you enjoyed them," she said with a smile. "I didn't know she was coming back to New York so fast, so I had them sent to her in California. I hope she gets well soon."

"Me too," said Eden then let Julia lead her down the path. "I think I'm going to be sick," said Eden with a trembling voice as she held on to Julia. "I should have answered the phone. I should have asked more questions. I should have." She couldn't say anything more because it was all she could do not to fall apart.

Julia was too stunned by what was revealed to speak at the moment, also. When they got out of the park, Julia hailed a cab and instructed the driver to take them back to the apartment owned by her parents. They rode there in silence.

When they got up to the apartment, Julia led Eden to her father's office where Eden sat on the couch, and Julia looked up phone numbers and made some calls. While Julia was on the phone, Eden looked up and saw the photos of Julia and Rafe pinned on the wall.

She got up and went over to look at them. She held her hand to her mouth trying not to let out the sound on the sob waiting there. She had never seen this many pictures of Rafe when she was so young in one place. There were only a few at the house of Rafe and her parents and some graduation photos of her. All those photos were gone now.

Eden wiped away a tear as she studied the pictures. Rafe looked so serious in most of them. Only in a few was she holding still or in proper focus. It seemed like all but three or four of the photos were taken to intentionally have only Julia in focus and as the actual subject. Even out of focus, Eden could see Rafe was a beautiful teenager.

"Rafe took all those," said Julia as she walked up behind Eden, wanting to put her arms around her. It was getting harder to hold back her feelings, but Julia knew it was only a matter of time before she would be able to make love to Eden like she did in her dreams. Julia cleared her mind and focused on the photos. "She was awful at getting into the shot before the timer went off and took the photo."

"I was wondering why they were all so blurry," said Eden and took a shaky breath. "Why are they here?"

"One day, she brought her camera on our adventure and said we should make a game out of seeing if my father could figure out what we were doing," Julia explained. "She said he needed to play more," she said with a shrug and smiled. "So when we got home, Rafe came into the office and took a push pin from Daddy's desk and pinned this photo up on the wall," Julia said and pointed to a Polaroid photo. "I don't think she ever found out that I just told Daddy what we did. My mother was so angry when she came home and saw what Rafe had done." Julia laughed. "Mother had been gone a month, so there were a lot of photos up, and she didn't like Polaroid photos up there, or any other photos it turned out, or the pin holes in the woodwork. Daddy left them, despite Mother's annoyance, and soon even more photos were pinned up. Daddy and Rafe had a strange relationship. He's always had a soft spot for her." She didn't explain further because she didn't know if her father wanted what happened when Rafe went to work with him known to anyone.

"It looks like you two had a lot of fun when you were young," said Eden as she touched a photo trailing her fingers over the image of Rafe. "Did you find out anything?" she asked as she turned and went to sit on the couch.

Julia sat down beside Eden and sighed. "Yes and no," she said. "The apartment manager said the visitor logs were private and wouldn't give me any information. I called the funeral home to see if they remembered anything about her." She hesitated a moment. "The man I talked to said Rafe made a special request."

"A special request," Eden repeated confused.

"Yes," said Julia. "He said she brought a painting in and requested it be with her father when he was cremated. He remembered her being upset and thought she was just grieving like other clients who make those kinds of requests. He took the painting and made sure her request was honored." Julia watched as Eden's eyes widened in shock then looked down at her hands. "I asked him what the painting was and he said he couldn't tell because it had already been charred and melted. My guess is it was something of her mother's that she wanted him to have with him."

"Yeah," said Eden softly hiding her anxiety. She felt like she had to hide her feelings a lot more lately to keep from being pressured to talk when all she wanted to do was be alone. It was good not to be the focus of Julia's attention for a while. Knowing there was much more significance to the painting, Eden was torn over whether or not she should tell Julia about Rafe's mother and Maria. The fear of doing anything else that might drive Rafe further away stopped her.

6

WAVING TO SIGNAL her friends to the table at the Kiki Bistro, Abby Van Falkov waited impatiently for them to make it and sit down with her. It seemed like ages since they had met as a group, and all their friends needed to catch up with Eden. Abby was happy they were finally getting together at the same time for a change. Jude and Flynn sat down, and Abby couldn't hold back.

"What's going on?" she asked shrilly. "It's like everyone disappeared off the planet."

"We've just been busy," said Flynn with a shrug and sat a wrapped package on the table.

"Busy doing what?"

"Living life and loving women," said Jude with a little snark as she placed the beribboned box in the chair beside her.

"Oh, haha," Abby groaned. "Seriously, it's been months. I haven't seen you out at any of the bars or the events. I haven't seen Eden at all lately unless it's at lunch once in a while. What's going on?"

Jude just smiled at her but didn't answer. "There's Julia and Eden." She pointed toward them as they walked inside.

"It's about time," Abby complained as she watched Julia approach and Eden head toward Letty's office in the back.

Julia made it to the table and pulled out her chair. "Eden is going to let Letty know she's here and let Bronte see Ephraim," she said as she sat down. "She also wants to make sure Letty's still going over tomorrow to spend time with Bronte."

"So," Abby started hesitantly, "has she heard anything from Rafe?"

It had been about four months since 'the incident' as Abby called it, and they were still waiting to hear anything from or about Rafe.

"Not really," said Julia with an annoyed sigh. "Rafe's been sending videos and pictures to Bronte's email through Katheryn so she can see them on her iPad. But there's been nothing for Eden."

"It was nice of Rafe to get an iPad for Bronte," said Flynn as he examined the menu.

Abby rolled her eyes at him. "But nothing has been sent to Eden? It's her birthday, for fuck's sake!"

"No," said Julia as the waiter came and took their orders. When he left, she looked around at everyone at the table. "I'm still sending Rafe emails to all the accounts I know of, plus Katheryn. She's got to answer sometime."

"Why don't you just leave her alone and let her contact you when she's ready?" asked Jude with a frown. Jude wondered if some of the emails were as bad as some of the things they had been saying when they talked about Rafe. If they were, she didn't blame Rafe for not answering. "When I talked to Katheryn about school and the studio, she told me within a week that Rafe still intended to cover things."

"I doubt she talked to Rafe," Julia said, agitated. "It was probably *that man*, Gabri."

"So," Jude said with a shrug, not understanding why it mattered if Katheryn talked to Rafe or Gabri. "Here comes Eden," she said with a nod of her head.

Eden tried to smile as she made it to the table with Letty close behind her. "Hi," she said to everyone as she sat down.

"I made sure your orders were taken care of," said Letty as she put Bronte in a seat, sat next to Eden, and then nodded to the others.

"Happy birthday!" they all said to Eden and put their gifts and cards in front of her as Ephraim brought out a cake.

"Thank you," said Eden as she smiled at everyone in appreciation as they sang to her. After Eden blew out the candles, Ephraim cut the cake and passed it and the ice cream around. Eden opened her gifts and sat them out so everyone could see what she got.

"We know we've seen you, but we just missed everyone being all together," said Abby as she ate her ice cream.

"We've missed this too," said Eden as she gave the cake to Bronte. She knew the past four months had been hard for everyone. She wasn't ready to tell them the other reason she wanted to see them all. Eden gave Abby a small smile then turned to Jude. "Where's Susy and Stacey?"

"Oh, right, you don't know," said Flynn as he ate his cake. "Stacey got the gig in New York, and she left Wednesday. She was really excited and wanted me to tell you thanks for the recommendation."

"It was nothing," said Eden. "If it weren't for Rafe asking me to recommend her to our studio, I'd have never known how artistic she is at doing makeup and mask making. I'm glad I could help her."

"I'm glad she's gone," said Abby disgruntled. "She's so annoying."

"She's got a good heart," said Jude and then she sipped her drink.

"Whatever," groaned Abby and stabbed her cake.

"Come on," said Jude with a mischievous grin. "She helped get you in contact with that Brooklyn singer you think is hot."

"What singer?" asked Eden, smiling at Abby's disgruntled look.

"Okay, the singer's good, and it was just business," she admitted hotly. "Her name is Julia Weldon, and she's not just a singer! She's got screen credits too!"

Julia rolled her eyes. "You sound lame," she said. "Stop trying so hard."

"Screw you—" Abby cringed realizing Bronte was at the table. That kid repeated everything. She looked at Eden apologetically. "Sorry."

Jude shook her head then spoke to Eden. "Susy had to work. She said hello and happy birthday."

The waiter brought out their food orders, and everyone ate in awkward silence for a while because they still felt the absence of Rafe.

Abby peered up at Jude suspiciously. "Why are you suddenly carrying messages from Susy? Are you dating her or something now?" She watched as Jude said nothing, but her smirk spoke for her. "You are! Why didn't I know this?" she demanded.

"Just because you have a 'need to know' doesn't mean I have a need to tell," said Jude and went back to eating her food.

"Well, we have some news you may find fun, Abby," said Letty with a smile. "Ephraim and I are looking into opening a second location."

"Really?" screeched Abby. "Fantastic. Where?"

"We haven't found the location yet," Ephraim explained, "but we're seriously looking."

"Ephraim's been putting feelers out for another chef too. It's exhilarating," said Letty as she smiled at Ephraim proudly.

"Is it gonna be another gay place?" asked Abby hopefully.

"Abby," chided Jude with a laugh, "what do you mean another gay place? This place isn't even a gay place."

"Well, it is, sort of," she said and frowned. "They have a ladies only night."

"But it doesn't mean one will go over in their new location," Jude pointed out. "Stop trying to make everywhere gay."

"Why should I? I think everywhere should be gay," she spat back miffed.

"No you don't," Julia joined in. "You just think everywhere should be a place where you can pick up girls and gossip."

Everyone laughed, and Abby couldn't help but smile. She couldn't deny those were two of her favorite things, and she liked having them together.

"Maybe you can look in the area where Jude's massage company is located for your new place," Eden suggested to Letty and Ephraim.

"Oh, yeah," agreed Jude. "Being closer to me would be great. The rent is really cheap right now, and it's an up and coming area. Getting in quick would be smart. Rafe even talked to me about investing in the area and suggested I try to buy the building with the space I'm renting."

"We'll definitely look into it then," Ephraim said enthusiastically. "Well, I'm needed in the kitchen. Happy birthday, Eden," he said again. Eden smiled in thanks, and he headed back to work.

"If Rafe thinks it's a good area to invest in, then it's worth checking out," said Letty. Rafe owned the building they were in now so she might help them get another. Letty sighed as she thought about Rafe and was disappointed Rafe hadn't contacted her. She had sent a few emails to Katheryn for her to forward to Rafe, telling her she was there for her, but she hadn't heard anything back.

"Speaking of investing," said Julia proudly. "I've finally convinced Daddy to diversify into the entertainment industry. We're going to create an investment product for film industry investing. We'll be looking for some people in the film production business to form a board of advisors along with a financial team. We hope it will be a product beneficial to investors as well as the industry."

"It sounds interesting," said Eden wondering just how the product would work. She knew the film industry was volatile and very hard to predict. She hoped Julia wasn't star blind and really looking into things before selling to investors.

"It is so far," Julia said excitedly. "I'm really hopeful Daddy will approve everything once we put the package together."

Julia wanted Eden to be interested because she hoped Eden might be part of the board. They had become much closer over the last few months. Julia was now sure this situation was exactly what her dream was all about. It was like Rafe still had hold of Eden even though she was gone. Since Rafe had disappeared, the dream as well as spending time with Eden had left Julia finding herself wanting to take care of Eden even more. Rafe disappearing on them was something else they had in common. She had felt guilty at first because of the accusation Rafe had made and because Rafe was sick. But Rafe had left and was now treating Eden like crap, plus Julia believed, now more than ever, her dream was a premonition, so she had pushed the guilt aside.

It seemed like they talked about Rafe less and less when they were together too. She hoped it meant her presence was finally filling the void Rafe had left in Eden. She was sure when Eden realized she wanted to be there for her, both their lives would be better. Julia would just keep subtly hinting so Eden would know she would love to be a family with her and Bronte if she would only give her a chance. Right now, Eden needed someone she could depend on, and Julia felt like she could be the one to easily step into the role. She knew Eden was not over Rafe yet, but it looked like Rafe wasn't coming back.

Julia leaned back in her chair, holding her warm cup of tea close to her body. Out of the corner of her eye, she subtly took in the object of her desire. Eden's golden hair was longer now and a lock had fallen forward into her face. The shirt she wore was askew from moving Bronte out of the stroller and to the chair, revealing a small amount of cleavage. Just enough to get Julia's imagination jump-started and a tingling sensation thrumming between her legs. *God, I want her*, Julia thought as the erotic ache grew more intense. Julia wanted to touch her, hold her—make love to her. Images flicked through her mind of Eden's body under her as they kissed and touched. She just needed the chance to prove to Eden that she didn't need Rafe anymore. Then Eden would see they could work and be happy together. Julia fought down the desire she was feeling, leaning forward to douse the tingling. Julia tore her eyes away from Eden to prevent herself from exposing her feelings.

"So what's going on with you, Eden?" Abby asked as she chewed her salad. "Are you doing okay?"

"Oh, I'm fine," Eden answered softly. She looked around the table and decided it was time to give them her news. "So, I just want you all to know the reason I haven't been around. I've been doing part-time work," she said, taking in all their shocked faces. "I needed to make some extra money."

"Is everything all right," Letty asked concerned. "Ephraim and I can help you."

"Yeah," agreed Julia surprised by the news. She had been spending a lot of time with Eden and never knew she was doing any part-time work. "Why do you need extra money?

Have you told Katheryn so she can contact Rafe? Let me help you," she said and put her hand on Eden's hand that was resting on the table.

"Everything is fine," Eden assured them and gently pulled her hand from Julia. She patted Julia's hand appreciatively then picked up her fork. Eden could see Julia wasn't happy with the news. It was another thing she knew she couldn't talk with Julia about until now. Eden had attempted once, and Julia tried talking her out of it and began being negative about Rafe, so she stopped. "I haven't gone to Katheryn," she answered softly. "I don't want to go to her." She took a breath, bracing herself for her friends' reactions. "I've decided I have to go to Italy and see Rafe. I want to see if she'll come home."

Eden shifted nervously under everyone's silence. "Well, anyway, it's why I need the extra money. I've already started saving. I have some vacation time I can take, and if I keep working part-time a bit longer, it'll help me get the rest of what I need so I can go sometime around May."

Abby was the first to recover from the news. "It a great idea," she said trying to be enthusiastic. "Hey, I'm trying to write a screenplay. I could hire you to help me out."

"I'd love to help," said Eden hopefully. "Maybe we can work out a schedule over the weekend."

Julia exchanged looks of concern with Letty and knew she would have to be the one to ask. "So," she said hesitantly, "did you hear from Rafe? Does she know you're going to see her?"

"No," she said quietly looking at everyone with determination. "I'm just going. I know that once she sees Bronte and me, she'll want to come home."

"You're taking the baby," asked Letty with concern.

"Of course she is," said Abby when she saw the look of incredulity on Eden's face at Letty's question. "Bronte is Rafe's baby too, and she's right, Rafe would want to see her."

Julia gave Abby a hard look. She didn't want her encouraging Eden to do something that might possibly send her into a tailspin. It had taken a long time to get Eden to the point where she didn't come home from work, go straight to bed, and cry.

"Are you sure you want to do this," Julia asked tentatively. "I just don't want you to set yourself up for disappointment." She saw Eden shift nervously and toy with her glass. "It's just, I know Rafe. If she hasn't contacted you—" She stopped, not wanting to say Rafe didn't want Eden, even though it was what she believed. "What I mean is, showing up unannounced could upset her and her friend Gabri. What if they don't agree to see you and you go all the way there for nothing?"

Eden was disappointed her friends weren't more receptive to her plan but not surprised at Julia's attempt to try to talk her out of going once again. "It won't be for nothing," she said softly. "Even if I don't see her, I'll at least get to find out how she's doing. I can't take the silence anymore," she said hoping they would understand. "I love her." It was the only thing that really mattered. She looked up and saw they were all watching her, waiting for more reasons. "I need her, and Bronte needs her too," she said giving them what they wanted. "I need to know if she's getting better and if she's being taken care of there. I just—" She stopped herself, controlling her emotions determined not to cry. "I just need to try."

"Of course you do," said Jude gently. "I think Rafe would want to see you. She loves you."

"Thank you," said Eden to Jude gratefully.

"I don't think you should go alone," said Julia firmly, not liking the way Jude was encouraging her. She definitely didn't like the idea in the slightest of Eden running around Italy after Rafe who would just hurt her again. "We should go with you."

"No," said Eden. "I don't think us all showing up there would go over well. Gabri might move her again, or she might think we're ganging up on her."

"Well, I can't go anyway," said Flynn as he sat down his drink. "April and May is a busy time for us, and I don't think I could get the time off."

"I think Eden's right. It shouldn't be all of us," said Jude. "I'm not going without an invitation. It's different for Eden. We don't really have a right to push in on Rafe."

"I have the right," said Julia upset they didn't agree with her. "I'm going." Someone had to be there for Eden, and she would not give her over to Rafe again without a fight. She had invested too much time and effort to lose Eden now. "What about you?" she asked Abby.

Abby flicked her eyes up at Eden, who was shaking her head in the negative, and then Abby looked over at Jude who kicked her under the table. "No," she blurted as she jumped at the kick. "No, I can't go, uh, I have... stuff," she stammered.

"No one else needs to go," said Eden. "I'll be fine." She saw Bronte was getting fussy in Letty's lap. "Thank you all for the wonderful birthday party, but it looks like I need to get Bronte home." She began packing up everything including her gifts then, with Letty's help, got Bronte into her stroller. "I'll see you when I can." She turned and walked toward the takeout counter to pick up dinner and pay for her food order.

"Eden," said Letty as she followed her. "You don't have to pay," she said softly and gave her the money back. "Come in with Bronte when you can and eat with us. I'll talk to Ephraim to see if we can help you get some money for the trip."

"Thank you," she said and hugged her as her tears flowed out. "I'm sorry," she said as she wiped her eyes. "I'll be grateful for any help I can get."

Letty walked Eden to the door, and when Eden left, Letty rejoined the others at the table. "Well, I say we all support her," said Letty firmly. "I know she's doing this for herself and Bronte, but we all want to know what's happening with Rafe."

Julia sighed and shook her head remembering the shape Eden was in when Rafe was taken away. "I just hope the price of us encouraging her isn't devastating for Eden. I'll try to talk her out of it. If I can't, then we'll have no choice except to support her and help her if the worst happens."

"You don't really think Rafe wouldn't want to see her, do you?" asked Abby with concern. "Rafe loves her."

"It may not be up to Rafe," said Julia with a frown. "Eden may have to go through a lot of trouble and people to even get to Rafe. Who knows where *that man* placed her," she said frustrated. Her reasons for calling him 'that man' with such disdain were much different from Abby's reasons, Julia convinced herself. "She'll have to speak with him to even find out where she is, and then, if he tells her, who knows if they'll let her in. It's Italy, and they won't recognize Eden as family, or anyone of importance."

"I read somewhere Italy had passed civil partnerships for same-sex couples," said Abby, "but who knows if it is still legal."

"It wouldn't help Eden anyway," Julia scoffed. "All she has is a cohabitation agreement."

"Do you think she's doing the right thing?" asked Letty.

"She's following her heart," said Jude thoughtfully.

"I'll talk to her again," said Julia. "She may be following her heart, but it could lead to more heartbreak. If I can't talk her out of going, I'll go with her." She shook her head thinking Eden should follow her heart away from Rafe and to someone else—preferably to her.

Julia looked around the table and debated on whether or not to tell them her intentions with Eden. The problem was she hadn't even told Eden her intentions yet. It was so frustrating to think about how much hold Rafe had over her, or really how much hold Eden allowed Rafe to have. Everything Julia had been doing lately was for Eden with the goal of them being together. Like helping her with Bronte and the house, holding her when she cried, and now even creating an investment product for the movie industry so

Eden could quit her job and work for Hawthorn Financial. With more money, Eden could move out of Rafe's house, hopefully into her condo, and they could be happy with each other.

Finding out all this time that Eden had been working on a plan to go see Rafe meant her efforts were not working the way she had hoped. She would just have to talk Eden out of going somehow. If Julia failed to get Eden to stay, then she would have to try to help Eden see who Rafe really was. She would be there for her when Rafe broke her heart again. She always knew it would have to be Eden's choice to leave Rafe. Maybe this trip would show her walking away from Rafe was the right choice. Then she would tell Eden how she felt, and they could finally be together.

Julia smiled at the thought.

7

When I look on you a moment, then I can speak no more, but my tongue falls silent, and at once a delicate flame courses beneath my skin, and with my eyes I see nothing, and my ears hum, and a wet sweat bathes me and a trembling seizes me all over. — Sappho

ON THE OUTSKIRTS of Florence, Italy, the car carrying Eden Kingsley turned off the narrow street and onto a long shaded driveway. Eden looked out the window as the car climbed the hill to the villa. She could see the red dome of the Cathedral Duomo and *Giotto's Campanile* standing like a tall sentinel beside it in the distance. The entire city, with all the colorful marble on the buildings, the statues, and art everywhere seemed surreal to her, even though she had seen it before when she visited with Rafe.

As the car moved forward the sprawling villa came into view. The villa had a grand entry with arches, columns and other architectural details Eden knew Rafe could name but, to Eden, it looked like a miniature palace or one of the many museums she had seen in Florence. She nervously wiped her sweaty palms on her pants then straightened her clothes as the car slowed to a stop in front of a large archway too narrow for the vehicle to pass through.

"Miss," said the driver in heavily accented English as he looked back at her, "you walk from here. It is a nice walk through the garden just there," he said and pointed her in the direction she should go. "I wait."

"Thank you," said Eden softly as the driver got out of the car and opened the door for her. She picked up the canvas bag and the notepad beside her and slid out of the car. She put the pad in the bag then took a breath and began her walk through the garden to see Gabri De Angelis.

Eden was nervous because she hadn't told Gabri she was coming, and Eden didn't know how she would be received by him. She hadn't heard from Rafe directly at all. Rafe had sent gifts for Bronte, and several times a month, Katheryn forwarded video clips of Rafe talking to Bronte or reading her a book, but there had been no messages specifically to her during the six months of Rafe's absence from their lives.

She sent emails to Katheryn to forward to Rafe, but she had no idea if she got them, so Eden sent them to every email account she knew Rafe had ever had. Most of the accounts were undeliverable, but a few were, so she used them hoping Rafe would respond but without result. Thinking back, some of the emails she regretted sending, but she had been desperately trying anything to get a response.

After her trip to New York with Julia, and then talking with her Dr. Cathcart, Eden felt she had to make the trip to Italy and find Rafe to bring her home. Julia insisted she come with Eden, but only after she was unable to talk Eden out of it. Eden convinced Julia to stay at the hotel with Bronte today because Eden wanted to talk to Gabri alone. She hoped that if Rafe was there, Gabri would let her talk with her today. If she was in a sanatorium or somewhere else, she hoped he would tell her where so she could see her.

She needed to see Rafe and talk to her about so many things. She hoped Rafe somehow might have some small amount of love for her left, and she would agree to come home. She looked up and saw she was already at the entrance. She straightened herself again, went up to the large ornate door, and rang the bell.

"*Buon pomeriggio*,"[1] said the woman who answered the door with a smile.

"*Boun pomeriggio*," Eden answered back nervously then glanced at the notepad she had taken out of the bag. "*Uhm*, Eden Kingsley, *un amico dall'America, a vedere Gabri De Angelis*," she said and tore the page from the notepad and handed the women the paper with her information on it.

---

[1] Good afternoon,

The woman took the paper, examined it, and then peered at Eden with confusion. *"Americano?"* she repeated and watched as Eden nodded and shifted nervously.

"A vedere Rafaella Salvaggio," Eden said hesitantly hoping she was pronouncing the words correctly.

"Venite, venite,"[2] the woman said and beckoned Eden into the villa.

Inside, Eden found herself overwhelmed by the marble floors and columns, painted ceilings, enormous ancient paintings and statuary, gold-leafed furniture, and a massive spiral staircase built as a focal point and leading to a mezzanine above. It was as if she had walked into the house of royalty, and she wasn't even sure how to move in the space.

"Venite," repeated the woman as she smiled and led Eden into an opulent waiting room. She motioned to the couch and said something Eden couldn't understand before leaving the room.

Eden sat down, afraid to move or touch anything. She had no idea Gabri lived in such a lavish home and felt intimidated by it. She took a deep breath then let it out slowly and tried to focus on one thing, the reason she was there—Rafe.

---

[2] Come, come,

8

GABRI DE ANGELIS WALKED angrily down the hallway toward his office to meet with Eden Kingsley, who he was told was waiting in the sitting room. He had no idea why she was here uninvited, but he would soon have her on her way if possible.

He sent his assistant and translator Stefano to bring her to his office. He wanted to understand why she was here and knew between Stefano and himself, they would be able to make it clear she must go. It seemed he wasn't clear enough before he left America.

He sat down at his desk and put his head in his hands then got up and made himself a drink. Rafaella was doing so well these past months, and he did not want this woman tearing down what had been rebuilt. Rafaella needed time to think about herself and getting well. She needed calm and to fill her time with things working her mind in positive ways. She did not need this woman punishing her and demanding things from her she might not be ready to give.

There was a tap on the door, and Stefano came in leading Ms. Kingsley and directing her to the chair on the other side of his desk. He took his drink over, sat down behind his desk, and observed her for a moment. He could tell she was nervous and thought it was good. It meant she knew she should not be here.

"Why are you here?" he asked in halting English as Stefano took the chair next to Eden.

"I've come to see Rafe," she said softly.

"No," Gabri said with a wave of his hand. He needed no translation to know what she had said.

"Gabri," Eden said and swallowed back her anxiety, "I've come a long way. It's been a long time, and I've not heard from Rafe. I need to see her and talk to her."

Gabri listened to Stefano and gave his reply for Stefano to translate. "Rafaella has sent gifts to the baby and video, so you have seen her," Stefano said calmly. "I will not allow you to interfere with her now."

"I don't want to stop her from getting better," Eden insisted. "I want to..." She hesitated. "I need to see her in person. I need to see for myself that she's doing better."

"You are selfish!" Gabri yelled out in English and banged his fist on the desk, startling both Eden and Stefano. "Selfish woman!" he retorted then continued in Italian.

Stefano translated nervously because he could see Gabri was upset about this woman's visit. He knew of the golden-haired woman because Rafe and Gabri had spoken of her. Gabri had not said many positive things about her, especially when he first brought Rafe to the villa.

He was sure the woman could see Gabri's anger, so he spoke calmly to her. "He says you pushed her and punished her until she was very sick, and now you come and expect him to put her in your hands again. No. He will not allow you to take away all her progress. She is not ready to talk to you. When she is ready, she will contact you. Then you can see her and talk with her. Not before."

Eden glanced up at Gabri shakily. Stefano's calm words did not reflect the anger Gabri was showing. She looked down at her notepad and tried to focus, but the things she wrote down as reasons she needed to see Rafe seemed weak. She looked up and steeled herself.

"I have things I need to tell Rafe, and they're things I need to say in person," she said firmly. "Also, I need answers from you. You never told me what happened to Rafe when you said she had to get help before. Rafe and I have a child together, one you helped us make, and I deserve to know what's happening with her for Bronte's sake if no other." Eden tried not to waver under Gabri's stare.

"Why should I talk to you about those private matters," Stefano continued to translate, "when it is you who has caused her harm now?"

Eden looked up at him confused. "Me?"

"Yes," said Stefano in English for Gabri. "Do you not understand anything at all about what was happening with Rafaella?"

"I," Eden stammered, "I know she was having phantom pains from what happened at the school. She was having nightmares a lot, more than I knew about I guess. I now know she had a breakdown in New York brought on because of her grief for her father," she hesitated, leaving out the painting of Maria, "and it was what brought back the memories of what happened to her when she was younger. I know she felt like I was still punishing her for what happened in New York." Eden swallowed her nervousness and tried to think of more. "I know Jake and the Stewards said and did things to make her think I was lying to her and trying to hurt her. Some I know about, others she's never told me," she said softly.

Gabri sighed heavily at Stefano's translation of her words. He could tell she had given no thought to what was happening with Rafaella and her part in everything. Maybe it was because she genuinely didn't understand how things affect people or perhaps she was just blind and selfish. He did not know. He motioned to Stefano so he would translate.

"Rafaella told me she did not tell you about things in her past because she did not want you to look at her with pity," Stefano said calmly for Gabri. "Her father and I, we don't look at her with pity because we lived through things with her and have similar scars, but you," Stefano paused and waited for Gabri to continue. "Rafaella tells me you don't see life as a challenge or adventure to overcome like she does, and it is one of the reasons she loved being around you. You saw things differently, and Rafe wanted to see things the way you saw them. But now she thinks you will see her differently than you did before, and she's right. So the question is, could you look at her without pity now if you knew all about her past?" Gabri watched Eden shift uncomfortably in her chair taking in the words Stefano was telling her. "If you can't, you should consider not seeing her."

Eden looked up at Gabri and shook her head. "I have to see her," she said softly. She was determined she would not let him talk her into leaving Italy without seeing and talking to Rafe.

"But Rafe has not said she wants to see you," Stefano translated. "She needs to have calm. She needs to be away from you. She needs this time to heal."

"Why," said Eden confused and upset, "why does she need to be away from me?"

"Are you blind? In her dreams, death was mocking her and demanding that she choose between her own death and yours. Do you understand how difficult you made life for her demanding she touch you, kiss you, be with you while she was fighting the demon in her mind? If you and those so-called friends would have just listened to her and left her alone or let her come to Italia, she may have been able to stay well, but you pushed, and you punished her until she could no longer function." Gabri spoke angrily, in contrast to Stefano's calm translation. "You are all so self-important and selfish. You are all so blind when things are put plainly in front of you. I don't understand why she calls you and the others 'friends and family.' You are more like strangers. You say you care, but only when it is convenient or when it is not hard."

Eden's face flushed red with anger and guilt at Gabri's words because they were similar to ones Rafe had said to her. "That's not true, Gabri. You said yourself she kept things from us. She kept a lot of things from us. I knew she had dreams, but even if she told me everything in them, I wouldn't know what was really happening to her because I knew nothing about all the things that happened to her when she was young! How is it selfish to tell her I love her and want her to know she's wanted and needed? How is it selfish to ask her to tell me what's going on and beg her to get help? How is it selfish to live with her tearing me apart constantly while trying to help her when she was pushing us all away?"

"She was pushing you away because of all those things!" Stefano translated putting more emotion in as Gabri had become upset. "She was tearing you apart to try and carve out space for herself to breathe and get away from all the things in her mind! Listen! Think! All those are things she asked you not to do! You didn't do all those things for her! You did them for yourself! She told me she asked you to move to Italia with her. Didn't it cross your mind why she would want to do something so drastic suddenly? She wanted to bring you, but even then, you couldn't see her wanting to move back here as a sign you should contact me, the one she is so close to that she chose to be the father of your child. You just saw how it affected you! She told me how you made excuses like your job or friends and other things. She is right when she says you don't see her anymore!"

"I was trying to keep her home to get her help!" Eden insisted. "You're right. I saw leaving the country as a bad idea. If I agreed to move here with her, I would have even less of an idea about how to get her help than I had at home, and I would have had no support or people I could call on for help! I don't speak the language or know anything about Italy!"

"Of course you don't!" scoffed Gabri, and Stefano tried not to copy it in his translation. "I am the one who could have helped you with everything! Even now, I have to tell you things you should know!" He fumed. "Another thing, how long have you known her? How many times has she brought you to visit Italy? You make no effort to learn her language or about her home or appreciate where she comes from and her heritage. You just walk through life wanting things handed to you and everyone to make life easy for you! Maybe this is the reason she is searching for the real reason you were so willing to leave her and think badly of her. She is not easy for you to be around anymore. You have to think about her too much, and it is inconvenient."

Eden gawped at Gabri in horror of what he was saying. He couldn't mean those things. She didn't want him telling Rafe those things. She calmed herself and could only think he was saying such horrible things to get the result he wanted and for her to leave without seeing Rafe. She was not going to let it happen no matter how much he hurt her with his words and tried to scare her.

"I hope you really don't think those things are true," she said holding in her anxiety. "I would never intentionally hurt Rafe." She took a breath and let it out slowly to control her emotions. "I've brought Bronte to see her," she revealed. "I know she wouldn't want to miss seeing her. Will you tell Rafe we're here, and we'd like to spend time with her? Or just tell me where she is so we can visit her?"

Gabri frowned and shook his head as Stefano translated her words. He should have known she would use the baby for leverage to see Rafe. He also knew if Rafe found out Bronte was here, and he prevented her from seeing the baby, Rafe would be angry.

"You are selfish and cruel," Gabri said in heavily accented English, "to do this to Rafaella now and to use the *bambina* in this way." He nodded to Stefano then let him translate the rest.

"He says he will talk to Rafe. Leave your information and where you are staying," relayed Stefano.

Eden felt a surge of hope as she tore off a page from her notepad with her hotel information and her phone number.

"Thank you, Gabri."

"Don't thank me," he said through Stefano. "I want you to think about what you're doing. If you can't see her and not look at her with pity, or if you can't stop yourself from emotionally pressuring her to get what you want from her, or if you can't stop yourself from doing things she asks you not to do, then you should not see her. If you can't think about her instead of yourself, you should let her see the baby, but you should not be there."

Eden swallowed and forced back the pain of his words then stood up understanding she was being dismissed. "I am thinking about Rafe. She's all I've been thinking about for months, whether you believe it or not."

"Mr. De Angelis says the discussion of Rafaella is now over and asked me to tell you not to come here again without an invitation," said Stefano.

"Of course," said Eden shakily as she walked toward the office door.

Gabri motioned for Stefano to follow her and make sure she found her way out then went back to his desk and picked up the phone to call Rafe's doctor. He had to make sure all was ready if Rafe became lost again.

Stefano led Eden from the office down to the front door. She was determined to hold back her tears as she walked down the path toward the car waiting to take her back to the hotel.

9

JULIA HAWTHORN DECIDED to pass the time while she waited for Eden by going through the Uffizi Gallery. She didn't know how long Eden would be gone, so since Bronte was with the au pair and finally taking a nap, she took the opportunity to get out of the hotel. She walked through the long hallway looking at statues on her way to find the next gallery room free of a crowd of tourists. She didn't like bumping elbows while looking at her art.

As she approached one of the art-filled rooms, a large crowd filed out, and Julia thought she caught sight of someone familiar. She stopped and looked again to be sure and knew then that she wasn't mistaken.

It was Rafe.

Rafe's hair had grown longer, and she looked a lot healthier than when Julia had last seen her. Rafe was dressed in black leather pants and a red V-neck T-shirt with cap sleeves with 'Ciao Bella' printed on the front, and she was carrying a drawing pad. Julia shook her head in wonder at the fact Rafe would dress in such a way to come into the gallery. She looked like a tourist or worse—a poor college student.

As the group of tourists walked down the hallway, Julia followed along at a short distance. She wasn't sure if she should talk with Rafe or wait to make contact. Julia knew at that very moment, Eden was probably asking Gabri about seeing her. Julia imagined, if she could talk to Rafe, she might be able to go around Gabri. On the other hand, if Rafe didn't want to see Eden, it might be better not to let Rafe know she was here, too.

Arriving at the next room, most of the tour group filed inside. Rafe stopped just outside the room. She spoke softly to a lovely dark-haired woman while a more matronly woman looked on. Julia presumed the older woman was the mother of the younger. After a moment, Rafe shook their hands. She then tore out a page from her drawing book, handing it to the beautiful dark-haired girl. As the pair went into the art-filled room, Rafe continued down the hallway alone.

Julia discretely followed Rafe. Soon, they approached the exit. Rafe began speaking with a girl at the information desk. After the girl handed Rafe some things from behind the desk, Rafe walked out of the museum. Following her outside, Julia watched as Rafe put on a black leather jacket matching her pants. Rafe put away her notebook in something similar to a messenger bag that she slung across her body then started walking across the plaza.

Julia decided to keep following her for a while, hoping Rafe would stop somewhere. Finally, Julia decided she shouldn't waste the opportunity to talk with Rafe—just in case Eden got nowhere with Gabri.

"Rafe!" Julia called. "Rafe Salvaggio. Is it really you?"

Rafe turned at the sound of her name, and the smile on her face twisted into a frown of confusion. "Julia?"

Julia caught up with Rafe and gave her a hug. "You look really good. What are you doing here?"

Rafe squinted suspiciously and backed away from her. "What, did you think I'd be locked away somewhere spinning around a lightbulb?" she asked defensively.

"No, no," she said holding her hands up. "I didn't mean any such thing. I'm just surprised to see you here."

"Really?" asked Rafe as she crossed her arms. She wondered why it would be so surprising to see her in the city where she lived now. "Well, I'm here, and I have to go. It was nice seeing you. Hope you enjoy Florence," she said with a wave then turned and walked away.

"Hey, Rafe, wait," Julia called out and went after her. "It's been a long time. Don't you want to talk?"

"Not really," said Rafe as she walked. "I left to get away from you and everyone for a while. I'm not sure I'm ready to deal with you."

"Deal with me?" asked Julia offended by Rafe's attitude and trying to keep up with her. "I've been your friend half your life. You could show me some courtesy."

Rafe stopped and scowled at Julia. "I thought I did. What do you want?"

"I just want to know how you're doing and what you've been doing," said Julia earnestly. "You know, catch up."

Rafe held her arms out from her sides. "As you can see I'm doing fine. As for what I've been doing," she shrugged indifferently, "getting better." She could tell Julia was expecting more. "Why are you in Italy?"

"I'm here with... a friend," she said not wanting to mention Eden just yet.

"Oh," said Rafe when it was plain it was all the response she was going to get. "Well, be sure to take your friend to

Pisa and Siena. It should be nice weather for a visit." She turned and began walking away.

Julia watched Rafe walk away for a moment then began following her again. "Is that all? Don't you want to talk to me? Maybe we can get coffee or lunch."

"I don't know what you want from me, Julia," said Rafe as she stopped to look at her. "I'm not sure what you want me to say. I wasn't expecting to see you, and I really do have to be somewhere." She walked up to a motorcycle and unlocked a saddle bag, retrieving a helmet.

"I guess I just want to talk," said Julia as she watched Rafe climb on the bike, put on the helmet, and then begin to buckle it. "I'm just as surprised to see you. I'm happy you're doing better, and you look good." She looked closer at the bag slung across Rafe's back and could see it wasn't a messenger bag but a compact paint box and easel.

Rafe glanced over at Julia and gave her a forced smile. "Thank you," she said politely and turned the key to start the bike. "Hope you have a good vacation," she said and pulled out of the space and sped down the narrow street.

Julia watched Rafe ride away and shook her head. "Typical hard-headed Rafe," she mumbled to herself then began walking toward her hotel. At the very least, she could tell Eden that Rafe was healthy enough to be out running around on a motorbike and going to museums.

Across the Arno River, Eden was being driven away from the villa and down the narrow street leading them back to the city and over the bridge to get to the hotel.

Unknowingly, Eden watched Rafe on her motorcycle as she went past her car headed in the direction of the villa.

10

RIDING HER MOTORCYCLE slowly down the smooth garden path, Rafe Salvaggio pulled up in front of the small cottage on the professionally landscaped and picturesque villa grounds where she now lived. She moved from the villa into the cottage a few months ago for privacy, and to get away from all the commotion always going on in the main house. Cutting the engine to the motorcycle, Rafe took off her gloves and shoved them into the pocket of her black leather jacket. She got off the bike, took off her helmet, stowed it in the saddle bag, and then made her way into the cottage.

Inside, she took off her jacket, depositing it on the table by the door, and then took her paint box to the room she was using as an office and painting studio. She went into the modest but efficient kitchen and made a glass of water. Sitting down at the small wooden kitchen table, she looked out at the garden as she sipped her cold drink.

The unexpected run-in with Julia was still on her mind. She knew she may have been brash with Julia, but she was surprised. She was worried Julia might be there to try to talk her into going back to America before she was ready. Plus, she promised Gabri she wouldn't see anyone from home until they both thought she was ready. At the right time, they would talk to the doctor about whether or not Rafe was prepared to add more stress to her life or not. Until then, she was to focus on working with the doctor and spending time doing small projects to keep her mind busy.

She finished her water and took the glass to the sink. Through the open window, she heard the echo of laughing and splashing from the direction of the pool up at the villa. She smiled and went to her room where she put on her bikini and grabbed a towel to go join everyone for an afternoon swim.

"*Ciao!*" said Rafe cheerfully as she made it to the pool and put her towel on a chair. She saw Gabri and Stefano were already in the pool playing. Sitting in one of the loungers, Nora was watching them and laughing.

Nora turned and smiled as Rafe walked over to her. "There you are! How was your day?" she asked in Italian.

"It was so hard," answered Rafe in her childhood language. She loved the fact Nora was an American who could speak fluent Italian. Rafe gave a false pout, and Nora's eyes sparked with mischief. "My eyes saw so much art, I'm exhausted." She chuckled unable to stop her smile. "But now I get to look at you, and I'm healed," she said to the dark blond woman with sparkling brown eyes.

"You're such a charmer!" Nora laughed and blushed. "No wonder everyone loves you."

Rafe smiled at her as she bent down and kissed her on the lips then kissed her pregnant stomach. "Hello, my little one," she said and kissed Nora's stomach again. She looked up at Nora and winked. "Did they take good care of you while I was gone?" she asked then looked over at Gabri as he swam.

"I don't think I was too much trouble for them," she said and added a roll of her eyes. "Will you show me what you did today?"

Rafe gave a short laugh and smiled at her sheepishly. "I gave it away."

"Rafe!" Nora chastised her. "You're always giving away all your beautiful work. I hope it was appreciated."

"I think it was," said Rafe with a nod. "I like giving it to people who see beauty in it."

"You mean you like giving it to beautiful women," she teased with a knowing smile.

"She was very beautiful!" Rafe laughed and held out her hand to Nora. "Are you getting in?"

"No, I think I'm sitting out for now," she answered. "I'm having a nice cool lemonade, and Gabri said lunch would be out soon. Go play," she said tapping Rafe's nose with her finger playfully.

"Okay!" Rafe ran, hurled herself forward, and dove into the pool. Coming up from under the water Rafe swam over to Gabri. "I need to talk to you after lunch," she said softly, wiping the water from her face with her hand.

Gabri frowned with concern. "Is everything okay?"

Rafe avoided his eye contact. "I think so. Let's talk later."

"Okay," he agreed. "I need to talk to you about a few things too."

"Great!" said Rafe as she held on to the side of the pool. "Let's race. Ready. Set. Go!" They were off freestyling across the pool as fast as they could swim.

After exhausting themselves in the pool, lunch came, and they all enjoyed eating and talking with each other until Gabri signaled to Rafe that they should go talk.

Rafe helped Nora up from her chair. It wouldn't be long before Nora had her baby, but it seemed she was still not slowing down though she looked tired. "Are you going to take a nap?" she asked softly.

"You read me so well." Nora smiled and kissed Rafe as they passed then made her way inside to take a nap.

"Let's go change then walk in the garden," Gabri suggested. "Stefano, you can take care of things here and continue the work in the studio, okay?"

"No problem," he said with a nod as they all went their separate ways.

11

GABRI DE ANGELIS FOUND Rafe already waiting for him in the garden sitting on a wooden bench. He was still not sure how he was going to break the news to her about Eden being at the house and bringing Bronte to Italy for an unplanned visit.

Gabri had made a call to the doctor right after Eden left his office. He told the doctor what was happening. She advised short visits or if they needed to be longer, monitored visits to make sure Rafe was not put into a position that might derail her progress. Rafe had made great strides since she got back home to *Firenze*. On the outside, it looked like Rafe was back to her old self, but Gabri knew looks could sometimes be deceiving. Right now, Rafe had no pressures or stressors to cause her problems. *No so-called friends who might cause her problems*, Gabri thought.

When Gabri brought Rafe home in November, she was very weak, so she spent time keeping her mind busy with positive things. She read books from the library, looked at art, and took paints and notebooks to paint or draw in gardens. Rafe loved talking to the workers in the olive grove. As she gained strength, Rafe helped the workers lay out nets and shake the branches of the olive trees in the olive grove. She began wandering the vineyards, tasting wine with the winemaker, and watching him test the soils and wines. She even tried helping with the beehives and collecting honey and watching the beekeeper make candles from the honeycomb. On good days, she would exhaust herself helping with jobs around the estates. On other days, she would spend her time working with her therapist and drawing to help chase away the demons.

The nights and days Rafe didn't have positive thoughts were agonizing. There were times when Rafe wouldn't sleep for days because of dark thoughts and dreams. Gabri and the doctor tried several things to help her sleep and finally had to resort to medication. It was a difficult decision because of the worry Rafe would become addicted. They even agreed that Gabri would hold the pills to make sure Rafe didn't take them too often.

Eventually, Rafe ventured out of the estate holdings and into the city. She walked the streets of her childhood again and visited the shops and museums. Rafe even traveled to construction sites that interested her to look over and talk to the people on the sites. This inspired her to write a paper and a couple of articles she said she might let someone actually look at someday. So far, Rafe would only show them to Nora.

She spent a lot of time with Nora, and it was clear to Gabri they loved each other, which made him very happy.

Rafe had even been out to a few parties and made some new friends. But there were still days when Rafe did nothing and couldn't get out of bed without help and encouragement. It had been a long time since she had such a day, and Gabri hoped it meant she was out of the worst part of her illness and back to her bright life and future. Then today, with the appearance of Eden, his hope was put on hold. He was worried the situation would pull Rafe back down again.

Gabri sat down next to Rafe and sighed as he patted her leg. "This garden is inspiring," he said with a slight smile.

"I think you're right," said Rafe thoughtfully as she looked out over the beautiful garden. "I'm thinking of painting it for Nora," she said softly. "Do you think she'll like a painting of it?"

"I think she would love anything you gave her," he said, knowing it was true. He chuckled. "I think she is even more in love with you than I am."

"I'm still irresistible!" Rafe laughed then leaned into Gabri and closed her eyes, grateful for his comfort. "Something happened today," she said softly. "It was kind of a shock, but I handled it."

"Tell me everything, *Eroina*," he said softly and put his arm around her.

"I saw my friend Julia from America outside the Uffizi," she revealed and felt Gabri stiffen at the news then relax. "She said she was here with a friend. I got away as fast as I could. I think I was rude, though," she said with a sigh. "I was just caught off guard."

Gabri took a moment to calm himself before speaking. He should have known Eden would not be here alone. He refocused his mind on Rafe. "Do you want to talk with her again? You can, you know, if you think you're ready."

Rafe shrugged and shook her head. "I don't know. All I could think was—I needed to get away. I've been trying not to think about her... and the others. I've been doing what you and the doctor tell me. Just focusing on me and getting well. I think about Bronte all the time, though. I think Julia could tell me how she's doing."

"You know how she's doing," said Gabri softly. "We have the videos Katheryn has sent and photos."

"Yes," Rafe agreed, "but I don't know if she remembers me or if she still loves me."

Gabri hugged her close and kissed the top of her head. "Of course she does," he said gently. He knew now there was no doubt he had to tell her Bronte was here. He could see not telling her would be the worst thing he could do.

"I think she could tell me how Eden's doing," Rafe said softly. "I know you don't want me to, but I think about her a lot too. I have to think about her to work through some of my problems. And I can't help it."

Gabri smiled and laughed softly. "I know you can't," he said and ran his hand over her hair. "It's okay to think about her. I know you're still searching for answers and have been working on them in therapy and on your own. Just remember you have to think of yourself too."

"I know," said Rafe with a sigh and closed her eyes again.

Gabri sat with her quietly for a while trying to reign in his anger and annoyance with Eden for possibly creating an unhealthy situation for Rafe. Gabri knew he had to tell Rafe, so he would just do it and help her as he could. "I have something to tell you, and it may shock you," Gabri said gravely.

Rafe sat up with concern on her face. "Is everything okay?"

Gabri could not help but smile at how deep her concern was for him. He didn't understand why people couldn't see how vulnerable she was and how everything affected her and made her want to make everything better.

"Everything is fine," he assured her. "I had an unexpected visitor today." He hesitated and looked into her eyes full of anticipation. "It was Eden," he said softly and watched Rafe look down and tremble slightly. "She said she needed to talk with you." He waited for a response, but Rafe just sat silently. "You don't have to see her. I can tell her to go home and to give you more time."

Rafe looked up at Gabri with searching eyes. "Do you think they're here..." she paused, "together? Eden and Julia?"

Gabri nodded. "I think it is most likely. Eden didn't mention Julia to me, but it makes sense."

"Julia didn't mention Eden," said Rafe. "Why do you think she wouldn't tell me Eden was here?"

"I don't know," he said and could see Rafe trying to figure out her own question.

"She should have told me," said Rafe with a frown.

"I have to tell you something more." He paused. "Eden has brought Bronte to see you."

"She has?" asked Rafe and wiped a tear away at the news. She took a breath and ran her hands through her hair. "I was hoping she could come after Nora's baby was born so they could meet," she said with a sad smile. "Do you think Eden will let her come back then?"

Gabri smiled to reassure her. "I hope so. They will be great friends," he predicted then hugged her. "I talked to the doctor about everything, and you should talk to her too." He watched Rafe nod her silent agreement. "She suggests short visits or monitored visits if they need to be longer, in case Eden pushes you."

Rafe looked up at Gabri again, not sure if she wanted to see Eden with or without time limits or monitoring. "Did Eden say what she wanted to talk to me about," she asked shakily. "Maybe if I knew, I'd be more prepared."

"She didn't say," he said with a shrug. "She just said she needed to talk with you in person."

"In person," Rafe repeated and rubbed her temples.

"Don't worry about what she wants to say," he said gently. "If you want, I can look through the emails she's sent. I've kept them all for you. Maybe she mentions what she wants to say in one."

"No, no," said Rafe with concern. "You shouldn't read them."

She didn't want him to read the emails Eden and the others had sent. She knew most of them were probably pleading for her to come home or were full of angry words about Gabri. She stopped reading them after a few weeks because Gabri and the doctor threatened to take away her computer and phone if she didn't stop reading them and stop listening to voice messages. The doctor said it was not good for her right then. She had forwarded all her email and voicemail accounts so Gabri had control of them. He, in turn, put all Eden and her other friends' emails into a particular folder without opening them. Others he took care of and forwarded important ones to her new account. Voicemails he listened to and handled how he saw fit. Rafe created new accounts for Italy but received very few calls or emails now.

"What else did she say?" she asked hesitantly.

"She wanted to know how you were doing and wants to see how you are for herself," he said unable to contain his exasperated sigh. "I told her you were doing well, but she still wants to see you in person."

"Is that all?" she asked softly.

"It is all she said to me about why she is here," he said with a nod. "She left her contact information. I can tell her no. You don't have to see or talk to her. I can see if only Bronte can visit. I'm sure Nora would love to meet her."

Rafe looked up at Gabri with worry. "Does Nora know Eden and Bronte are here?"

"No," said Gabri. "Only you, me, and Stefano."

"I don't think I want Nora to know yet," said Rafe shakily. "I don't want her to get upset if I don't get to see Bronte. I don't know if I want her to meet Eden if she doesn't let me see Bronte alone."

"Rafaella," said Gabri and took her shoulders then looked into her eyes. "It is not your job to keep Nora from being upset." He shook his head sadly. "But you will have to decide to tell her about everything or not. Just don't make it about her feelings. Make it about your own. Then, if you decide you want her to know, talk to her, and see how she feels. She can decide for herself if she wants to be there or not. She loves you deeply, and I think she may surprise you."

"Okay, I'll think about it," Rafe agreed. "I'll think about it." She felt the warmth from Gabri's hands go away as he released her. "Do you think Eden knows about New York?"

"I don't know," Gabri answered and was quiet for a while. "If you talk with her, are you going to tell her?"

"Yes," she said softly. "It caused her a lot of pain, and I think maybe knowing will help her."

Gabri leaned his head back trying not to show his frustration at Rafe thinking she should tell Eden about New York to help Eden rather than to help herself.

It had taken months to unwind Rafe's belief she'd had an affair. During those months, they had to reconcile what had actually happened and what was false and manifesting as her memory, then showing up in her dreams. It was the first time anyone ever had to challenge Rafe's truth because it was hurting her. It was terrifying and messy and one of the hardest things Gabri had ever had to see Rafe go through.

Holding onto the belief that she'd had an affair seemed the root of most of her issues with Eden. Once they took those beliefs away, it was easier to help her with other things causing her torment, especially her thoughts she had to protect Eden from death.

They had also worked on a few of the things to do with Eden and the Stewards still haunting Rafe's dreams and caught in her mind. Gabri gave the doctor all the information from the attorney and Rafe's doctors in America, and it was decided most of those things could be worked on when Rafe was able to think more clearly about them. When her memories were corrected, and her PTSD was under control, they began to work on those issues, but they were far from resolved. There were still other issues with long roots not so easily traced and addressed without causing more grief.

They hadn't talked about if Rafe would try to reconcile with Eden or if she would only work to be a good co-parent to Bronte. But now, with Eden's unexpected visit, they might have to delve in before Rafe was ready. This filled Gabri with worry.

Gabri could see Rafe's thoughts were starting to get dark, and she was withdrawing. He gave her a nudge to get her attention. "Think tomorrow," he commanded. "We've been invited to a party tonight. The music festival will be starting soon, and everyone is meeting for a party to celebrate," he said, grinning and forcing himself to sound excited. "I need you to come and dance with me," he said as he pulled her up from the bench. "I will be the most famous musician because I have you by my side!" He laughed and drew her into a dance move.

Laughing, Rafe danced with Gabri down the path to the villa. "All *Firenze* will celebrate us!" She laughed. "The angel and his wild dancer!"

12

IN THE HOTEL room at the Palazzo Vecchietti, Eden Kingsley was cleaning up the lunch plates from room service to keep busy. She had reluctantly let Bronte go play with the au pair again at Julia's urging. As Eden worked, Julia watched from the other side of the room. Eden had told Julia about her visit to Gabri De Angelis and was still upset about the meeting. Eden could only hope Gabri would tell Rafe about Bronte, and he would call to set up a time for Rafe to see them.

"The hotel staff will get those," Julia pointed out, wishing they had gone out to one of the many restaurants nearby. They stayed in because Eden was in no shape to go out.

Eden looked at the plate in her hand and sighed as she sat it down. "I'm just trying to do something with myself so I don't lose control and cry again," she said and sat down in a chair at the table. She looked across the room at Julia desperately. "He called me selfish and cruel. Am I? Is showing up to see her selfish and cruel?"

"No," said Julia reassuringly. "You're here because you love her and want to help. You're here to make sure she sees her daughter."

Julia watched as Eden brushed crumbs from the tablecloth. She wasn't sure if she should feel guilty or happy about being right regarding how they would treat Eden. Julia wanted to be supportive. She knew Eden loved Rafe and wanted her back. Julia remembered her own pain when her feelings for Rafe weren't returned. She still felt that pain at times and could sympathize with Eden. But now, her romantic feelings had shifted to Eden, and Julia wanted them returned so they could both be happy. She was walking a fine emotional line, and it was a little confusing at times. Other times, it was very complicated to think about Rafe and the feelings she had for her for so long.

When they first met, Julia felt a bit like a sister to Rafe. Moving to New York with no friends had been hard and meeting Rafe made things easier. But even sisters get jealous or compete with each other.

The problem was, Julia always felt she lost at everything. It seemed like Rafe always got the best grades, had the most friends, more allowance, and more freedom in general, and of course, she always had a girlfriend. When they were younger, Julia always tried to think of Rafe as a sister, but it all changed when she started feeling and wanting Rafe to be more.

The rejection she got from Rafe when they were teenagers still blanketed Julia with frustration. When she finally came out to Rafe and told her how she felt, Julia was sure Rafe would feel the same, and they would be happy together. Instead, she was haunted by Rafe's mirth at the suggestion they date, and the memory of Rafe telling her they were better off as friends. Every day seemed to be a struggle after that, but she did her best to stay friends and keep a sisterly relationship with Rafe.

Years later, when they reconnected in college, Rafe just had to show off with all the degrees she was working toward and the business she had started. Julia had to hear about it constantly from her own father all the time. It was maddening. The most crushing part of finding each other again was Rafe still being uninterested in her. No matter how many times she humiliated herself by suggesting the possibility, or the trouble she went through to be there for Rafe to try to show her they could be good together, Rafe remained unmoved and thought of it as a joke.

Now Rafe was throwing away everything, including their friendship, and letting some man take over her life. She knew Gabri was Rafe's childhood friend, but she was Rafe's friend too. Rafe should have allowed her or her father to help. If she had, then Rafe would still be in America with the best care in the world.

Julia wasn't sure if she should be angry about Rafe throwing away everything, including Eden, or if she should just sit back and reap any benefits that might fall her way. The last time Rafe's antics ended up ruining a relationship was with Andrea.

Rafe had been dating Andrea for months then just disappeared and broke up with her in an email. Andrea was devastated and hurt. Julia couldn't believe Rafe would break up with her. Andrea was perfect. She was talented and smart and breathtakingly beautiful. Julia wasted no time in consoling her and letting her know she was available and interested.

Julia had dated several girls Rafe had dated, but it never worked out. She really thought things would be different with Andrea. It seemed like they were compatible in every way. They liked a lot of the same things, and the sex was great. A year into their relationship, so sure things could only get better, Julia had been ready to ask Andrea to get married.

They had already moved in together, and Julia convinced her father to hire Andrea to be an art curator for Hawthorn Financial. She was even hoping she and Andrea could start a subsidiary for clients who wanted to invest in fine art. Then Andrea announced she got a job offer in France. It wasn't even a better offer than what she was getting at Hawthorn Financial, but, for some reason, Andrea chose going to work in France instead of staying and making a life together. It was heartbreaking. In a sisterly way, Rafe had been there and helped her get through the pain of losing Andrea. The problem was Julia did not want a sister then—or now.

It seemed Rafe was breaking up with Eden like she had broken up with Andrea. The only difference was Rafe had her friend Gabri involved this time. She just wished Eden could see what Rafe was doing. She didn't want Eden to be hurt like Andrea. But this was different. Unlike Andrea, Eden had a child and needed Rafe so she could have a real dependable relationship and give Bronte a stable home life. Julia knew she could step in and be a reliable parent and give Bronte everything she needed, and she would do anything to make Eden happy.

For months, since her realization Eden should be the focus of her romantic attentions, Julia had been making subtle gestures to let Eden know she would be there for her. So far, Eden had not picked up on any of them. Eden hanging onto Rafe like a dog with a bone was very frustrating. Eden was still living in the fantasy that Rafe would come back.

Julia knew now, based on her own dreams and feelings, she must have known subconsciously that Eden was who she had wanted to be with for a long time. Her feelings for Rafe had just been in the way. Now all those old feelings for Rafe were in the past. She hoped this trip would open Eden's eyes to the truth about who really cared about her. The crux was the feeling of guilt she sometimes felt. She didn't want to be disloyal to Rafe, but she wanted Eden and the happiness they could have together. Switching loyalties was never easy, especially when the feelings were not yet mutual.

"He says I should have waited," said Eden breaking the long silence. "But I don't know how long he'd make me wait. What if Rafe thinks I've forgotten about her? What if she thinks I've done what she said and let go? I don't want her to think I did."

"You've been waiting and giving Gabri everything he's asked for," Julia reminded her. "You've sent videos and photos of Bronte. You've made sure Bronte got to see the videos he sent, and she got all the gifts they sent. They, on the other hand, haven't sent you anything about Rafe and how she's doing."

"Gabri said I could see how she was doing in the videos," said Eden softly. "But it's not the same."

"Right, and she hasn't answered emails or calls from any of us," Julia said annoyed. "It's like he's holding her prisoner."

Eden looked up at her with concern. "You don't think he's really holding her prisoner, do you?"

"No," said Julia thinking of her earlier run-in with Rafe. "As a matter of fact," she hesitated, "I actually saw her today."

"What?" Eden said looking up at her in surprise. She got up and moved to a chair closer to Julia. "You saw her? Where? How was she? Did you tell her I'm here? What did she say? Why didn't you tell me?"

"Hold on, hold on," said Julia at Eden's barrage of questions. "I saw her when I was at the Uffizi Gallery. She looked fine and sounded like she was fine. She didn't say much."

"What was she doing?" asked Eden wanting every detail she could get. "What did she say?"

"I saw her as she was leaving the museum," said Julia, seeing Eden was burning for all the information she could get, and it stung a little. "She was really quite rude. I asked her how she was doing, and she said she was fine and had to go. She said she didn't want to deal with me. Can you believe her? Then she got on her motorcycle and rode away."

"Her motorcycle?" asked Eden and then dismissed the information. "Did she say anything about me? Did you tell her I was here?"

"No," said Julia shaking her head. "I didn't say anything about you. I didn't know what was happening with your meeting. I didn't want to say anything, just in case there was some reason Gabri wasn't going to tell her about you, and we were leaving. I wasn't sure how much to tell her, so I just didn't tell her anything. I told her I was here with a friend is all."

Eden stared at Julia and didn't know how to react. The only reason they came was to see Rafe, and Julia saw her but didn't tell her about it right away. "Why didn't you tell me sooner?"

"I wanted to," said Julia seeing Eden was upset. "You just had so much you wanted to tell. I was waiting for the right moment. I wasn't going to keep it from you, I promise."

"No, I know," said Eden obviously jealous. "It's just, you saw her, and I want to see her so much."

"Well, it wasn't exactly a long or pleasant visit," she said wryly.

"Tell me how she looked," Eden pleaded intently. Her brown eyes burned bright with desperate curiosity. "Tell me whatever you can remember."

"Like I said, she looked fine," she said warily. "Healthy. Her hair was longer. She was wearing leather pants and a jacket. It was motorcycle riding clothes and boots. Her T-shirt was one of those touristy things with *Ciao Bella* on it. She was carrying an artist paint box." Julia tried to think of more details to make up for the guilt she was feeling edged with jealousy. "She wasn't happy to see me. She got away as quickly as she could. She said she had to be somewhere."

Eden was hoping for more but could see Julia struggling to think of things, so she knew Julia was at the limit of what she could tell. "I wonder where she had to be," she said softly. Eden wondered if Rafe had to go back to a hospital or sanatorium. "Do you think if we go back to the museum tomorrow, she'll be there?" she asked hopefully, thinking maybe Rafe was allowed out for some reason every day.

"I don't know," Julia said gently. "If Gabri tells her you're here, she may not go anywhere until she decides what to do." Julia didn't want Eden getting her hopes up about seeing Rafe out on the streets of Florence.

"What if he never calls?" Eden asked worriedly. "How will we be able to see her?"

"Let's not think about it now," Julia said with a shrug. "I told you, Rafe looked and sounded fine. Give them a while to process the news that we're here. Rafe will want to see you and Bronte," she said trying to sound positive even though she was doubtful.

"What if Gabri will only allow Bronte to see her and not me?" Eden asked, afraid it was exactly what would happen. "What do I do? Do I just let him take her? I don't know if I can," she admitted nervously, remembering Jake's words again about all the children taken from their mothers and spirited away to foreign countries. "You don't think they would keep her from me if they take her, do you?"

"No," said Julia reassuringly. "Rafe wouldn't do anything to hurt Bronte. I don't think she would let Gabri do it to you, either."

"I need to lic down," she told Julia as she felt her anxiety building. "Can you take care of Bronte for a while when she gets back?"

"Of course," said Julia. She gave a reassuring smile as Eden made her way into the bedroom. Someday, Julia would be able to hold Eden and tell her how she felt and not just give subtle hints. Sometime soon she hoped.

Eden lay on the bed, hoping Julia was right about Gabri. She closed her eyes picturing Rafe as Julia described her. It seemed like Gabri wasn't only limiting the time Eden could have, but he was also going to limit the conversation Eden could have with Rafe. Eden didn't know if she could talk to Rafe without telling her how she felt and telling her she loved her and wanted her to come home. Eden knew Rafe may want to stay longer if her doctor was helping her, and she did want her to get better, but she missed her. Eden needed to talk to her and hear her voice and look at her and just be in her presence. If she didn't get to see her, it wouldn't matter if she could look at her without pity or not.

Eden took a deep calming breath and did her relaxation techniques to keep her anxiety under control. As she breathed and thought about Rafe, she fell asleep and dreamed of her.

13

MUSIC FILLED THE air while food and drinks flowed freely and the people who filled the square sang, talked, and laughed. It was a perfect Saturday night to celebrate all the musicians coming together before the beginning of the local music festival. All the musicians were showing off to each other, and some were collaborating and writing new songs on the spot. Spirits were high and everywhere were beautiful sounds of voices and instruments that were a gift to all experiencing them.

Rafe Salvaggio watched as Nora finished singing and couldn't help but notice the beautiful blush on her face and the glow surrounding her as she took her bows to the cheers and admiration of the crowd. Rafe stood with the crowd and clapped for Nora then rushed to her to help her from the stage and escort her proudly to their table.

"You were wonderful!" Rafe said as she leaned close to talk directly into Nora's ear so she could hear over the crowd. "You have the voice of an angel."

Nora laughed and kissed Rafe promptly on her lips. "I think you're my biggest fan. How did I look up there with my large stomach? Was I grotesque?"

"You're beautiful," said Rafe with a laugh because Nora was, very. "How can you think you're anything else? Look, they all love you and would die to be in your presence."

"You're so dramatic!" Nora laughed at Rafe and her teasing.

"Look, Stefano is carrying the guitars, and Gabri is just behind him," said Rafe as she pointed to the two men. "They should be playing soon. Let's get you something to eat," she said and called the waiter to order more food and drinks for the table. Rafe turned back to Nora. "Will you clap and cheer for me as much as I did for you if I dance for you?" she asked with a laugh. "All *Firenze* means nothing to me if you are not pleased with all you see," she said dramatically and opened her arms in the offering.

"You're very drunk," exclaimed Nora laughing at Rafe's antics, "but yes, I will be your biggest fan!" She kissed Rafe briefly as everyone at the table laughed and cheered them on.

"We are all very drunk on our love for you!" she shouted, and everyone cheered again. "Look," Rafe pointed to the stage. "It's Gabri! It is the *Angelo di Firenze!*" she yelled and made her way to the stage with others who had been waiting for him to perform. She got to the stage and waved at Gabri who smiled and laughed. "Gabri, you promised we would dance!" she reminded him as he began to play.

Gabri and his band played and sang while Rafe and everyone on the square danced to his music, feeling the beat and singing his words. Nora came out and found Rafe and danced a few steps with her then went back to her seat, laughing in amazement, as always, at the excitement Gabri brought to the party. Soon, it was close to the end of his song, and he set his guitar down. Jumping out into the crowd, he danced with Rafe as he promised. Stefano didn't let the music end so they could all dance a little longer. Gabri and Rafe laughed and danced to the cheers and encouragement of the crowd until the music finally ended, and they were exhausted. Gabri kissed Rafe to the cheers of the crowd and leaped back onto the stage to play his next song as Rafe made her way back to Nora.

"Did you cheer and clap?" Rafe asked breathlessly.

"Yes, I did!" Nora laughed and kissed Rafe again playfully. "You two are so beautiful together," she said as her eyes sparkled. "I still think if he put a photo of the two of you on his next album, it would sell out!" she declared for probably the hundredth time since she had first seen them together.

Rafe laughed. "The cover won't sell the music, and his music is what the people want." Rafe picked up her glass of wine and quenched her thirst as they listened to Gabri sing the rest of his set, and the crowd cheered him as he finished. Rafe leaned close to Nora. "Gabri says that when he's finished, we're invited to a private party with some big music producers. I think they believe they can romance him. He said we should meet him at the car."

"Oh, Rafe," Nora groaned. "I was hoping we were going home. You know I'd stay out later but look at me. I'm huge and tired."

Rafe saw she did look tired. "I'm sorry," she said with concern. "I'll see if we can take the car home, and they can get a ride to the party and home later."

"Now that sounds like a great plan." Nora smiled in appreciation but could see she had taken down Rafe's excitement for the night. "But first, I'd like to see you dance again. I don't think I've seen all you have to offer." She winked as another band began to play on stage.

"Oh, really?" asked Rafe and arched her brow seductively. "The fact you could see I have more to offer than anyone here is what makes me love you more," she said then stood up and offered her hand. "I will dance you into the night." She took Nora's hand, and they danced through the crowd to get to the other side of the plaza. Gabri and Stefano had already gone with their instruments where the car waited further down one of the side streets.

Nora laughed as they danced and held tightly to Rafe who was still feeling her wine. Rafe would break away and dance for her then come back and take her arm and hold her close as they made their way to the car.

"You'll be feeling this night tomorrow!" Nora claimed teasingly as Rafe kissed her cheek and pulled her along gently.

"I feel everything now," she said as they walked. "I feel the music and how you captured me with your voice and your beauty. My love for you will make me live for you forever," she teased elaborately

"That will be a first," Nora joked, loving Rafe's attention. "Where were you when I was a gangly teenager?" She tried to take a step forward, but Rafe stopped dead in front of her. "What are you doing now?" she asked playfully.

Rafe had stopped suddenly at the vision in front of her. She watched as the two women, one golden and one silver-haired, sitting at the sidewalk table, talked to each other and one held the others hand across the table. Then they shared bites of food and laughed. They looked very happy. Rafe heard Nora's questioning, and she turned to look at her.

"It's nothing," Rafe said and began to lead Nora away. She had recognized Eden and Julia immediately. Rafe knew now the reason Eden wanted to see her. It was to tell her she and Julia were together. Rafe had pushed them together before she left so she shouldn't be surprised. At least now she would be prepared.

"Rafe!" a voice called out as Rafe led Nora away.

Nora pulled on Rafe to stop her. "Rafe, someone's calling you. Do you know those women?"

Looking over at Nora sadly, Rafe sighed. "Yes," she said softly. She hesitated a moment then held Nora's arm as she walked them to the table. Rafe looked from Eden to Julia, finding it difficult to look directly at them. "Hello," she said, trying to sound happy, forcing a smile to her face. "You both look wonderful. I'm so happy for you. I would stay and talk, but I have to get Nora home. Hope you enjoy your time here," she said and began to pull Nora away.

In confusion, Eden looked from Rafe to the very pregnant woman next to her, barely hearing what Rafe was saying. As Rafe began to walk away, she snapped her head around looking Julia in shock then stood up. "Rafe! Rafe, I need to talk to you!" she called to her.

"Shit," said Julia under her breath. She tried to wrap her mind around the situation and stood with Eden.

"Who are those people?" Nora asked as Rafe pulled her away.

"People I used to know," Rafe said shakily. "I need to go home."

"Okay," said Nora. Seeing the immediate change in Rafe's mood and appearance made her worry.

"Rafe!" Eden called out. "Wait, please. I just want to talk to you! What are you doing?" She turned to Julia, "What's happening?" she asked shakily. Eden went after Rafe and the woman she was with and was holding onto so closely. *This cannot be happening*, she thought. *Maybe this was why Gabri didn't want me to see Rafe—because she's with someone new.* She caught up with Rafe and called her again, "Rafe, stop!"

Nora pulled Rafe to a stop. "I think the American woman wants to talk with you," she said in Italian. "Is there something wrong? Is she someone from a museum you gave a drawing to and now you're trying to avoid?"

Rafe frowned at Nora then turned as Eden came upon them. "I'm sorry, I can't talk to you right now," said Rafe politely in English but avoided looking up at Eden. "Please, call Gabri and set up a time tomorrow, or whenever."

Eden couldn't believe Rafe really wasn't going to talk to her. "Why are you doing this?" she asked in disbelief then pointed at Nora. "Who is she? I don't understand what's happening."

"I'm not doing anything. I was just polite," said Rafe doing her best to stay calm. "This is Nora," she said as she held tightly to her hand. "I'm just taking her home," Rafe said shakily. She was not ready to have a conversation with Eden. Rafe just wanted to get away before things escalated in the street. "We have to go," she said and started to walk away again.

"Stop!" said Eden and grasped Rafe's arm, pulling her back around, and Nora caught herself as she was pulled off balance at the sudden movement because Rafe had been holding her hand.

Gabri was at their side, it seemed from nowhere. He took Nora's arm and steadied her then took Rafe's arm pulling her away from Eden. "What are you doing," Gabri said in his accented English as Stefano took Nora and walked her away. "Don't touch them!" he barked. "If you cannot control yourself, you should not talk to her!" he yelled at Eden and then tugged on Rafe's arm, leading her away.

"Wait, Gabri! I just wanted to talk to her," said Eden desperately.

Gabri released Rafe and turned on Eden angrily. "Yes, and she said to call me for a time! Listen! Now you go back with your friend," he said pointing to Julia who had been watching things unfold. Then he turned and caught up with Rafe and retook her arm. "She will not talk to you this way," said Gabri reverting back to Italian. "I'm sorry this happened."

"I'm sorry," said Rafe shakily. "I could have ignored them when they called to me, but I didn't want to be rude again in front of Nora."

"What did they want?" Gabri asked with concern. "Why were they chasing after you?"

"I don't know," said Rafe uneasily. "Everything was just a blur. I was just trying to walk away."

"I'm glad we decided to come back to walk with you after putting the instruments away in the car instead of going straight to the party," said Gabri. "My heart nearly stopped when I saw Nora almost fall."

"I tried to hang on to her," said Rafe and tears threatened to come to her eyes. "I'm sorry, Gabri."

Seeing Rafe upset, Gabri's heart hurt for her. He wanted to be confident that she was calm. "I know you tried," he said and put a calming hand on her. "It's not your fault. I know you love her and want to keep her and the baby safe," he said firmly. They made it to the car, and Gabri opened the car door. "Let's get in the car and go home."

"What about your party?" asked Rafe. She recovered from the moment and was happy no tears actually fell to reveal her weakness. "It's important. Nora and I can go home. We'll be fine now," she said and turned to Nora who was in the driver's seat. "You're fine, right? Gabri shouldn't miss the party. We'll be okay now, won't we?"

Nora looked from Rafe to Gabri. She could tell Rafe didn't want to be the reason for Gabri to miss meeting the people who would be at the party. "We'll be fine," said Nora reassuringly.

Gabri sighed and nodded his head. "Okay," he said as Rafe closed the back door then walked around and got into the passenger's seat. He walked around the car and leaned on the driver's door. "Be careful," he said softly to Nora. "Stefano and I will be there after the party."

"Bye," said Nora and Gabri kissed her through the car window.

"Goodbye," he said and smiled at her. "Drive carefully." He looked past Nora at Rafe. "We'll talk tomorrow."

"Okay," said Rafe as Nora put the car in gear then drove them toward home. "I'm sorry about what happened," she apologized to Nora softly.

"Do you want to tell me who they were?" Nora asked gently.

"I don't want to talk about it right now."

They drove home in silence.

14

JULIA HAWTHORN TOOK care of the check at the restaurant and walked back to the hotel with Eden who was upset, crying, and trying not to let her anxiety overtake her. It may have escaped Eden's notice, but Gabri seemed to speak excellent English for someone who needed a translator.

"Why wouldn't she talk to us?" Eden asked the night as her face glistened with tears.

"She was the same way when I saw her," Julia reminded Eden.

"Who was the woman with her?" asked Eden as she wiped her face. "Did you see she was pregnant?"

"I saw," said Julia evenly. All kinds of scenarios ran through her head about who the woman could be. She decided not to give into conjecture because Eden was already so upset. "She's probably just a friend."

"What if she's more? What if Rafe's over here starting a new family, and Gabri's helping her?" asked Eden upset. "I can't take this!"

Julia took Eden by the arm and stopped her. "Eden, that's nonsense. Rafe's only been here six months. She may be good at picking up women, but I don't think she could talk someone into having a baby for her in such a short time."

"I don't know," said Eden, pulling her arm away from Julia in frustration. "Back when the article about her came out, women were propositioning her all the time and telling her they'd have her baby."

"Yes, and all those women were either half-crazy or lying to get Rafe in bed," Julia argued, though she wasn't sure why. "Rafe never took any of it seriously—no one took those propositions seriously."

"Why was she telling us to have a nice time here?" Eden asked at a loss. "She must know I'm here to see her. Why is she telling us she's glad we're happy?"

"I don't know," said Julia. "She was using her 'I don't want to be here, but I have to be polite' act on us too." Julia followed Eden as she started toward the hotel again. "Maybe she was just caught off guard," she suggested. "She did tell you to call Gabri so it seems like she may want to talk to you."

"She could have talked to me right then," she retorted. "This is just so frustrating, Julia. I can't just talk to her. I have to make an appointment through someone. I never thought she would treat me like this. Is she trying to tell me it's really over? Is she still trying to push me away?" Eden couldn't hold in tears that she was fighting any longer. "Is she telling me there's no hope, and she really doesn't love me anymore?"

Julia stopped and pulled Eden into an embrace. Her opinion was 'yes' to all those things, but she knew to say so to Eden wouldn't help the situation.

"Don't worry. I'm here for you," Julia said softly. "I'll always be here for you."

15

TAKING HER GLASS of wine to the small wooden kitchen table, Rafe Salvaggio sat down, opened her drawing notebook, and began to draw. After getting home from the festival, she made sure Nora was safely in her bed. Then Rafe unloaded Gabri's instruments and put them in the studio. After Rafe had taken care of things in the main house, she made her way back to her cottage. She took a shower, hoping it would relax her so she could sleep, but sleep eluded her.

The vision of Eden and Julia filled her mind, and she tried to convince herself that the two of them being together was probably for the best. Rafe knew she had a long way to go before she could resolve all the issues she was struggling with, and Eden deserved someone who could take care of her. She knew it was too much to expect Eden to wait on her, especially being a continent away.

So much had happened that it felt impossible for Rafe to imagine any resolution between them. Being here, far away from everything, made Rafe feel disconnected from it all now. It was like a bad dream she couldn't shake. Sometimes, it was literally a nightmare, and it made it hard for her to want to go to sleep.

Gabri could help take Rafe's mind off things during the day, but when she was alone, especially at night, the things she struggled with came flooding into her mind. It would not be so bad if just one thing came into her mind at a time, and she could focus and be able to resolve the issue. But it wasn't how things were working. Her thoughts and issues seemed to tangle together and come out as a big knot. It seemed with every advance at untangling things, another knot was there to add to the tangle. It sometimes became too much, and she had to do anything she could to stop herself from thinking. Tonight, she found it impossible to push her thoughts away.

She had known Eden was in Italy because Gabri had told her. She even guessed Julia was with her. But seeing them together made it real. She wondered what Gabri had told Eden about her problems if anything. She tried not to think about it. She agreed months ago to allow Gabri to handle everything where communication was concerned so she could focus on getting well. Maybe Eden didn't want to be with someone with problems like hers. She could not blame her. She couldn't blame anyone. She wondered how long Gabri would be out at the party and if she should ask for a sleeping pill when he came home.

Papa made sure to keep everything quiet about the time she spent with the doctor when she was younger here in Italy. They even hid the few times she needed help while living in New York. For a while, it seemed every serious relationship Rafe was in had to be evaluated and picked apart. It had to be decided if the person was trustworthy and would be able to handle the responsibilities of knowing about her illness and what it entailed.

Sometimes, it felt as if she would always be on the cusp of a relationship, never to have anything complete and real. No one ever seemed worthy to her father, and Rafe always agreed with him to break things off—until Eden. It was harder with Eden. When things started getting serious, her papa would broach the subject of whether or not Eden was worthy enough to tell about her past. At the time, she struggled with the fact she didn't want to make her past the reason for ending a relationship again. Rafe felt she couldn't end the relationship because she was in love with Eden. But she couldn't tell Eden about her past, either. In fact, she begged her papa not to tell Eden about what had happened in her childhood.

Rafe finally convinced her papa, and herself, telling anyone about her past would hurt more than help at that point in her life. She was older and hadn't had any problems for a long time. Plus, Rafe thought with Eden's anxieties that it would make her have doubts and second thoughts about being together. She knew it was dishonest, but she swore to her papa she would tell Eden if she ever had to. He had been insisting she tell Eden since they were planning to have a child, but Rafe still couldn't bring herself to do it. He died, then Eden left, and everything else happened. None of those secrets seemed to matter anymore.

When Eden came back, Rafe thought that telling her about the past would only complicate things more. She did try to tell Eden before she left home with Gabri. She told her a lot of things, but she just couldn't stand the look in Eden's eyes afterward. Now it was too late to come clean, and it probably didn't matter anymore anyway.

Rafe looked up at the knock on her door. Putting down her pencil, she got up and answered the door wondering if Gabri had come home already.

"Nora," Rafe said with surprise. "Is everything okay?"

"I was going to ask you the same," she said as she stepped inside out of the night. "I got up to use the restroom, and I saw your light was still on."

"I'm fine," Rafe said with a small smile to reassure her.

"Good," said Nora and gave her a hug, "then you can make me some tea to help me get back to sleep."

"Sure." Rafe chuckled and led her to the small kitchen. She closed her drawing pad and moved it off the table then went to the stove to start the water for tea as Nora sat down. She set out everything for tea then sat down across from Nora. "So, why can't you sleep," Rafe asked with concern. "Is the baby moving too much?"

"The baby's fine," she said and took Rafe's hand across the table. "I was worried about you and what happened tonight. Who were those women and why did they upset you?"

Rafe looked down at their hands, gave Nora's hand a squeeze, and then sighed. She didn't want to tell Nora what was happening. She didn't want Nora to be upset if Bronte couldn't visit. Nora loved watching the videos of Bronte with her. She said it was like getting a sneak preview of what her baby would look like. She helped Rafe pick out gifts and helped her and Gabri make videos to send to Bronte. They made a lot more videos than they sent, but someday, Rafe hoped Bronte would see them all, especially the ones all three of them were in. She looked up into Nora's eyes and could see she wouldn't take no for an answer.

"It was Eden," she said softly.

"Eden? Your Eden?" Nora asked in surprise. She put her fingers to her temple and shook her head in disbelief. She berated herself for not recognizing Eden from all of Rafe's drawings. "Why didn't we talk to her? We could have stayed and had a coffee with her, or invited her here. Did she bring Bronte?"

"Gabri is going to set up a time for me to see them," said Rafe as the kettle whistled. She got up and poured the water into the teapot to steep the tea, then brought it to the table as Nora watched her.

Nora wrinkled her brow in disbelief. "Gabri? What are you talking about?"

Rafe shrugged. "Eden came to see Gabri today. She asked him to tell me she was here with Bronte."

"Wait. She was here at the house today?" Nora asked confused.

"Yeah." Rafe nodded and hung her head. "Gabri told her he would talk to me and set up a time for us to meet and spend time with Bronte."

"Okay, I'm confused," she said with a frown. "Why does she have to have an appointment to see you, and why does Gabri get to decide when it is?"

"I don't know," said Rafe feeling helpless under her unhappy gaze. Now there was someone else she was disappointing. "It's just better if he handles it. The doctor told him I should have short or monitored visits to make sure I don't get too pressured or stressed."

Nora stared at Rafe for a moment not understanding the situation. "What do you have to feel stressed or pressured about? The way you talk about Eden, I would think you'd be happy she's here." Nora watched as Rafe poured their tea but said nothing. "Why aren't you happy she's here?"

Rafe fidgeted with her cup a moment then looked up at Nora sadly. "I think she's here to get closure... maybe." She shrugged and shifted uncomfortably. "The other woman she was with is Julia. I think they're together now." She stopped not knowing what else to say.

"You think?" Nora repeated. "What makes you think they're together? Did she tell Gabri something?"

"No," said Rafe softly. "It's just things they did, things I saw."

"Like what?"

"Just things," said Rafe and took a sip of her tea. "Drink your tea."

Nora shook her head at Rafe then took a sip of her tea. "Aw, is this chamomile?"

"Yes." Rafe smiled because Nora recognized the tea.

"Why do you and Gabri always make this?" she asked annoyed. "I swear between the two of you I've had more chamomile tea in the past seven months than I can stand."

"But it's good for you," said Rafe with a frown. "It helps with everything and helps you relax."

Nora sighed heavily and shook her head. "First, it doesn't cure everything," she insisted, "and second, there's only so much of the stuff a girl can take, especially a pregnant one."

"We don't give it to you all the time," said Rafe with a sulk. "Just when you say you're not feeling well or need to relax. I know it doesn't cure everything, it just helps, and it's fine to drink in moderation when you're pregnant. I use to make it for..."

Nora frowned at Rafe's hurt expression, knowing she meant to say Eden. "Fine, don't worry, I'll drink it." She took another sip of the tea to prove her words. "Now, tell me why you think she's here for closure. What things are you talking about?"

Rafe took a deep breath and let it out slowly. "I guess one thing is I saw Julia outside the Uffizi today, and she didn't tell me Eden was here. Why wouldn't she tell me?" Rafe looked down into her cup. "I think maybe it's because she knew Eden was here asking to see me. She probably didn't want to say anything until Eden could talk to me."

"Okay," said Nora as she considered Rafe's words. "What else?"

"Tonight," said Rafe, "you saw them. They were holding hands and sharing food and looked so happy together."

Nora sat back in her chair and thought about the two women and what she remembered about them. "They looked like two tourists enjoying dinner in Italy," she said thoughtfully. "They shared a bite of their meal, so what? They knew each other, so they touched hands, so what? I don't think it means anything." She saw Rafe wasn't convinced. "Well, what do you think they saw when they looked back at us?"

Rafe frowned then sat back in her chair and wished Nora had not come down. "I don't know," she said edgily.

"Let's think about it," she said seeing Rafe was uncomfortable. "Between you and Gabri, neither of you think I can take a step on my own, especially over the cobblestone, so I was holding tightly onto your arm, and you were holding on to me when you weren't dancing around. You were a little drunk, and we were joking, laughing and even shared a few friendly kisses. We're very good friends, but do you think, to her, it's all it looked like?"

"But you're pregnant. Eden would know I'm not with you," Rafe scoffed.

"Oh, please," Nora reproached with a weary groan. "Just because I'm pregnant doesn't mean I couldn't be your lover. I'm sure you made love to Eden while she was pregnant. If you didn't, then she *should* leave you," said Nora with a small laugh. "But I think I know you, so I'm probably right." She watched Rafe try not to smile, knowing she was right. "She could think you're the one who needs closure." Nora watched as Rafe considered her words. "So, don't you think you should talk to her before you jump to conclusions?"

"Maybe," Rafe asserted then looked up at Nora. "Before I left," she paused, "I kind of pushed them together, so I wouldn't be surprised if I'm right."

"You were sick," she countered. "I'm sure you did and said a lot of things you didn't mean. I remember Gabri having to deal with some of the things you were saying. But now you're getting better. Did you mean the things you said? Do you really want them to be together?"

Rafe threw up her hands in frustration. "I don't know if what I want even matters. I don't know why she's here or what she wants." She couldn't hide the misery in her eyes. "I'll just be happy if she lets me see Bronte and will let her come back when the baby is born." She put her head in her hands. "I'm just having a hard time right now. Too much is running through my head," she said sadly.

Nora stood up and went to Rafe. She took Rafe's face in her hands. "One thing you shouldn't have going through your mind is what Eden might have to say. You should meet her and let her tell you. Good or bad. Don't torture yourself when you can know by asking." She kissed Rafe's forehead. "Come on. Let's get you in bed," she said and pulled Rafe up then led her to the bedroom.

"You know it's easier said than done, right?" said Rafe as Nora pushed her gently into the bed.

"Yes, because you love her," said Nora and sat on the bed next to Rafe.

"No, because I need a pill," shot Rafe.

Nora frowned. She didn't like Rafe asking for pills again so she pretended to ignore the comment for the moment. "If you didn't love her, you wouldn't think so much about her."

"No, I think about her so much because I'm fucked up and confused," said Rafe crossly.

Nora sighed and shook her head. "Scoot over," she said, and Rafe moved to give her room in the bed. She lay down and got herself into a comfortable position. "Try to sleep. I'll tell Gabri to check on you when he gets home to see if you really need a pill." She put her arm around Rafe. "I know you love her," she whispered into her ear."

"How?" Rafe asked softly as she stared at the wall.

"Because I know how much you and Gabri are alike," she said softly. "I see how you two are together. It's scary how even when you're apart you think alike. I see how much you love each other. I'm positive about how Gabri loves you. I was so jealous when you first came," she confessed. "I was his pregnant wife, and he was spending every moment with you. Then I saw you two one night, and you were both drunk and crying as you held each other. You could have ended up in bed together, but you didn't. Then I knew there was something else going on. I put my jealousy aside and got to know you. I talked to Gabri about you, and I really listened to him. You two went through so much together and are so close because of it all."

"Then you found out I was gay," Rafe reminded her with a chuckle, "so you knew I wasn't a threat. I don't do men."

Nora laughed softly. "There is that," she agreed. "But it's not what I'm talking about. I'm talking about how you two love. I think because of your love for each other, and the things you went through together, you can't help but pour all your feelings and love into the person you decide to give your hearts. You both even picked blonds from America," she teased. "He showed me your drawings of Cyprian the Fair from when you were young. You drew her blond and fair, and he told me she was also called Venus by some."

"He showed you those drawings?" Rafe shook her head and rolled her eyes. "Those are terrible."

"You were a teenager, and actually, they're excellent," said Nora. "He was thinking of using one on his CD cover." She listened to Rafe groan about the news and smiled. "I think you two fell in love with Eden and me because of those drawings and your American mother. Otherwise, you would have fallen in love with each other."

"My mother?" asked Rafe confused.

She chuckled. "Yes, Gabri told me how he was in love with both you and your mother when he was young."

"I don't know anything about that," said Rafe trying to wrap her head around the information. "We couldn't fall in love with each other. I'm gay, remember?"

"Anyway," Nora said ignoring her stubbornness, "don't think you can change the subject." She shifted to get comfortable again. "I know Gabri loves me more than he loves his own life, and he proves it in every move he makes, every decision, every look or touch. It's like this cloak he puts over me." She moved her lips close to Rafe's ear. "I think you love the same way. I can feel it and know you love me. Not like you love Eden, but it's like your love for Gabri covers the baby and me now. I think you love Eden like Gabri loves me. I think you can't help yourself." She took a calming breath. "I believe it's why she's here," she said softly.

"I do love you," Rafe said quietly. "I'll always love you."

"I believe you." Nora smiled to herself. "I think, if Gabri ever left me, you'd be by my side taking care of me."

"He would never leave you," she whispered.

"I think you're right," she said feeling a surge of love for Rafe and her reassuring words. "But, if he ever did, I don't think you'd have any problems convincing me to become a. . ." She hesitated as she searched for the Italian word.

"*Lesbica*," said Rafe helpfully. "But don't say it too loud. We're in Italy." She chuckled. "Not everyone here would stay in love with me if they knew."

"I don't think anyone who knows you would care," she said laughing softly. "My god you smell good." She breathed in Rafe's scent. "I think you may smell better than Gabri," she quipped.

"It's my sexy lesbian smell," Rafe teased. "I'll buy you the soap I use to give to Gabri." She turned her head to look at Nora. "You wouldn't have to be gay for me to take care of you."

"No, no," Nora said as she laughed. "That's not what I'm trying to say. I mean, in that scenario, I would probably fall in love with you because of the way you love. Like I said, I can feel it from you, the love you have for me."

"Yes," Rafe pretended to yawn, "I'm irresistible, just like Gabri, but I smell better."

Nora laughed again. "You both also have big heads. I'm trying to show you how Eden might feel," she said with a sigh. "I'm failing, I think." She kissed Rafe's head.

"I think you're doing fine," said Rafe softly. "You have a voice like an angel. Keep talking, I should fall asleep soon," she chuckled lightly.

"Just remember I'm talking metaphorically and don't go telling Gabri all this," she said and tapped her on the head.

"He already knows you're madly in love with me," said Rafe with a shrug.

"Oh, he does?" she scoffed as Rafe nodded her head into the pillow. "Well, I guess I'm as bad as the two of you at hiding who I love." She kissed Rafe's head. "You love her. Just maybe she loves you too." She listened as Rafe sighed but said nothing. "If you promise to talk to her, and be nice, and listen to her, I'll sing to you," she said softly. "I know how you love to hear me sing."

Rafe knew Nora had her best interests at heart and wanted her to be happy. She just didn't know everything going on and what had happened. She also knew Nora could keep talking all night, and she was right, she did love it when she sang. "Since you're making fun of me, you have to sing Venus," said Rafe and grinned into her pillow. "The one by Frankie Avalon

"Seriously?" Nora groaned.

"Oh, did I pick a song you don't know?" Rafe chortled.

"No," said Nora, resigned to her fate. "I know it." She shook her head and took a breath then sang. "Hey, Venus, oh, Venus..." Nora began.

After the first verse, Rafe laughed and turned over to join her in the song. They sang with gusto then finished it together.

"Make my wish come true—"

The last note was sung, and they laughed. Then Nora kissed Rafe on her forehead. "Yes, it's definitely your love song. You just remember when you talk to Eden."

"You sing beautifully." Rafe smiled then closed her eyes, purposely not responding to her about Eden. "Now will you sing Soft Kitty?"

"No!" Nora laughed and gave her a playful slap on her arm. "Go to sleep."

"I love you, Nora," said Rafe softly trying not to grin as she wrapped her arms around her.

"I love you too," she said and held her close.

Nora fell asleep and Rafe's mind kept her from the same peace.

16

IT WAS EARLY Sunday morning, and Nora De Angelis was up, answering the call of the baby pressing into her bladder. She came out of the restroom and looked over at Rafe, who was asleep. She wondered how long Rafe had laid awake before her mind allowed her to rest. Nora still couldn't believe how beautiful Rafe was, even after all these months of looking at her. She was tempted to draw a mustache on her in her sleep, but then she would probably look like the most beautiful boy she had ever seen, and it would just make things worse.

She laughed at herself at the thought. Gabri would have some competition then. The two of them together were like something Michelangelo or Bernini would have carved or like they were exquisite people who walked out of a beautiful painting from the Renaissance. They only needed the clothes. Somehow, they enhanced each other. She thought that maybe it was because of how close and comfortable they were with each other. She still believed if Gabri put a photo of the two of them on his CD, it would make it sell even more copies, though they both laughed at the idea.

Nora made her way to the kitchen and cleaned up the tea set and wine glass from last night and then looked over and saw Rafe's drawing pad. She loved looking at the drawings Rafe made and the paintings she seemed to make with such ease. She picked up the pad and thumbed through it looking at the illustrations.

"Oh, Rafe," she said with a sigh as she closed the pad and put it back. She took one last look around and then quietly went out the door to go back to the main house.

Walking into her bedroom, Nora found Gabri had dragged himself home sometime in the night. She went over to the bed sat down and kissed him gently. He was so beautiful. Nora knew the moment she saw him that she wanted to be with him, and the first time he kissed her, Nora knew she would marry him. She was so happy he felt the same way.

He was upset when Rafe missed the wedding, but he knew she was busy starting her new job at the time. He emailed Rafe about the baby due in May, but she didn't answer his emails or calls. Not long afterward, Rafe sent an email telling him she had been in a hospital. No one had contacted Gabri about it, and he was distraught. The next email was everything about transferring Rafe's power of attorney to Gabri. Gabri was so concerned that he couldn't get to America fast enough. It was fortunate he happened to have taken a job there, and he was able to check on her in person.

Nora had no idea who Rafe really was when she first arrived. She knew nothing about her except what she learned from Gabri in his stories about Rafe and her father, Ettore. She knew Rafe was a big part of Gabri's life, but she didn't know her personally. Nora was telling Rafe the truth about her jealousy when Gabri brought the beautiful woman home, and it seemed he spent every waking moment with her. Then the doctor showed up, and she knew something was wrong. Gabri finally got to a place where he would talk to her about everything. It was then she decided to get to know Rafe. She was so glad she didn't react first and think later. Otherwise, she might not have Rafe as the friend she loved so much now.

"Hey, beautiful lady," said Gabri in Italian as he opened his eyes and saw Nora looking down at him.

Nora smiled down at him. "Good morning," she said speaking to him in his native language. "What time did you get home?"

"Late," he said with a yawn. "I saw your note. Was Rafe okay last night?"

"She was fine," she said and kissed him gently. "I stayed with her because she was having a hard time and not sleeping. We had tea then I lay down with her. She made me sing Frankie Avalon." She smiled at the memory.

Gabri laughed. "Venus?"

"Yes." She laughed with him.

"Be thankful it wasn't the one by Bananarama," he said with a chuckle.

Nora smiled at the thought. "Are you getting up or staying in bed? I'm starving." She got up and started changing her clothes.

Gabri watched her from the bed and couldn't help but smile knowing she loved him. He remembered the first night they had met. He had not yet seen her but heard a beautiful voice singing and had to know who sang so sweetly. He made his way through the crowd and saw a vision standing next to the piano. The piano player was terrible. He went up, tapped him out, and then played for her. When he saw Nora smile, he knew his heart was lost before even knowing her name. He was so happy when she met with him again, and finally, he had to kiss her. From that moment, she was all he lived for, and they sang so many beautiful songs together.

"I'll eat with you." He yawned then got out of bed and dressed. "Maybe I'll try to come take a nap with you after lunch to catch up on my sleep."

They went down to the kitchen where Gabri made cappuccino and Nora got out the fruit and brioche with jam. When everything was ready, they sat down and enjoyed their breakfast.

"Thank you for not making chamomile tea," said Nora as she sipped her milk-heavy cappuccino. Gabri smiled at her as he chewed his food. "Why didn't you tell me Eden was here yesterday?"

Gabri stopped chewing and shifted in his chair. "It was up to Rafe, and it looks like she told you." He shrugged as if it was nothing.

"Why did you send her away? You knew Rafe would be home for lunch. Why didn't you ask her to stay?" she asked looking at him sternly.

"Because I don't want her derailing Rafaella's progress," he said tensely.

"How can seeing the woman she loves derail her progress?" she asked with an arched eyebrow. She knew when Gabri called Rafe by her full name, he was in protective mode.

"You don't understand, Nora," he said then sipped his coffee.

"Help me understand then," she insisted, "because it seems to me you're interfering where you shouldn't."

Gabri put his coffee down and sighed in frustration. "Eden and her friends are why Rafaella was in the shape she was when I brought her here. They pushed her further into her sickness and were making her worse. I won't allow them to do it again."

"Well, Rafe loves her, and I think Eden is here because she loves Rafe," she said firmly. "I listened to you complain about how Eden knew nothing about Rafe's problems, so, if it's true, then she didn't mean to do anything to hurt her." Gabri was frowning, but she continued despite his displeasure. "Maybe you should consider telling her what happened to Rafe so she'll understand."

"No," Gabri said sharply. "She is not Rafaella's family. Even Rafaella told her nothing."

"She is her family," said Nora firmly. "Eden is Bronte's mother, and she has the right to know."

"I told her I'd make an appointment when Rafaella is ready," he said hoping to end the conversation.

"Well, I think she's ready. You should call her," Nora informed Gabri.

"She's not ready," he said flatly. "Eden is here to push and pressure to get whatever it is she wants, and I won't allow it."

"You won't allow it?" scoffed Nora. "How do you know she wants something? What did she tell you?" She watched as Gabri scowled at her. "What did she say?"

"She only said she wanted to see Rafaella," he said in exasperation. "Stefano and I made sure she didn't stay long."

Nora eyed him suspiciously. "Stefano and you?" She put down her fork with a bite of brioche still on it. "Gabri," she said in annoyance, "what exactly did you do? Did you double team and scare her with your angry Italian man and translator act?" She caught his guilty face. "I can't believe you! You intimidated her! You speak perfectly good English. Why would you pretend you don't?"

"So she would listen," said Gabri affronted by her chastising. "I don't want her to see Rafaella if she is going to do the things she did before. I don't want her to hurt her again and send her into a trance. I am protecting her!"

"You're protecting her? From Eden? The woman who loves her?" Nora demanded. "Have you seen Rafe's notebooks? They are full of drawings of Eden and Bronte. Don't you think seeing them would help her?"

"How do you know she loves her?" Gabri demanded. "Even Rafaella isn't sure!"

"For a man who writes such beautiful love songs, you are so blind!" she yelled back. "What woman travels thousands of miles, with a baby, puts up with a bully like you, and waits by a phone in a foreign country for a call that may not come, unless she loves someone? I swear you and Rafe are so hard headed!" She fumed with flashing angry eyes. "You are not her father, and you have no right to interfere in her relationship."

"I may not be her father, but you are not her mother!" he yelled back. "I have every right! I have her power of attorney!"

"I guarantee you the paperwork says nothing about you dictating her love life!" Nora yelled. "I may not be her mother, but at least I can see she loves Eden!" She picked up her fork. "You need to fix this," she said trying to calm herself.

"Fix—" Gabri choked out.

"Yes, this is your fault," said Nora. "If you hadn't put yourself between them, this wouldn't be happening."

"Nora, Nora, Nora," Gabri said pleadingly. "Even her doctor thinks she's not ready for this. I have to make sure she stays well."

Nora shook her head at him. "I know the doctor made her decision based on whatever you told her," she said and knew she was right by the guilty look on his face. "You can't protect her from everything. She has to live again. Keeping her from love will hurt her more than help her, and you know it. She couldn't sleep last night and even talked about asking for a pill. She needs to know so she can put her mind at ease."

"This is why Eden should have stayed home," Gabri insisted.

"If it turns out Eden doesn't love her, we can help Rafe find love again," said Nora hoping Gabri would see reason "But she deserves to know why Eden is here, and she deserves to see Bronte."

Gabri took a short breath and tried to hide the tear forming in his eye. "I can't see her so sick again," he said sadly.

Nora could see he was getting upset, and she got up and went to him. He turned and pulled her into his lap, and she took his face into her hands. "I know you love her," she said softly. "I love your tender Italian heart. It's why I know you'll be a wonderful father." She kissed him and laid her head on his shoulder. "We really have been treating her like our child," she said softly. "But she's not a child. She's getting better, and Eden is in her heart. You know she won't be better until things with Eden are resolved. Would you want someone to turn me away if I traveled so far to see you?"

"No," said Gabri as he held her and ran his hand over her pregnant stomach.

"Rafe trusts you to do what's best. It's why she turned to you for help," said Nora. "But it's not your job to take this responsibility from her. She knows it's true. She's just afraid of the unknown." She kissed Gabri again.

"What if it hurts her?" he asked with worry. "I don't want to do anything that might get her hurt again."

"We can be there for support if she needs us, okay?" Nora said softly. "It's possible she might get hurt. But Eden is here now, so you can't let this chance slip away if they love each other." She kissed him and looked into his eyes. "You'll talk to Rafe and fix this?"

"Okay," Gabri relented. "I'll fix it."

17

WALKING DOWN THE garden path, Gabri De Angelis made his way toward the cottage Rafaella had moved into a few months after he brought her to the villa. He worried when she wanted to move out of the main house, but Rafaella said she wanted to be more independent. At first, Gabri thought she might want to bring lovers home, and Nora told him he thought too much like a man.

It turned out Nora was right because, as far as he could tell, Rafe never brought a lover home. He ran his hand through his thick black hair. Nora was right again. Rafe must still have feelings for Eden. He really was blind. Though he was not so blind that he would let Eden take advantage of the feelings Rafe may have for selfish reasons. He still blamed her for the things he learned were published about Rafe. He still could not believe everything that happened in California, but it was all true.

Gabri shook his head and knocked on the cottage door. When there was no answer, he checked the door and found it unlocked, so he went inside.

"Rafaella!" Gabri called. "Rafe, are you awake?" He heard a groan from the back room and knew she was still in bed. "I'm making espresso for you. Get up and come in," he called back to her then began making the thick coffee.

Rafe dragged herself out of bed, shuffled into the kitchen, sat down at the small table, and yawned. "Why are you here? Why are you awake this early? It's too late to take a pill."

Gabri finished the espresso and brought it along with some biscotti he had found to the table and sat it in front of Rafe. "Drink your espresso," he said and sat down in the other chair. He watched her take her first sip before saying anything more. "I didn't bring a pill. I have been informed I may be overstepping my place," he said formally.

"What?" Rafe asked in a confused haze.

He pulled a slip of paper from his pocket and put it on the table. "This is Eden's information. I have to tell you," he said hesitantly, "I was rude to her." Rafe was looking back at him with confusion. "I was worried about you, and I may have told her," he paused, "no, I told her, she should not come if she couldn't think of you first." He looked away sheepishly. "Nora said it was not my place to tell her if she could see you or not and to put conditions on her visits."

Rafe looked from Gabri to the slip of paper. She downed her espresso and sat the cup on the table then looked at Gabri again. "So, Nora got to you too," she said softly and smiled at him.

Gabri smiled back. "She is a very hard-headed woman. It's a good thing she loves us."

"She loves me more," said Rafe with a sly smile. "I smell better than you."

Gabri burst out laughing. "I am always second to you, even with my own wife!"

Rafe looked down at the piece of paper and bit her lower lip. "I'm not sure what to do," she said softly as her moment of joy faded. Rafe looked up at Gabri as a rush of thoughts and emotions filled her. She couldn't hide them in her eyes. "I feel like I've stepped outside my life, and I've wasted all my time because I haven't tried to figure out how to fix things so I can make everyone happy."

"You've been working on getting well," said Gabri and put his hand over hers. "It's not your job to make everyone happy."

"I just don't know how to face them now," she said and looked away from Gabri.

Gabri reached out and lifted her face by her chin so she would look at him. "You face them with your Salvaggio pride," he said with a smile. "You fought your demons again, and you are here now. You are still with us, you are strong and smart and beautiful. No one burns with life more than you do. No one is blessed with the love of so many like you are."

Rafe chuckled. "I'm not a song."

"You are!" insisted Gabri. "You are in every song. Everyone who sings is singing about you. You are the heroine who has overcome and now walks in the wild light again."

"And Nora thinks *I'm* dramatic." Rafe chuckled and shook her head. "Thank you."

"What do you want to do?" he asked. "I'll help you. Do you want to start small? Nora is worried we don't have much time before Eden may have to leave." He sat back in the chair and tapped the tabletop nervously. "She also said, if Eden comes again, I'm not allowed to send her away."

"Hmph," breathed Rafe, "she told me I have to be nice and listen." She frowned up at Gabri. "I think she's trying to control us."

"She is very bossy," Gabri agreed. "But what can we do?" He shrugged.

Rafe imitated his shrug. "Love her despite her flaws."

"Yes," Gabri said thoughtfully. "The bossy ones need the most love."

Rafe glanced down at the piece of paper with Eden's information on it again. "I think you're right. I think I should start small." She looked up at Gabri. "Maybe Eden would agree to let me see Bronte alone first. This way, if what she wants to tell me will hurt me, I'll at least have been happy for my time with Bronte."

"Do you want me to call this morning," he asked, "or do you want to call?"

"Did Eden call you before she came?" asked Rafe as she considered what to do.

"No," said Gabri. "She only made a personal visit."

"Then, I think we should send Fausto with a car around nine o'clock with a message," said Rafe pensively. "This way it's more personal and not just an impersonal call from you. It'll make things more convenient for her too, if we send a car, so she doesn't have to bring Bronte herself."

"Excellent," said Gabri. "This way she will also know you acknowledge her visit and you know where she is staying. This will also tell her you appreciate her coming out in person to inquire. I think this is a good idea."

Rafe got up, went to her desk, and got some paper. "Okay," she said softly as she wrote. "Will you give this to Fausto?"

"Yes," said Gabri as Rafe finished writing then folded the note and put it in an envelope. She wrote Eden's name on the envelope and handed it to him. He held up the note. "I'll give him this and the name of her hotel."

Rafe took a nervous breath and glanced up at Gabri. "I hope she remembers me," she said softly.

"She will." Gabri smiled and hugged her then left to deliver the note to the driver.

Rafe watched him go then looked over at her drawing pad. She opened it to the drawing she did of Eden holding Bronte. "Please, remember me," she said softly then closed the book.

18

AFTER A BUSY morning checking schedules and confirming arrangements for the guests coming to stay at the villa tomorrow, Nora De Angelis made her way to the kitchen for a light snack. She was excited about all the musicians who would be showing up this weekend to stay for the week of the music festival. Nora ran her hand over her stomach and smiled because the baby should be born not long after the festival, and Nora couldn't wait. She was happy that the sounds of music and joy would surround him just before he would be born.

Nora looked up as the housekeeper, Lyka, rushed into the kitchen frantically speaking in a mix of her native Filipino mixed with Italian and looking very upset.

"Lyka, slow down," Nora said firmly. "What's happened?"

"They are bad again!" she said in halting Italian. "They have done no good!"

Nora sighed knowing she was talking about something Gabri and Rafe were doing. They were always doing something to upset Lyka. The last time they upset her was when Rafe wanted to check the roof tiles, and she and Gabri decided it would be a good idea to use the safety rope to swing down on to the top floor balcony and into the room. Lyka just happened to be in the room cleaning and thought the villa was under attack. She didn't come back to work for three days.

"Calm down," said Nora. "Sit down and tell me what happened."

Lyka sat down and looked desperately at Nora. "They have stolen a baby!" she cried. "They have it. They have no business with a baby! They will," she sobbed, "they will be no good!"

"A baby?" Nora repeated not sure if she understood Lyka correctly. "Okay, just have some coffee and calm yourself. I'll go see," said Nora and left to go see what Lyka was talking about.

Nora stepped out of the kitchen door and saw precisely what Lyka was talking about. Gabri and Rafe were speeding down the garden path in the golf cart, and Rafe was holding onto a dark-haired toddler and grinning with excitement. They pulled up to the door and smiled up at Nora.

"Bronte's here!" Rafe called happily as she climbed out of the cart with the little girl. "We just took a quick tour of the garden," she said happily and headed back to the garden to play.

Gabri pulled a backpack from the back of the golf cart and rushed up to the door. "Nora," he called with a smile, "come see the baby. She just got here, and we are going to play in the garden. Come with us!"

Nora looked from Gabri as he grinned at her over to the baby clinging happily to Rafe as she walked along the garden path. "Where's Eden?"

"She's at the hotel, of course." Gabri shrugged and carried the backpack into the kitchen and put it on a chair. "Lyka, put the baby's things in the nursery," Gabri said happily. Lyka grabbed the backpack then ran out crying. "What's wrong with her?" Gabri asked Nora who had followed him inside.

"She thinks you stole a baby. Why would she think that?" asked Nora suspiciously. "Where's her mother?"

"Rafe is her mother," Gabri said with a smile. "You should have seen her eyes light up when she saw Rafe. She remembers her! Come, let's go see her."

Nora took Gabri by the arm to stop him. "Wait," she said firmly. "You're not answering my questions." She gave Gabri a stern look. "If Eden's not here, how did the baby get here?"

"We sent Fausto," said Gabri happily. "This morning we sent the car and a personal note, and now she is here."

Nora shook her head at Gabri in disbelief at what she was hearing. "You sent Fausto? Our Fausto and a car?" she asked in confusion.

Gabri nodded. "Yes and a message. Come," he said and tried to pull her along.

"I think you had better give me more details," said Nora as she pulled her hand from Gabri. "Again, why is Eden not here, and why does Lyka think you stole the baby? She's very upset with you two, and I don't want you upsetting her so she won't come into work again."

Gabri took Nora by the shoulders and kissed her. "Everything is fine," he said happily. "I fixed everything like you told me," he explained. "I talked to Rafe this morning, and we gave a message to Fausto for Eden asking to send the baby. I told Lyka we were getting a baby today so make the nursery ready." He shrugged. "And now she is here."

"So, Eden isn't here?" Nora asked still trying to figure out what the two had done.

"No," said Gabri as he walked out the door. "Rafe is waiting."

"Wait, first tell me what you wrote to Eden," said Nora as she caught up with Gabri and held him back.

Gabri glanced at her and then toward Rafe impatiently. He turned back to Nora resigned to his fate. Ignoring Nora was not healthy for his marriage. "Rafe sent a note thanking Eden for bringing Bronte and sent a car to bring the baby here. We told her to pack a swimming suit and change of clothes for the baby. We told her the baby would be returned tonight. We don't have much time, like you said," Gabri reminded her, "so we asked for the baby this morning."

"So, you just sent Fausto with a car this morning, without any warning, and expected Eden to send her baby to you?" asked Nora in disbelief.

"And we sent a message," Gabri reminded her. "This way Rafe acknowledged her visit here and tells her she knows where she is staying. The personal message, and the convenience of our sending a car, also tells her Rafe appreciates her coming out in person to inquire. It fixed everything," said Gabri proudly. "Come see the baby," he said and went to find Rafe.

After watching him walk away, Nora rubbed her temple and shook her head. "I swear you two would drive a saint mad," she mumbled. She turned on her heal and headed inside then up to the nursery where she found Lyka worrying over Bronte's backpack. "Lyka, it's okay. The baby's mother knows she's here. I just need you to make sure lunch is made so they feed her, okay?"

"I'll make the lunch, but then I am going home," said Lyka upset. "They should not be taking babies!" Lyka ran out of the room, and Nora hoped it was to the kitchen.

Nora left the nursery, stopped by the office to grab her purse, then made her way back downstairs. She met Stefano as he was just getting up and around, carrying his breakfast from the kitchen. "Stefano, I need you to drive me down to the car in the golf cart," she said as she took his breakfast, sat it on the table, then rushed him past Lyka and out the door before he could protest.

They made it to the garage, and Fausto came out to meet them. Nora looked over at Stefano as she was getting out of the cart. "Keep an eye on Gabri and Rafe," she said rapidly.

"They have Rafe's daughter out in the garden. I think Lyka may leave after she makes lunch, but I doubt she'll be here when it's time to serve it, so you may be on your own for finding plates and drinks."

She went to the car where Fausto had the door open for her and looked inside. "We should take the other car since this one has the car seat," she told him. "I want to make sure the baby is safe if they decide to take her somewhere." Fausto opened the door to the other car, and Nora got into the front passenger seat.

When Fausto got in, he waited for her instructions.

"Take me to the hotel where you picked up the baby," she said firmly and noticed as he cringed. She had no doubt Fausto knew she was beyond angry.

19

THE ROOM IS *too quiet*, thought Eden Kingsley as she looked out the window at the city street below. It was quiet because Bronte wasn't in the room playing, laughing and talking. Bronte had learned so many new words over the past six months, and Eden loved listening to her talk about her day and talk to her stuffed toys. Having Bronte with her was what kept Eden going every day since Gabri carried Rafe out of the house, and then out of the country. With Bronte gone, it felt like her reason for holding it all together was gone too, and she was struggling.

The note Gabri and Rafe sent said Bronte would be back later tonight, but she still worried about the possibility they might change their minds about returning her. Even worse, though she had expected Rafe to want to see Bronte and not her, was that it still hurt.

Eden could tell Gabri didn't want her to be in Italy. She also knew he was angry about what had happened last night when they saw Rafe as they were having dinner. Eden was still worried about the woman Rafe had been with, even though Julia said it was probably just a friend. She worried about who she was and why Rafe seemed so happy with her. Eden was concerned Rafe had found someone else to start a family with. Though she knew Rafe would always be there for Bronte, she wondered how much they would see each other if Rafe was focused on a new baby.

Julia took another sip of her tea trying to calm herself as she watched Eden look yearningly out the window where she had observed the hulking, burly Italian man get in the car and drive away with Bronte. Eden had stopped crying, but Julia could tell she was still upset. Julia was upset for Eden, but her primary feeling was deep anger toward Rafe, something Julia had never felt before. She included Gabri in her rage.

How they could do this to Eden was beyond her. The other thing making Julia angry was the fact Eden had read their note demanding Bronte, and she actually packed a bag for the baby, helped put the car seat in the car, and sent her with the hulking driver. It was as if Rafe thought she had to send a huge hairy bodyguard because Eden might make trouble. Julia never thought she would see Eden send Bronte off as she did. She wasn't sure if it was a testament to how desperate Eden was to see Rafe or if she really felt threatened by the driver. Maybe she was more afraid of Gabri because of him calling her cruel and selfish.

"Eden," Julia said softly feeling a surge of protectiveness for her, "come and sit down. Are you sure you want to wait in the room all day? They said she wouldn't be back until tonight."

"I don't know what I want to do," said Eden as she sat at the table and wiped the traces of tears from her eyes and face. "I just want to be sure I'm here when she comes back."

"Maybe we should do something to take your mind off everything," she suggested as she reached out to hug Eden. She wished she could hold her and comfort her in a more personal way but knew it would be inappropriate right now. She let her go and sat back in her chair. "We could go to a museum or go shopping, or we could even take a cooking class if one's available."

Eden sighed and put her head in her hands. "I can't think about doing anything right now," she said softly then looked up at Julia. "Did I make a mistake coming here?'

"No," said Julia as she shook her head. She had to stop thinking of herself and help Eden get through this nightmare. There would be plenty of time to think about where things might go with Eden once the relationship with Rafe ended. It looked from where she was sitting that their relationship was over and Eden just had to finally accept the hard truth. Now she only had to try to be helpful and positive and let Rafe be, well, Rafe. "At the very least, Rafe got to see Bronte, and you made it happen," she pointed out. "Plus, we've only been here two days. Maybe after spending time with Bronte, they'll change their minds about talking to you."

"I don't think Gabri will change his mind," Eden said sadly. "I'm pretty sure he would prefer I leave as soon as possible. It's probably why he asked for Bronte today."

Julia sat her teacup down in frustration. She just couldn't hold in her feelings any longer. "It makes me so angry Rafe's allowing you to be treated this way. She must know what he's doing," she insisted. "The note was in her handwriting."

There was a knock on the door, and they looked at each other in surprise. "Did you order more room service?" Eden asked as she looked from Julia to the door.

"No." Julia got up to answer the door. "Just stay there," she told Eden, "I'll see who it is." If it was anyone else delivering a note full of demands, she was going to give them a piece of her mind. She went to the door and opened it a crack. "*Si?*" she asked through the opening.

"I'm looking for Eden," said a woman's voice in English. "I'm not sure what her last name is. It may be Salvaggio."

Julia jerked the door open and stared into the eyes of a blond woman heavy in her pregnancy. "Who are you?" she asked in surprise as she recognized her from last night. She looked tentatively over her shoulder at Eden then back again, worried this woman had come with bad news.

Nora stood her ground wanting to speak directly with Eden. "I'm looking for Eden Salvaggio. I'm sorry if I have the wrong room, but this is the number I was given by our driver."

"Her name isn't Salvaggio," Julia snapped with irritation at Rafe and the situation. At this moment, she also didn't like Eden being given Rafe's last name. "Her name is Eden Kingsley," she said firmly.

"Oh," said Nora, aware by calling Eden by Rafe's last name it was upsetting to the woman with the British-sounding accent. "I really wasn't sure. I just knew the baby's last name was Salvaggio, so I thought maybe hers was too."

"Who is it?" Eden asked as she approached the door. She stopped in her tracks as she saw the woman from last night.

Over Julia's shoulder, Nora saw Eden and recognized her from Rafe's drawings and by her light golden blond hair. "Eden," she said with a friendly smile and held out her hand. "My name is Nora De Angelis. I hope I'm not intruding, but I'd like to talk with you."

Julia looked from Eden to Nora then opened the door and stepped aside so Nora could come into the room. "I'm Julia Hawthorn," she said with authority. "What is it you want?"

Nora took a moment to gather herself, understanding the platinum-blond British-sounding woman was who Rafe thought Eden was in a relationship with now. The protectiveness and the anger the woman was showing could mean Rafe was right, but it wasn't why she was here.

She glimpsed at Eden who stood silently looking back at her. "Hello." She put out her hand, but Eden didn't take it. "I'm here to talk to you about the things my husband has said to you," she said as she put her hand down. "I talked to him today, and I don't think he handled things well with you. Do you mind if we sit?" she asked and put her hand on her stomach and smiled kindly. "Standing for long periods is getting difficult at the moment."

"Of course," said Eden as she snapped out of her shock. "Come in. We were having some tea. Would you like anything?"

"No, thank you," said Nora as she followed Eden to the table and sat down with the two women. She could tell Eden had been upset and knew it was because of Gabri and Rafe's idiotic stunt this morning. "This is probably very strange for you," she said trying to find common ground. "It's strange for me too. It's a bit surreal to meet a woman who has had my husband's child but doesn't really know him and never actually had sex with him. When Gabri told me about Rafe and you, before we were married, I never thought about if I'd actually meet you until Gabri brought Rafe home. Then I thought Rafe would get better, go back home, and I'd never meet you. But, here we are," she said looking at each woman in turn.

Julia could see Eden was anxious. Eden could barely look at the woman sitting across from them. "You said you wanted to talk to Eden about what your husband said to her," Julia reminded her, wanting the woman to get to the point.

"Yes," said Nora. "First, I want to let you know the baby is at the villa with Rafe and Gabri. They're playing, and she should be fine," she revealed and saw a small amount of relief settle on Eden.

"Thank you," said Eden softly.

Nora took a breath sure she would feel just as bad as Eden looked if someone had done to her what Gabri had done. "I'm sorry about the way Gabri treated you. He cares deeply about Rafe and is very protective of her. After getting to know her, I care about Rafe just as much as he does. She's a wonderful person. But," she added, "we don't really know anything about your relationship or how you might feel about Rafe." She watched as Eden shifted in her seat, and Julia just glared at her coolly. "Still, it's no excuse for how he treated you. I told Gabri he had no right to interfere in your relationship with Rafe, and he won't do it again."

"So, what exactly do you mean?" Julia asked suspiciously.

"I mean Gabri won't be deciding if Eden can see or talk with Rafe," she said firmly. "Only Rafe will be making those decisions from now on."

"Was it Rafe's decision to send a hairy minion and demand we send Bronte to her this morning?" asked Julia trying to hold in her anger.

Nora grimaced because she could see they were angry about this morning, and she didn't blame them. Fausto did look intimidating, but he was a gentle man. "It was the two of them together," she admitted. "Sometimes, when they're together, it's like they revert back to being twelve-year-olds." She sighed at the truth about the two childhood friends. "They somehow think what they did was polite."

"How the hell was it polite," asked Julia annoyed to the point her voice raised an octave.

"The way they explained it, they sent a personal note showing Rafe was appreciative of Eden bringing Bronte for her to see. By sending Fausto with the car, they think they made everything convenient for you because you wouldn't have to take Bronte out to the villa or pick her up yourself,"

Nora explained. "I know, it's idiotic, but, like I said, when they get together, sometimes they have strange ideas of what's polite or even what's reasonable at times."

Nora wasn't sure why Eden was not talking or responding. "I think, since Gabri and Rafe went through so much with each other when they were young, they sometimes regress a bit when they're together. At times, since they were only children, they can seem very entitled, and sometimes even their good intentions come out wrong to everyone else because of it."

"Don't let Rafe hear you say those things," Julia scoffed. "I know she was entitled, but she believes she has had some sort of hard life."

Nora frowned at Julia's comment. "She actually did have a hard childhood," she said in defense of Rafe. "But maybe you don't know much about it. Gabri told me you didn't know a lot about her history. Even I don't really know everything because Gabri has a hard time talking about things without getting emotional, but from what he's told me, Rafe has been through a lot."

"She has," Eden agreed softly finally able to speak as she worked to control her anxiety and shyness.

"I know it may be hard, but try not to be too angry with them," Nora said gently. "Rafe was so happy to see the baby, and I know it means a lot to Rafe that you brought her all the way here. I think this will be good for Rafe. She's been working so hard on things and has made some vast improvements from when she first came."

"She looked happy when we saw her last night," said Eden softly.

"She was." Nora smiled as she nodded. "Gabri and I were performing last night, and Rafe was enjoying the music and had quite a lot to drink. It was wonderful to see her feeling good for a change. I just wish she were so happy all the time."

Nora scrutinized Eden but couldn't see what Rafe apparently saw in her. It seemed like the woman was so unresponsive and must be extremely shy while Rafe was the complete opposite. Maybe Eden was acting like this because Rafe was right—Eden was here for closure.

"She wasn't so happy all night," Nora informed Eden. "She had a hard night after we got home. She tries to act like she's fine, but if you really look, you can see she isn't. This is why Gabri is so protective of her, and I guess I am too."

"Eden had a hard night, too," said Julia curtly. She didn't want this woman to think Rafe's feelings were any more significant than Eden's were.

"Oh, I'm sure she did," said Nora as she looked from Julia to Eden. "It's one of the reasons I'm here. After what happened last night, and what Gabri told me about your meeting, not to mention this morning, I thought it would be a good idea to come and let you know what was happening. Gabri will be giving you an apology in person if you meet with him again."

Eden nodded nervously as she tried to meet Nora's eyes. She felt relief knowing Nora was Gabri's wife and not someone Rafe was in a relationship with. She was grateful the woman was showing her the first kindness about the situation she had experienced since they had come to Italy.

"Can you tell me how she's doing?" Eden asked nervously. "I haven't been told anything about her and what's been happening with her medical treatments. You said she was getting better. Does it mean she might be coming back soon?"

It was Nora's turn to shift uncomfortably. She heartily disagreed with the way Gabri treated Eden, but she did not think he was wrong not to discuss Rafe's medical issues with her. For all they knew, she was here to get information that could lead to taking the baby away from Rafe, or she could want information so she could sue Rafe for more support. Gabri treated Eden the way he did because he didn't trust her. Besides all those things, Nora really didn't know anything more than what Rafe and Gabri were willing to tell her, and it wasn't much.

"I just know she's doing better," Nora said sympathetically. "They don't talk a lot with me about her medical treatment. I think it's a matter of pride for both of them, so they handle things privately."

"Oh..." Eden sighed, feeling a bit deflated. She shouldn't have been surprised. Rafe hadn't shared what was going on with her therapy at home either.

Julia watched Eden and knew she had to help her. For some reason, Eden wasn't asking the questions she needed to ask. Julia turned her gaze on Nora, determined to get answers. "Rafe has responsibilities at home," she said firmly. "Eden needs answers to a lot of questions. She can't live in limbo forever. They really haven't been fair to her. They don't answer her emails or send her any real information at all. It's not unreasonable to want to know something, anything.

Then, when she comes all this way, they are rude both times they see her."

Nora could feel the anger coming from the English woman, but she couldn't do anything about what information Rafe gave to Eden. She was only here to make sure Eden knew Gabri would not be interfering in their relationship. After meeting them, she was beginning to see why Gabri might feel he should interfere.

"I'm sorry you feel Rafe hasn't been taking care of her responsibilities. Gabri has been making sure Rafe is well taken care of, and all her financial obligations are taken care of as best he can. I would hope, if you needed anything, he would help you if it's in his power. Is something wrong Gabri should know about?" she asked with concern. "If there is, I'd like to help if I can."

"No," said Eden and put her hand on Julia so she would keep silent because it was clear she was too angry with Rafe right now. "Everything's fine. I just need to talk to Rafe. Do you know if she'll meet with me? Has she said anything?"

Nora watched the two women and the way Eden touched the other with familiarity. She felt a lot of tension in the room and wondered if they really were here to deliver bad news to Rafe. If they were, maybe it would be better for Rafe to get the news sooner than later so not to get her hopes up. She felt guilty for the conversation with Rafe last night because she might be wrong about this woman being in love with Rafe.

"I talked to her last night," she said softly. "She told me she would meet you and listen to whatever you have to say." She watched as the two women quickly glanced at each other. "Listen," she said hesitantly, "why don't we go out, and I'll take you to a few sights, and we can get lunch. Then, after Rafe has spent a few hours with the baby, I can take you to the villa. This will give you a chance to talk to Rafe, and you can ride with Bronte back to the hotel afterward. What do you think?"

"You," Eden stammered, "you would take me to see her?" She flicked her eyes toward Julia then back to Nora as her heart beat hard.

Eden's reaction and the red flush blooming over her face surprised Nora. It was the most responsive she had been since she got here. "Yes," she nodded, "after Rafe gets to spend some time with the baby."

Eden turned to Julia. "I want to go," she said shaking with anticipation. "Do you want to go?"

Julia wasn't sure what to think of Nora's offer. On the one hand, it was what Eden had been asking for, but on the other, she was worried about the shape Eden would be in when she returned if the meeting didn't go well. "How do you think she'll feel about me being there?" she asked Eden. "The last time I saw her, she wasn't exactly glad to see me."

Eden had no idea what to tell Julia. The last thing on her mind was how Rafe felt about Julia. She was too focused on her own feelings and the possible feelings Rafe might or might not be having for her. "I-I don't know," she stammered and looked at Nora then back at Julia.

Julia could see Eden wanted to go no matter what she decided. She reminded herself Eden was here because she wanted Rafe to come home. Julia knew it was a possibility. If it was going to happen, then Rafe might be more receptive to Eden if she didn't tag along.

"I think I'll stay and go out on my own and do some shopping," said Julia. She knew seeing them reconcile would be hard for her to watch right now. "Maybe after you talk with her, she'll want to meet us all together." She gave what she hoped was a confident smile. Julia's vision for keeping Eden for herself was in the balance and letting Eden go alone was a significant risk. She hoped all the time they had spent together and things she had said to Eden would mitigate her susceptibility for allowing Rafe the chance to hurt her again. Julia felt she had spent enough time picking up the pieces Rafe had left behind and didn't relish the idea of doing it again and waiting longer for Eden to see the truth about who she should choose.

"Okay," said Eden and squeezed Julia's shoulder in appreciation as she got up. "I just need to gather my things."

20

HAVING SPENT THE afternoon touring Florence shops and sites, Nora De Angelis was happy to see Eden Kingsley coming out of her shyness. Fausto was trying to be especially kind, hoping to get a smile from Eden so he felt forgiven for his involvement in this morning's antics. Nora and Fausto told Eden about some fun places she could take Bronte like the *Piazza dell Republica* right outside the hotel, where there was shopping and an antique carousel, the famous toy store where Rafe had gone to get some of the wooden Pinocchio toys she sent Bronte called *Bartolucci,* and the Children's Museum next to the *Uffizi.* Nora took Eden to lunch at one of her favorite places in the middle of the shopping district. After a long lunch, and a little more therapeutic shopping, Nora bought some gelato to take home and share with Gabri and Rafe, maybe with Eden and the baby too if they stayed for dinner.

Nora could see the change in Eden as soon as they headed toward the villa. She became quiet and distracted as she held tightly to the canvas bag slung across her body that she seemed to use as a security blanket. Fausto pulled the car into the private driveway leading to the car barn in the back of the villa. They were soon gathering things from the car and getting into the golf cart Fausto would use to take them to the house. They rode silently to the villa then gathered everything and headed toward the kitchen entrance.

Nora led Eden into the kitchen where she put the gelato into the freezer. "Please excuse the mess," said Nora as she saw all the dishes and the mess from lunch left there. It was clear Lyka had gone home, and Nora could only hope she would come back tomorrow. "The housekeeper was upset this morning, and it looks like she went home early."

"Oh, no problem," said Eden softly. She looked around the large commercial kitchen and at the long wooden table where Rafe, Bronte, and the others had lunch. The kitchen was almost as intimidating as the marble foyer she had walked into the day before.

The sound of muffled screaming came from somewhere in the house. "Oh, what now," groaned Nora as a look of concern crossed Eden's face. "Come on," she said and led Eden out of the kitchen.

They walked through the house and came to the main hall. As they entered, they saw Gabri running down the marble hallway pulling something behind him as fast as he could. Stefano was using the video camera to record it all and had Rafe's camera hanging from his neck. As Gabri got closer, they could see he was pulling a blanket and sitting on it was Rafe holding Bronte.

"*Corri, Gabri!*"[3] Bronte and Rafe were yelling and laughing as he pulled them down the hall and around different large pieces of furniture.

The entire hallway had been cleared of most of the smaller furniture, and the furniture in the formal living room, as well as the rug, had been pushed to the sides so they would have a place to run and turn around as the blanket slid across the marble floor.

"What the hell are you doing?" yelled Nora and her voice echoed through the hall.

Gabri stopped short, but the blanket that carried Rafe and Bronte kept moving forward over the slick floor and ran into the back of his legs. Gabri fell backward, but he caught himself and rolled to a stop not far from Rafe and Bronte. Stefano looked up in surprise, and all three gave Nora a guilty look.

"*Corri, Gabri!*" Bronte called. She kept laughing, not ready for the game to end. "*Corri, Mama!*"

Gabri scrambled up and grabbed the blanket. "*Penso che siamo nei guai!*"[4] he yelled as he quickly pulled them back

---

[3] Run, Gabri!

down the hall where they had come from. Stefano followed, and Bronte and Rafe laughed, not noticing Eden was behind Nora.

"You *are* in trouble!" Nora yelled as she followed them. "I'll be right back," she said to Eden. "Just make yourself at home. If it's even possible right now," she grumbled.

Eden stood stunned as she watched Nora stomp down the hallway after them. It was definitely not how she expected to find Rafe. She looked around, found a seat on an opulent chair, and waited.

Nora made it down the hall and into the room where Gabri had dragged Rafe and Bronte. They were untangling Bronte and couch cushions from the blanket when she walked in. "Gabrielli Braulio De Angelis, what do you think you're doing?" She glared at Rafe who was laughing. "You too, Rafaella Salvaggio! Look at this place! We have a house full of people coming this week, and you've destroyed the place!"

"We'll fix it," promised Gabri desperate to please Nora and not feel her wrath. He looked over at Rafe and couldn't help but laugh with her.

"We were just having fun," Rafe offered innocently. "What use are marble floors if you can't slide on them?"

Nora was about to yell at them about what use a broken bone or a cracked skull would be if they crashed, but then she caught sight of Bronte who was sitting on the cushion waiting to go again. "Look at what you're teaching her," said Nora softly, but the anger could still be heard in her voice. "She could get hurt and then what would you tell Eden?"

---

[4] I think we're in trouble!

"We had cushions all around her," said Rafe with a frown. "I wouldn't let her get hurt."

"Right," said Gabri with a nod. "We were careful. I wasn't even running as fast as I could."

"*Corri!*" Bronte called out and jumped up then tried to pull the blanket. "I wanna go again!"

Rafe swooped Bronte up and kissed her. "*Siamo male!*[5] We've been caught misbehaving," she said as she laughed and kissed her again then held her on her hip.

"*Samoo malay!*" Bronte yelled, trying to repeat Rafe's words. Rafe, Gabri, and Stefano couldn't help laughing.

Rafe tried to control her laughter. "We'll fix it," she promised Nora with an unconcerned grin.

Nora looked over at Gabri's guilty face and then at Rafe, who didn't look guilty at all and sighed with frustration. "I expect it fixed today," she said firmly and looked at Stefano. "You help!"

"Of course," Gabri agreed in relief.

"Of course," Stefano repeated guiltily. He took the cameras he was carrying, put them on the table swiftly, and then ran out to start fixing things, but mostly to get away from Nora's anger.

"Rafe," said Nora the tone in her voice serious. "Eden is here. She'd like to talk with you."

Rafe's look went dark at the news. "Why is she here? I told her I would have Bronte back to her tonight. She always does this! She always makes it hard for me to have time with Bronte!" She walked over the cushions with Bronte, grabbed

---

[5] We are bad!

her camera, and then brushed past Nora angrily and went out of the room.

"Why is she here?" asked Gabri irritated. "Why couldn't she wait?"

Nora sighed sadly. "It's my fault," she admitted. "I invited her."

"Why? Rafe was having such a good day," said Gabri upset.

Nora walked into the room and sat down on the cushion-less couch. "Sit down with me," she said, and Gabri sat next to her. "I went to see her because of what you two did this morning." She saw Gabri's look of confusion and shook her head. "What you did wasn't polite," she informed him." I know you think you were fixing things, but you can't send Fausto and ask a mother to send her child to you with a note. She is in a foreign country and barely knows us. Fausto probably terrified her."

"Fausto?" asked Gabri shaking his head. "He's a teddy bear and wouldn't hurt anyone."

"We know that, but Eden doesn't," she insisted. Fausto looks like a burly scary mobster unless you know him. "I wouldn't have blamed her if she hadn't sent the baby. I think she only did because she felt intimidated. She was distraught."

"But she is Rafe's baby, too," Gabri reasoned.

"I know," said Nora, "but you could have asked in a better way." She watched as Gabri frowned looking in the direction Rafe had gone. "I talked with Eden and the woman she came with, Julia," she said hesitantly. "I'm not sure Rafe's wrong about why Eden's here. Julia seemed very possessive of Eden and angry at Rafe. I think they should talk sooner than later. If she's here to get closure, then I think Rafe's better off knowing right away rather than worrying about it for days. She's already started to lose sleep over Eden being here, and it's not good for her." Gabri leaned over and put his head in his hands. Nora rubbed his back. "We'll be here for her no matter what," she said softly. "I hope I'm wrong. Eden is hard to read because she's so shy. Maybe it's best for both of them if they can start talking now."

Gabri sat up and gave Nora a worried frown. "I hope you're wrong too. Let's go talk to Rafe."

21

NORA DE ANGELIS FOLLOWED Gabri outside. They found Rafe taking pictures as she and Bronte played. As they approached, they saw Rafe and Bronte were tearing off petals and throwing them in the air, so they floated down on them. The petals landed on their heads getting stuck in their hair and covering them. There were so many it looked like they were sitting in a bed of flower petals.

"The flower garden too," Nora complained to Gabri as they got closer.

"Little girls love flowers," said Gabri with a shrug. "They grow just for them to enjoy."

"Who's logic is that?" she asked with a sigh. "Don't tell me," she muttered as they got to Rafe and Bronte. "Hello," said Nora as Gabri helped her sit on the grass next to Bronte. "Look at all these beautiful flower petals," she said giving up her anger when she saw how happy Bronte was as the little girl walked up to Rafe and put petals in her hair.

"You look pretty now, Mama," said Bronte then went to get more petals.

"Hey," said Rafe and tossed some petals on Nora then took her picture. "Do I have to send her to Eden now?"

"No," said Nora as she watched Bronte for a moment. The little girl was trying to keep playing and fighting sleepiness from all the excitement of the day. She looked so much like Gabri and was such a beautiful little girl. Bronte sat in Rafe's lap, and it was clear she was worn out. "Maybe we can take her to the nursery and put her down for a nap."

"I don't need a nap," Bronte informed them and took off running through the flowerbeds laughing.

"I'll get her," said Gabri and rushed after her.

Rafe watched Gabri and Bronte with a smile and Nora struggled with her decision to bring Eden home. It was too late to change things, plus Gabri had gone about his actions wrong too, so she could only hope for the best. "We can take care of Bronte so you can talk to Eden. Maybe she'll agree to let Bronte stay the night or come back again tomorrow."

Rafe shook her head doubting it would happen. "I guess I really don't have a choice," she said trying to hold in her frustration.

"You do have a choice," said Nora. "I invited her because I thought, if you're right, it would be better to talk to her now so you don't keep worrying about what she wants to say." She could see Rafe wasn't happy. "What you did this morning was wrong," she said firmly. "You really upset her, and you both should have known better. I know you're Bronte's mother, but Eden is in an unfamiliar place surrounded by unfamiliar people. I can guarantee you, if someone did it to me, I would not have sent my child. I think she only did because Fausto and Gabri intimidated her. If you love her, you can't do those kinds of things to her—even if she doesn't feel the same."

Rafe frowned darkly at Nora. "I wasn't ready to see her," she said softly. "I just wanted one good day." Bronte came bounding back, with Gabri close behind and jumped into Rafe's lap. She gave Bronte a kiss on her cheek. "Your mommy's here to take you home." She picked Bronte up from her lap and put her in a pile of flower petals to play. "Bye-bye," she said then stood up.

"Bye, Mama," said Bronte with a wave then started to play with the petals.

"I'll be in the garden near my cottage," Rafe said and walked away.

"Rafe," Gabri called, but she kept walking. He looked over at Nora. "If we are going to let *that woman* talk to Rafe, there are a few things I want to tell her first." He stood up and helped Nora to her feet.

"Just don't intimidate her, and you better speak to her in English," she said with concern as Gabri picked up Bronte.

"Since you invited her, you should be there too," he said gruffly and started to the house as Bronte held on to him fighting sleep and telling them how she didn't need a nap.

Inside the house, Eden was waiting. When Nora and Gabri made it back to her, Gabri put Bronte down.

"Mommy!" called Bronte as she ran to Eden.

"Hi, baby," Eden cooed to Bronte and picked her up. "Were you having fun with Mama?"

"Yeah, she lives in a garden," Bronte revealed as she nodded. "Gabri said I have to take a nap now," she said with a yawn.

"It looks like you need one," she said and hugged her. Eden looked up at Nora and Gabri. "Where's Rafe?"

"Rafe is still out in the garden," said Nora. "We thought, since it looks like Bronte needs a nap, we could put her in the nursery before you go see Rafe. Come on, I'll show you the way," said Nora and led Eden up to the nursery with Gabri carrying Bronte close behind.

Bronte wasn't always good at naptime because of all her energy. Eden put her into the crib and spoke to her, convincing her to get into her sleeping position. Bronte didn't like the fact she was in a crib but finally settled. Eden tucked Bronte in and rubbed her back for a while as she told her a good night story and answered lots of questions. "Rest your body and your eyes," said Eden softly.

"But I don't have to sleep," said Bronte softly.

"No, just rest," whispered Eden. "We'll play more after quiet time." When Bronte was settled, Eden and Nora went out of the nursey quietly. "It may take a while for her to fall asleep, but she usually does."

Nora nodded and smiled as the sound of Bronte's singing followed them. "Gabri has some things he needs to say to you," she said and led them to Gabri's office. Nora sat down and indicated for Eden sit next to her. She looked up at Gabri. "Go ahead," Nora said firmly.

Gabri frowned at Nora. He was frustrated Nora had brought Eden and that he had to apologize. But Rafe didn't tell him to send her away, so he saw no other choice but to comply. "I am sorry if you felt intimidated and for interfering in your relationship with Rafe," he said in clear English. "Also, as you can see, I can speak English."

Nora nodded her approval. "He likes to pretend he doesn't speak English to intimidate and get his way sometimes. It's a very annoying habit," said Nora and gave Gabri a frown. "In this case, he was doing it because he thought he was protecting Rafe, but it was impolite and inappropriate."

"I already apologized," said Gabri annoyed. "You don't have to do it again for me."

Nora looked up at Gabri sternly. "Yes, sometimes I do," she said and turned to Eden who was looking at them both nervously. "We also want to tell you that we love Rafe very much and hope, after you talk with her, you'll let her see Bronte again and maybe let her spend the night with us while you're here. We understand it may depend on how your conversation goes, but we wanted to let you know what we hope for Rafe."

"Can I speak now?" Gabri asked impatiently. Nora rolled her eyes at him then nodded. "Thank you." He settled his attention on Eden. "Rafe has been getting better, but I want you to remember she is still not well. As I told you before, I don't want you to pressure her and make her sick again."

"Eden," Nora interrupted, "Gabri is just trying to tell you we care about Rafe and don't want to see her hurt.

"So che quello che sto dicendo,"[6] said Gabri annoyed. *"Non ho bisogno si spiegare le mie parole."*[7]

"English!" Nora chastised him. "And yes, you do."

Gabri threw up his hands in frustration. "Nora is the one who invited you," he said sternly, "but you remember the things I told you and don't be cruel or selfish!"

"I'll remember," said Eden softly. "I didn't come to be cruel or selfish."

"Of course you didn't," said Nora and gave Gabri a disapproving glare.

They watched Gabri go to a cabinet and unlock it, then take out some small packages. He walked back to his desk and sat the boxes on the edge of the desk and then sat down. "Since I'm being told I can't interfere anymore, I guess I must give you these. They are gifts to you from Rafe. I didn't send them because I thought they might make you come when she wasn't ready. But it seems you've come anyway." He pushed the packages forward. "When you see one of them, you may understand how sick she was at the time. I don't know the reason she wanted to send those things to you."

Eden took the packages nervously. "Thank you," was all she could think to say. She knew she probably should not have been, but she was shocked Rafe had wanted to send her gifts. She was not shocked Gabri had not sent them, though.

"Gabri," Nora said with a sigh. She shook her head at the fact he hadn't sent Eden the things Rafe wanted her to have.

---

[6] I know what I'm saying
[7] I don't need you to explain my words

"She was sick," he said defensively. "She needed time." He glowered at Nora. "I don't like this. She is not ready," he said and walked out the door.

Nora watched Gabri walk out upset, then turned to Eden. "As you can see Gabri is worried about Rafe and about what you have to say to her."

"I'm not here to hurt her," said Eden softly.

"Good," said Nora with a sad smile hoping it was true. Her interaction with Eden and Julia concerned her, and she was worried about Rafe. "Come on. I'll show you where to find Rafe."

Nora led Eden downstairs and out the back entrance to the patio. "See the little cottage over there," Nora pointed toward Rafe's cottage. "It's the cottage where Rafe is staying. She said she would be out in the garden. Just follow the path, and you should find her." She walked over to a panel with buttons. "This is the servant call bank. Only a few buttons are set up to work right now. If no one's here when you come back, just push this button, and Fausto will come up to the kitchen entrance to take you to the car. Do you think you can find your way to the nursery?"

"I think so," said Eden looking at the call bank and recalling the layout of the villa.

"Okay, I'll leave you to it then. We'll be upstairs. I'm exhausted and need a rest. I'll check on Bronte while I'm upstairs, and I'll put the gifts from Rafe in the nursery too. Hopefully, we'll see you later," she said and then walked back into the house, hoping things would go well for Rafe's sake.

Nora checked on Bronte who had fallen asleep then went to her room where Gabri was laying on the bed. "Well, she's going to see Rafe," she said as she climbed in beside him. "I'm sorry this is so upsetting for you both.

"Why did you invite her?" Gabri groaned. "Rafe would have seen her eventually."

"Rafe won't get any sleep or peace of mind until they talk," she said troubled. "When I met Eden and the other woman, Julia, I got worried I'd start losing sleep over it too."

Gabri sighed and turned to hold Nora. "We were having such a good day with the baby."

"I saw." Nora chuckled. "I really need everything put back. We have a house full of people who will start showing up tomorrow."

"I know," said Gabri and kissed her. "We'll fix it."

Nora took a deep breath and hoped she had done the right thing. She kissed Gabri on his cheek. "I think you should tell Eden about Rafe like we talked about. She should know so she doesn't make the same mistakes again."

"We'll see," he said and frowned. "I want to be careful about what we tell Eden. Rafe won't want her to know things if she's leaving her for the other woman, Julia."

"I understand, but you have to let her know some things no matter what."

"Rafe said she told her some things and her cousin Letty told their friends what she knows about Brettito."

"We can just see how things go then we can decide what to do," she said softly.

Gabri lay quietly with her for a while thinking about Rafe. "My heart is hurting for her."

"Shh, you don't know if it will be anything bad," Nora whispered. "Think positive." She stroked his face and smiled. "I checked on the baby before I came in."

"Was she sleeping?" he asked softly.

"Yes," she smiled and kissed him. "You make beautiful babies."

"Did I tell you when Rafe asked me, I thought she would have the baby?" he asked and smiled sadly. "I was very disappointed when she told me Eden was going to be the mother."

Nora beheld Gabri's handsome face and thought about how beautiful Rafe was. "Well, I'm glad they wanted Eden to have the baby."

"Why?" he asked with a frown.

Nora laughed. "Because if Rafe had your baby, I wouldn't have stood a chance at getting you."

"No," said Gabri, "she was in love with Eden."

"She may still be," said Nora with a yawn.

"Her father never should have taken her to America," Gabri pouted.

"Why not?"

"If she were here, she would not be with women," he insisted. "If she were here, I could have made her happy."

Nora looked away and sighed. She knew it was Gabri's 'machismo' speaking, wanting to solve problems with his ego and manliness. Gabri had confessed years ago that Ettore, for a long time, treated Gabri like he was Rafe's husband by putting him in charge of the estates and keeping him in the loop about Rafe's personal and medical issues. It made their relationship difficult to accept until Nora understood their love for each other was not romantic at all, for either of them. Gabri's childhood infatuation had morphed into protector. "She does love you."

Gabri groaned and felt like he could kick himself for being thoughtless. "I'm sorry. I'm only talking about the past. Right now, I would not change a thing because I have you. I love you," he assured her.

"It's okay," said Nora, reassuring him with a smile. "I know you worry about her."

"I just can't help sometimes thinking if she had stayed here, she would have never got so sick again, and I could have watched over her. Maybe Ettore made a mistake taking her to America."

"You do realize living in America is not what made her gay, right?" asked Nora with a small laugh. "She probably figured things out in high school, and even if she stayed here, she would still be gay."

Gabri shrugged. "Maybe. I just think she was sick and maybe she got confused. America is very confusing."

"Gabri, sometimes I think you have the weirdest thoughts," said Nora with a laugh of disbelief. "America isn't confusing." She paused. "Okay, sometimes it can be. But living there didn't make Rafe gay, I can guarantee it."

"If Rafe would have had the baby, we could have the baby here all the time," he said with a sigh.

Nora laughed softly. "Well, if she had, then you two would have been famous for having the most beautiful baby in the world."

Gabri laughed and kissed Nora. "Our baby will be the most beautiful baby in the world because we will love him with all our hearts."

"I'm glad she's gay," Nora whispered in his ear.

"Why?" He smiled at the sensation.

"Because it means I have you, and I get to have our baby. I love you," Nora sighed into him as she kissed him.

"I love you, too," he said and kissed Nora gently. "I'm glad Rafe is gay too, because now I have you, and I cannot imagine life without you."

22

CARRYING THE SMALL canvas bag slung across her shoulder, Eden Kingsley walked down the garden path. The garden was beautiful, and she could see how being in such a relaxing place would help Rafe. There were well-trimmed hedges surrounding fountains, small areas planted with flowers attracting butterflies, and shaded areas with benches and statuary.

Eden made it to the small cottage and knocked on the door, but there was no answer, so she knew Rafe was still somewhere out in the garden. She had been waiting for this moment for months. Eden had gone over in her mind a thousand times what she would say and all of Rafe's possible responses. After talking with Gabri, she knew a lot of the negative scenarios about what Rafe might say were very likely, and it made her anxious.

She continued her walk down the shaded path and came to a small park area with benches and statues. She saw Rafe from behind sitting quietly on one of the benches. As she got closer, she saw Rafe had a sketchpad out, but it was closed. Her heart beat hard at seeing her, and she stopped for a moment to calm herself. She wiped the nervous sweat from her brow, took a breath, and then stepped forward with determination to get her love and her life back.

Rafe had heard footsteps along the path and knew it was Eden because Nora would not have walked this far, and Gabri had much heavier steps. She had closed her sketchbook as soon as she heard the footsteps and waited for them to come closer.

She looked up and saw Eden come around the bench and stand in front of her. The sun shined down on her and made her golden blond hair shine. Rafe couldn't help thinking how beautiful she was and wished she could just sit and enjoy the vision and not have it spoiled. But she knew Eden had things to say to her, so she looked down, away from the image, and waited.

"Hi," said Eden softly as she sat next to Rafe, putting the canvas bag at her feet. "Bronte is taking a nap."

"Yeah, she was pretty worn out," said Rafe noting how much she missed hearing Eden's voice.

"Your friend Nora is nice," said Eden. "She looks like she's due any time now."

Rafe nodded her silent agreement but couldn't bring herself to look at Eden.

"She invited me because she said you agreed to see me," said Eden and watched Rafe toy with her pencil. "I have a lot of things I need to talk to you about, and since I'm here now, it seems like I can't think of them all," said Eden nervously. "You look good."

"Thank you," said Rafe softly. "You look good too."

Eden swallowed and cleared her throat. "I've missed you. Everyone misses you."

"I'm sorry," said Rafe. She could tell Eden was nervous and thought it was sad they had come to this. "I had to come here. I had to get away from everything."

"It's okay," she said softly.

"I am doing better," Rafe said softly as she looked down at her hands. "I don't have those phantom pains very much anymore. I do still get headaches and still have some other problems up here," she said and pointed to her head. "But I'm working on things."

Eden wanted to reach out and touch her but stopped herself. "I'm glad you're doing better."

They sat in silence for a while. Rafe could tell Eden was hesitant about saying whatever it was she needed to say. "I know you have some things you want to tell me," she said softly. "But there's something I need to tell you before you do."

Eden took a nervous breath. "Okay," she said and clasped her hands together anxiously, preparing for the worst.

"I know you think I did a lot of things that hurt you," she started, "and I admit I did hurt you but," she hesitated as she looked over at Eden but avoided her eyes, "I didn't have an affair when I was in New York." She looked up at Eden and saw her eyes widen. She used to love looking into her beautiful light brown eyes with those bright golden specks, but now it was just painful. She looked away before more pain came. "I know you may not believe me, but Gabri and the doctor are sure," she said hastily before Eden could protest. "They say all the stuff I thought was true, and what I told you about the affair, was just my brain trying to put together pieces missing in my mind about my time there." She ran her hands through her hair. "I know telling you I did, and believing I had an affair, caused you a lot of problems, and it may be too little too late, but I'm sorry." She waited for Eden to respond but she just sat silently. "I know it was what caused a lot of our problems, and it's why you left me and became so angry with me. You're probably still angry with me, and I understand."

"I'm not angry with you," said Eden softly. She watched as Rafe fidgeted with her pencil. "It sounds like you're not sure. Don't you agree with Gabri and the doctor?"

"I want to," said Rafe as she put her pencil down and rubbed her temple. "I never wanted to hurt you." She looked up at Eden to see if she believed her but still couldn't meet her eyes.

"I went to New York with Julia a few months after you left," Eden said shakily as Rafe glanced back with surprise and pain in her gray-blue eyes. "I talked with Lauren myself, and I think Gabri and your doctor are right. I don't believe you had an affair with her. If I would have just taken the time to think things through. . ." She hesitated. "I should have known you wouldn't," she stammered, "you wouldn't cheat on me."

"You couldn't have known," said Rafe relieved she believed her. "Everyone thought it was true. No one doubted it, so what does it say about me?" She shook her head and shrugged. "No matter what I do, or how hard I try, it seems like I can't outrun my past." She sighed and shook her head again. "I'm glad you believe I didn't do it." She glanced toward Eden, only able to glimpse her profile, and felt the loss painfully. Bronte talked a lot today about the things she and Eden did with Julia. It was clear Eden and Julia were traveling and spending a lot of time with each other. So it seemed Rafe was right about them being together. Rafe resigned herself to reality. Maybe it was all for the best. "I still betrayed you, even if I didn't have an affair."

Eden caught the pain in Rafe's voice. She wasn't sure why Rafe was still saying she betrayed her. "I'm just sorry it took all this time to find out the truth. If Gabri hadn't come, we might have never known," Eden said softly. "Back then, I was just so, I don't know, so caught up in listening to people I shouldn't have been. I think I hurt myself by believing you would do something so hurtful, and it hurt you too."

Rafe leaned back and stretched her body. She felt so exhausted from all the tension she had been holding onto at seeing Eden. Now it seemed like there was nothing left, and it was sad, but it was also a relief.

"We both messed things up pretty bad," Rafe said as she relaxed and fidgeted with her pencil. "Now I guess we can move forward and try to find some happiness." She gave Eden a smile she knew was weak, but it was all she could manage at the moment. "So," she said wanting to get the conversation over with, "why are you here?"

"I hope we can find happiness again, Rafe," said Eden feeling like the conversation was starting out well. "I'm here because there are so many things we need to talk about and so many things I need to say to you." She turned and picked up the small canvas bag beside her and opened it. She pulled out her notepad with all the things she wanted to talk to Rafe about.

Rafe frowned as she examined the bag Eden was closing. The bag was hers, she realized and dropped her pencil. It was the brown canvas school bag that she had left in the trunk of her father's car. It was supposed to be there, not in Eden's hands. "Where did you get this?" she asked looking from Eden to the bag. "Where did you get it?" she asked again harshly.

"I got it from your car," said Eden and held it out to her. "When Gabri was getting things out I took this. I wanted to give it to you myself."

"Give it to me," she demanded angrily. She snatched it from Eden's hands and looked inside. Pulling out an old drawing notebook she flipped through it then closed it and put the notebook back. "Why did you bring this here?" she asked angrily.

"I," Eden stammered, "I didn't read the letter. I swear, I only saw some of the drawings and the paper about your mother," she said shakily. "I didn't want to read the letter and make you think I was using it to get what I want."

Rafe clutched the bag tightly and glared angrily at Eden. "I didn't want this here! If I wanted it, I would have asked Gabri to get it!" She stood up and picked up her drawing pad and pencil.

"I just thought," Eden started.

"Well, you thought wrong!" Rafe fumed at Eden. "Don't think for me! You come here saying you just want to talk, but really, you do nothing but make things worse!"

"I don't understand," said Eden shakily.

"Of course you don't!" Rafe yelled. "You don't understand, you don't think, you don't listen, and you don't see me anymore! I don't know why I even expected any understanding from you when you're so blind and thoughtless!" Rafe turned on her heal and walked away from Eden, her anger getting close to its peak. She was angry with Eden and mad at the hope Nora stirred inside her, now just another painful reminder she could never outrun her past, and it would always haunt her.

"Rafe!" Eden called and followed her frantically not comprehending what had happened. "Rafe, I'm sorry! I didn't know if Gabri would let me see you, and I wanted to have something that might make him let me."

"Did he see this?" Rafe demanded furiously as she turned to face her. "Did you show this to him?"

"No," she stammered, "no, I mean he knew I took it from the car, but I don't think he thought anything of it. I didn't have to use it because Nora brought me to see you. I was just carrying my notepad in it."

Rafe tried to calm herself and take in Eden's words. "He didn't see it," she mumbled. "Good, good." She turned and started walking to her cottage again.

"Wait," said Eden as she followed. "Please, tell me what's wrong. What did I do?"

Rafe opened the door to the cottage and looked back at Eden with a frown. "I need some time alone now," she said firmly. "I hope you let me see Bronte again."

"But what about us, Rafe?" Eden asked pleadingly. "We need to talk and spend time together. Will you see me again?"

Rafe clutched the canvas bag tighter looking away from Eden. "I don't know right now. I just need to be alone and think." She went into the cottage and closed the door behind her.

Eden went up to the door and tried to open it, but Rafe had locked it. She leaned on the door and was at a loss about what to do. Eden knew she couldn't pressure Rafe to let her inside because of what Gabri had told her, but she was worried about what was happening with Rafe. She looked down at the notepad in her hands with the list of all the things she wanted to say and sighed. She wondered if she would ever get the chance.

"Rafe," she called, "I hope you want to see me again. I still have things I wanted to say to you in person." She waited to see if Rafe would answer. "I love you," she said softly when Rafe didn't respond. She made her way back up to the main house feeling like she had lost Rafe all over again.

23

IN THE NURSERY, Nora De Angelis rocked Bronte and tried to comfort her as she cried. She and Gabri had been sleeping when Nora heard Bronte's cries and came in to find her upset and asking for her mommy. Nora looked up as Eden walked into the room.

"Look, Bronte," said Nora as Eden approached them. "There's your mommy."

"Oh, baby," said Eden and held out her hands to Bronte who reached back. "Come on, my sweet girl. Everything's okay," she said and held her close.

"Sit down here," said Nora as she got up from the rocker. "She woke up in a strange place and is a little upset."

"Yeah, traveling on a long flight and waking up in different places has been hard on her," said Eden as she sat with Bronte. "Let's wipe those tears," she cooed to the baby. "We're okay now."

"I'm sad," Bronte cried as she nuzzled her mommy.

"I know. It's okay," Eden said softly. "Let's just relax together." She rocked as Bronte sniffled and snuggled close.

Nora sat down on the recliner and watched Eden with Bronte. The baby clung to Eden and calmed since her mommy was here. Their contrast in hair and skin was what Nora imagined her and her own baby might have if he took after his father.

"How was your visit with Rafe?" she asked curiously.

Eden took a calming breath as she stroked Bronte's hair and forced herself to look at Nora. "It went well at first," she said softly and couldn't help the tear of anxiety that welled in her eye. "Then I did something wrong, and she walked away," she said and wiped her tear before it fell.

"She walked away?" asked Nora with concern. "Where did she go?" She wondered what bad news the woman had given Rafe and knew Gabri was not going to be happy when he found out Rafe was upset.

"She went inside her house," she answered softly. "I don't understand what happened."

"Mama lives in a garden," Bronte interrupted her voice still hitching from being upset.

"You're right. I saw her house," Eden cooed and stroked her hair.

"Was she angry or upset about whatever you came to talk to her about?" asked Nora trying to grasp why Rafe would walk away.

"She was upset," Eden nodded. "She said she needed to think. I didn't know what to do, so I just did what Gabri said and didn't pressure her about anything."

"Did she say what she needed to think about?"

"No," Eden said softly. She was afraid to tell Nora how upset Rafe was about the bag. It was clear Rafe didn't want Gabri to know about it. She could tell Nora wasn't satisfied with her answers. Eden felt like Nora had been so helpful and nice. She needed her to know how much it meant to her that they were taking care of Rafe and how grateful she was about letting her come and try to talk with her.

"I, uh, I realize you and Gabri don't really know me, and I can see how much you care about Rafe," Eden said nervously. "You took her in and helped her with getting the medical help she needs, and you let her live on your estate in your cottage. She looks healthy, and she says she's doing better. I'm thrilled to know she's been so well cared for while she's been here."

"We do care about her," Nora said but hid her surprise at finding out Eden thought she and Gabri owned the villa and estate. She wasn't sure if she should reveal Rafe owned everything except their personal things. Gabri was the estate manager for this place and several other estates that Rafe's father bought back when real estate was relatively cheap in Italy.

Managing and working on the estates was how Gabri had made a living since he was in college. It was work he started doing part-time in college because it gave him time to work on his music career. Now he was the manager of all the estates, and he had a staff he managed to do the day-to-day work so he could go on tours and work on recording his music. It was something Gabri loved to do, and he had brought in people who could make the estates more than pay for themselves over the years. Gabri always talked about how Ettore Salvaggio made it possible for him to follow his passion.

Eden swallowed back her anxiety. "This is all very hard for me." She could not stop her tears this time. "I'm sorry," she said as she wiped her tears, "I'm sorry. I can't help crying. I suffer from chronic anxiety, and it's difficult for me when I'm under stress, especially in emotional situations."

She sniffed and swallowed then took some deep breaths. She didn't want to upset Bronte again.

"Rafe was always the one who helped me through things like this," she confessed. "I've been getting help from a therapist now, but it isn't the same, you know?" She could see Nora's eyes soften. "I don't know what she's told you about us. I made a lot of mistakes, and they hurt her deeply. We were trying to rebuild our relationship, but with both of us having so many problems, it was hard. Gabri probably told you how he found her. I knew she was having problems, but I didn't really know the extent. Rafe is tough to. . ." Eden hesitated and wiped tears from her face, "to control or convince about anything when she's made up her mind. She told me she was going to therapy, but really she had quit. She wouldn't talk to any of us and pushed us away. We really didn't understand why. I didn't understand what I was doing wrong until I talked with Gabri yesterday. I still feel like I don't really know everything that is happening with her."

Bronte looked up at her mommy and put her hand on her face. "Are you sad?"

"No, baby," she said as she wiped the tears from her face and was glad they had finally stopped. She looked up at Nora. "I know Gabri may not believe it, but I do want what's best for Rafe." Her words trailed off as she saw Gabri enter the room.

Nora looked up and smiled at the sight of him. "Gabri," she greeted him, "Eden was just telling me about her talk with Rafe."

"Where is she?" Gabri asked. It seemed to him if things went well she would be here saying goodbye to her baby.

"She's down in her house," said Nora. "Things didn't go badly, but they weren't the best, either. Eden wasn't sure what she had done, but she promised you she wouldn't pressure Rafe, so she came up here to be with the baby."

"She, she said she still thinks she betrayed me. I'm not sure why she thinks she did," said Eden hesitantly. She could feel his ire as Gabri frowned at her. "She just said she needed to think."

"I'll go check on her," said Gabri curtly. He gave Nora a quick kiss then left to go find Rafe.

"Let's go to the kitchen and see if Bronte wants some gelato," Nora offered and saw Bronte perk up and look at her. Nora hoped she would get more information from Eden about what had happened so she and Gabri could help Rafe get through the situation.

24

THE ORANGE AND blue flames left swaths of blackness as they ran across the thick paper, curling it and leaving only black ash in the small stone bowl. As the paper burned, Rafe Salvaggio tore out another page from the drawing pad to add to the flame before it went out. She watched as the faces, statues, and copies of art she had drawn disappeared into the blackness. If she focused, she could see the flame change color slightly as it engulfed the pencil lead where there was shading or dark filled spaces.

She thought it was too bad she couldn't choose which of her memories she could add to the flame so they would disappear into the blackness also. She wondered if her missing memories were worse than the ones haunting her. Having the memory of what happened in New York would have been helpful when Eden was accusing her of having an affair.

Rafe found the sketchbook she was slowly burning in the bag she took from Eden. It was very tiring trying to outrun her past, especially when it came back to haunt her at unexpected times. She thought everything was under control, but she was again dragged back into dark places against her will. She tore out another page and held it over the flame.

"Rafe," said Gabri as he came upon her burning paper. "Is everything all right? What are you doing?" He looked at the burning paper then at the drawing pad and the drawing on the open page. "Stop, Rafe," he said taking the drawing pad from her easily. "Why are you burning this?"

Holding the page she had torn out over the flame, Rafe ignored him.

"*Eroina*," he said softly and knelt down next to her chair. "Tell me everything," he pleaded as he always did when he saw she might be thinking about things she shouldn't think about.

Rafe reached down, took the drawing pad back, and tore another page out to add it to the flames. "Do you remember what we did to Brettito's notebook," she said softly as she watched the page burn.

"Yes," whispered Gabri. The page she was burning had a drawing on it that Rafe had done of several people. There was a dancing *zingari* girl and also Brettito, who looked so young but exactly how Gabri remembered him. He recognized a sketch of Eden, and there were other people he did not know. He thought they may be people from the museums or in the square where Rafe went to draw. "We burned it," he said softly.

"We burned it." Rafe nodded then turned her haunted eyes toward Gabri. "If you found out I did something horrible, would you still be my friend?"

"I will always be your friend, no matter what," said Gabri. "I will always love you."

"I hope so," she said as she let go of the paper so it could burn the rest of the way on its own.

"What did you do? Did you do something to Eden?" he asked, worried about what had happened between them. "Is it why you're burning drawings of her?"

"No, I didn't do anything to Eden," she said and got the lighter out to refresh the flame on the paper.

"What did she do to you?" he asked hating to see her this way. "I knew I should have stopped her from coming."

"It's okay," she said with a sigh. "Maybe it was good we talked." She thought about their conversation for a moment. "Well, maybe I did do something to her." Her eyes met Gabri's again. "I betrayed her."

"No," Gabri said and shook his head, hating she was repeating this. "Why are you saying this?"

Rafe avoided his eyes shrugged. "I didn't tell her," she said as she tore out another page, "so don't you think it's true?"

Gabri turned his face up toward the darkening sky then looked back at Rafe. He knew what she was talking about and it upset him. "You still believe you're the betrayer because you didn't tell her about," he hesitated, "about the things that happened with your mother and Brettito and about being sick."

Rafe nodded and tore out another page to burn. "I am," she whispered as the images on the paper blackened.

"No," said Gabri desperate to make her think differently. "No. I think you were just hopeful. You were hopeful you were well, and there was no need to worry her about anything."

"False hope." Rafe chuckled at the absurdity of ever having hope in any form. "Hope I could outrun my past, but I can't. There is not one person in my life I haven't betrayed in some way, including you."

"*Eroina*, please," Gabri begged. "Don't think this way."

"Don't worry, Gabri," said Rafe as seeing the concern on his face. "I'm still here. I'm just saying what's true." She tore out another page and used the lighter to make a new flame.

"You haven't betrayed me, *Eroina*," Gabri insisted. "Please, stop burning your work."

Rafe gave Gabri a sad smile. She knew he had always loved her and believed the best of her. He had followed her everywhere, even when he knew they would get in trouble if they were caught or there was a possibility of their adventures ending badly. She thought he was a much better friend to her than she was to him. She reached out and touched his face then put her hand on his shoulder. "Don't worry, I'm fine," she said and gave him a small smile.

"I'll talk with Eden," said Gabri wanting to help Rafe. "Nora says she should know everything so she understands what happened."

"I already told her most of it," she said softly, "but it was too late. It probably doesn't matter anymore." She tore out another page and added it to the fire. "Everyone is telling her my secrets and other things about me. Letty is telling her things. Julia and Abby tell her things. I guess you can tell her too. I have no control over anything anymore."

"You have control," said Gabri. "No matter what they tell her, only you can tell her if it's the truth."

Rafe shook her head at Gabri sadly. "Maybe I don't know what the truth is anymore. What else happened I can't remember, or I remember wrong? I just need to be alone to think," she said softly closing the drawing pad. She had burned all the pages she needed to burn.

"Eden and the baby are still here," said Gabri hoping the news would help her. "Do you want to come and spend time with them before they have to go?"

"No," said Rafe. "I'm going to take a walk and think." She got up, opened the door to the cottage and set the drawing pad inside. After closing the door, she started toward the garden path then turned back. "I'll help you put the house back together tomorrow," she called giving a small wave as she continued toward the path.

Gabri stood, and with concern and frustration, he watched Rafe walk away. He wanted to believe Rafe when she said she was okay, but sometimes, it was hard to tell if she really was or if she was just saying she was so he wouldn't worry. All he could do was watch closely and do his best to get Rafe help to fight the demons she faced alone.

25

IN THE LARGE industrial kitchen, Eden Kingsley had done her best to open up to Nora and answer her questions while Bronte enjoyed her chocolate gelato. Nora could tell it was hard for Eden. At times, it seemed like she was asking for help, but Nora wasn't sure exactly how much help they could actually be for her. They would not force Rafe to see Eden if she didn't want to see her.

As Gabri walked into the kitchen, Nora could see he was agitated. "Is Rafe okay?" she asked.

Eden looked up at Gabri hoping that he had good news.

"She says she is," said Gabri clearly not believing it.

"Is she coming to have gelato with us?" Eden asked hopefully.

"No," said Gabri and saw Eden's disappointment.

Gabri knew he would have to tell her about Rafaella. He did feel it was right she knew because of the baby. He also knew Rafaella's reasons for not saying anything at all about her childhood were not the best, though he understood her.

He would never know why Rafaella's father chose not to tell Eden anything. Rafaella had been well for so long, maybe Ettore thought she was finally happy and would never have any more problems. But she has issues now, and Rafaella hadn't told him that he couldn't tell Eden what happened to her when she was young.

Gabri sighed because Nora was right again. He decided he would have to do what Rafaella's father did not do and tell Eden everything. Maybe then it would make her understand why she should go home and let Rafaella heal. "I need to talk to Eden," he said firmly. He could see Nora understood what he was going to talk with her about.

"I can watch Bronte," said Nora and looked at Eden. "We'll be fine down here for a while."

Eden looked at Gabri nervously and wondered if something was wrong. "Okay," she said softly.

"Come," said Gabri. "We must go to my office."

26

TRUDGING HEAVILY UP the stairs, Gabri De Angelis led Eden to his office. As they walked inside, he motioned for her to sit down. He made his way to the small bar where he made himself a drink, hoping it would help him get through what he had to relive. The memory of Rafe burning her drawings and talking about being the betrayer again was fresh in his mind and had him on edge. It was painful to see the face of Brettito burning as they discussed the burning of his notebook. It was also hard thinking about all the reasons behind what they had done. Rafe had been convinced it was evidence against her and was sure the police would come after her for Brettito's death. Gabri couldn't convince her they didn't need to burn the notebook. So that night, they burned every page in the pizza oven behind Rafe's house.

Now Gabri had to think about it all again and talk about it because of this woman.

"Would you like a drink?" he offered Eden.

"No thank you," she said nervously.

He took his drink back to his desk and sat down. He took a sip of his drink while looking at Eden in silence trying to figure out where to start. He sat his glass down then got up and started toward a cabinet.

"I am going to tell you everything about what happened to Rafaella," he said as he unlocked the cabinet.

He took out a large file and some papers and then carried them to the desk. He took out a form from a drawer in his desk and filled it in then signed it and looked up at Eden.

"This is a confidentiality agreement," he said and handed Eden the form. "I want you to sign it before I give what could be sensitive information to you. I would like you to sign the agreement so I have assurances the information won't be repeated. This means you will not repeat what I tell you, and you won't talk to anyone about it except me and only when appropriate. You won't even speak to Nora or Rafe about this." He watched Eden look over the form. "If you put your name next to mine, then sign at the bottom, everything will be in order."

Eden looked up at Gabri for a moment then back at the form. Gabri was taking all this very seriously, and it was unnerving. "I don't understand why we need this," she said softly.

"As I said, it is for our confidentiality of this conversation," said Gabri and handed her a pen.

Eden took the pen nervously. "Okay," she said softly and began to read the agreement.

Gabri watched her look over the form. "You may not know this, but Rafaella and I sometimes call you the golden mother," his mouth twitched into a small smile. "It is a compliment to you and how much she loved you."

"I love her too, Gabri," said Eden nervously noting the past tense in his comment. "I love her with all my heart."

"Good." Gabri nodded wondering if she was truthful or if she was saying what she thought he wanted to hear. "Because of Bronte, and so you will understand why I'm so protective, I've decided you will now know things even Rafaella doesn't know."

Eden just stared, not understanding what was happening. "What things?" she asked softly.

"You will not discuss those things listed in the confidentiality agreement with Rafaella or anyone other than me," he repeated to reinforce his words. "Rafaella is better off not knowing," Gabri said sternly. "Knowing will cause her more pain and affect her health. Do you understand and agree for Rafaella's sake? You won't cause her pain or threaten her health by telling her some of the things I will tell you? Will you sign and agree?"

"I don't want to cause her pain or hurt her," said Eden not knowing what else to say and knowing she was making another promise that may tie her hands. "I won't tell anything for Rafe's sake. I promise. I'll sign the agreement." She took the pen given to her and filled in her name then signed the document and handed it back to Gabri.

27

TAKING THE FORM from Eden's hand, Gabri De Angelis looked it over and nodded. He put it into the large file on his desk and prepared himself to relive some of the most terrible times in his and Rafe's life. With what was published about Rafe in the American papers, and how it affected Rafe, Gabri felt much better having the agreement in place. If Eden repeated anything he told her about Rafe's childhood or medical history, then he would be able to take her to court and separate her entirely from Rafe if necessary.

"I will tell you about Rafaella and all the things she knows as well as things she does not know. This is an act of trust, and I hope you are worthy of my trust." He paused and regarded Eden for a moment, hoping he was doing the right thing.

"Everything started when Rafaella was very young," Gabri began. "You know Rafaella's mother died when she was twelve," he asked, and Eden nodded. "Well," he hesitated, "Rafaella was on the back of the bicycle when it was struck. She was not hurt badly," he quickly assured her. "Physically, she had a mild head injury, bruises, and scrapes. She was on the back and was thrown into people on the sidewalk but ended up in the street. She, to this day, thinks she rode her own bicycle to school that day, and she has no real memory of what really happened."

Gabri waited a moment to allow Eden to take in his words. "Rafaella was talking to her mother in the street as she died. When help came, she had to be dragged away from her mother by three teachers. No one really knows what her mother told her. Rafaella has a false memory of her mother taking her to the door of the school. They never made it there. The doctor said it was a coping mechanism her mind did for her. It was her true injury. Has she told you about going to the hospital and meeting her father?"

Eden wasn't sure if she should tell him she knew or not because it was another secret she was supposed to keep. "What happened?" she asked, deciding to play it safe, thinking he may be testing her.

Gabri sighed and ran his hand through his dark hair. "Rafaella tells a story about how she hugged her father in the hospital," said Gabri working to control his emotions. "The man she hugged was not her father. She ran out of the exam room, and the doctor thought she had seen a vision. She hugged an old man who was in the hospital crying over his dead wife, but not over her mother. The nurse realized Rafe was in a trance and thought the old man was her father. When she told the old man why Rafe was hugging him and begging to see her mother, he cried harder for the tears she shed. He is the one who told Rafe her mother was dead, and the old man told her his wife was dead too."

Gabri paused as the memory of Ettore telling him what happened ran through his mind. "Rafaella's father came, and he pulled her away from the man as gently as he could," he said softly. "Ettore Salvaggio was a great man." He wiped a tear from his eye and continued. "He paid for the old man's wife's headstone, and her flowers, for taking care of Rafaella. You see, what you called 'emotional blackouts' have happened to her before."

Gabri paused a moment remembering the past and all the things Rafe did after her mother died. "Rafaella ran away several times," he continued, "but she only remembers doing it one time. It seemed like Ettore had all of Florence on the lookout for her. Everyone we knew made sure to make a note when they saw her. See, we handle these matters differently here. When she ran away, and she knocked on a familiar door, she was welcomed in and kept, until either her father or her au pair or a friend could get her home. She slowly got better, and her mind came back to us with the help of her doctor, but she still has gaps and false memory, so we don't talk about it in front of her."

Eden was stunned at what she was hearing. "If she never talks about it, how can she resolve her problems and fears?"

Gabri nodded at the question. "As long as her memory is not challenged, everything is fine. If it is challenged, well, those were the times when she had problems," Gabri revealed. "The doctor said there is no harm with letting her mind protect her until the memory comes back naturally. Then she can get help with it again. She has always accepted the story she tells, and it has not changed even today. I have talked to her about it since she has come home," said Gabri with a sigh. "Her memory is very broken about things that happened back then, and she doesn't like to talk about it. She remembers some things right, and other things not at all. But even with all she's been through, she is one of the most intelligent and loving people you will ever know. I'm sure you will agree with me."

Eden nodded and wiped away a tear for Rafe. "Yes, she is brilliant and loving." She was still trying to take in everything Gabri was telling her. The things Rafe went through it seemed were much more severe than she knew. She could not imagine coping with such a significant loss and actually being in the accident and watching her mother die at twelve.

"Did she tell you about Brettito, our friend?" Gabri asked breaking the silence.

"No," said Eden softly, "but Letty told me what she heard Rafe's father tell her parents. She said Rafe fell into the street and into his blood and was covered in it. She said he told them Rafe was inconsolable for a long time."

Gabri leaned back in his chair and sighed. He took a moment to collect himself because it was still hard even for him sometimes to think about what had happened. "Rafaella tells the story fine until she comes to what happened to Brettito. We were all enthralled with the *zingari* and wanted to learn their magic. It was a game, and Brettito wanted to win and impress Rafaella because we were in love with her." He smiled sadly. "So he made friends with the *zingari* boys.

"One day, we skipped school to go to a festival and, the way Rafaella tells it, she and I were looking for Brettito and heard four gunshots. We ran and saw Brettito taken away in an ambulance, and she realized she was standing in his blood, and she lost control and was inconsolable. It's the story we all tell, but it's not the truth."

Gabri wiped his hand over his face sadly, took a breath, then continued. "What actually happened was we were looking for Brettito, and we caught him near a shop, a tabacchi. He was talking to some *zingari* boys. We called him over to tell him not to run with the *zingari* boys, to stay with us. As we stood there talking to him, some *zingari* boys rushed toward us in a group, as they do, and someone shouted out an alarm. It was from one of the jewelry stores, and the guards shot at the *zingari*. You have to understand, the jewelry stores were well guarded. Some were even owned by the Mafia. The other things you have to understand is the guards had machine guns, and there were not just four shots. There were close to maybe four hundred or even more it seemed because four guards were shooting into and around the crowd. It was like we were in a war with the loud machine guns and people screaming."

Gabri closed his eyes for a moment and shook his head at the memory. "The group of boys ran between us. I was still close to the shop and jumped inside. It seemed everything slowed and took so long to stop, but really, it was seconds. Rafaella and Brettito were on the street, and Brettito," Gabri hesitated, "he stepped in front of Rafaella. He was hit six times and," Gabri said huskily feeling the pain of losing his friend. "Several bullets ripped all the way through him. Rafaella was only grazed because Brettito's body flew back into her and knocked her to the ground saving her. But she was petite, and Brettito had grown faster than both of us, so when he fell on her, he broke her arm. When she was forced to the ground, she hit her head on the street was knocked unconscious for a time."

He paused for a moment to gather himself. "Brettito was hit in his stomach, chest, neck, and head," he continued softly. "If the bullets had been lower, or at a different angle, Rafaella would have died too. The bullet that grazed Rafaella came through the side of his stomach and put a small wound on her arm. You can't even see it now. She was knocked back away from the angle of the shots when Brettito fell back into her. It's the only reason she was not hit again. When Rafaella woke, she found herself trapped under him. She struggled to free herself as Brettito's body bled out on her but, because of his size and her broken arm, she couldn't lift him. It was how she got covered in so much of his blood and," he hesitated and felt sick at the memory, "other parts of him. We didn't know Rafaella was alive until after the shooting had stopped and she started calling Brettito's name and screaming for help.

"We were able to get through the crazed crowd and pull her out from under him. She was covered in more blood and gore than she even knew. It smelled terrible and was so thick it was almost black looking." Gabri looked up at Eden. He had gone slightly pale from the memory. "Two of the *zingari* boys were dead close by, their blood mingling with Brettito's. She still has no idea four others died, and many were injured that day from being shot or just trying to get away from the shooting. All the wounded and dead were the reason there was so much blood in the street around her."

Still living in the memory, Gabri continued. "We pulled Rafaella from under Brettito. She was covered in his blood, and her eyes were... wild," he said softly. "She held on to Brettito and just kept screaming. It is a sound I never want to hear again and wish I could forget. The ambulance came to help, and even with a broken arm, it took four of us to calm her and keep her from Brettito's body so we could get her into the ambulance. Just from touching her, we were all covered in blood."

Gabri sat silently for a moment then took a sip of his drink for strength. "She says her father came and got her at the tabacchi, but she was in a trance for a long time after she was put in the ambulance and taken to the hospital. Her father really came to her at the hospital. She thinks she was home for two weeks, but it was really almost ten."

Taking another sip of his drink, Gabri gave Eden time to digest his words before sharing another hard memory. "We took her to the funeral for Brettito. Her father had to drag her out because Rafe was frantic. She was trying to tell Brettito's mother she was sorry, and she had to be restrained. Rafe started running away again thinking that she had caused Brettito's death. She thought the police would come for her. The police never came, and the guards who were to blame were barely punished. It turned out nothing of real value was taken. If they had just stopped a moment to understand what was taken and see it was just petty *zingari* thieves, none of it would have happened. The *zingari* were pushed out of the city, and everything was blamed on the two *zingari* who were shot," he said bitterly. It was never mentioned if Brettito was involved with the heist. Gabri was sure he was meant to be a lookout.

"Ettore decided it would be too much for Rafaella to take if she started wandering the streets and people began talking to her about what had happened. So, as soon as he could, he moved her to Milano and got a doctor there to help her so she wouldn't run the streets. But she found a way to run them anyway." Gabri shook his head and smiled sadly at the memory of Rafaella calling and telling him to meet her at the train station and having to call her father to get the money for the train for her return or so he could get to Milano then back to Florence.

"My god," said Eden softly as she covered her mouth and tried to comprehend everything Rafe had gone through. Now she understood just how Rafe felt about Gabri, and why she had been so hurt about everything surrounding the insemination and pregnancy. Rafe's connection to Bronte was more than just Gabri being her friend. He was literally a lifeline for her when she was grieving for the tragedies surrounding her mother and her friend Brettito. No wonder she and Gabri seemed so close when they were together.

"When she was finally better," Gabri started again suddenly, "they moved to America so her father could keep her away from everything for a while. They took a trip back to Italy the next year and then came back often since everything was good. We were all happy she was able to cope and have a good life again."

Gabri opened the file and pulled out a packet. "When her father was sick, he sent me all the old paperwork and the photographs of Rafaella so she wouldn't find them when he died." He looked through the file and handed her three photos. "The one in the middle she has seen. The others she will never see," Gabri said softly. "So, you see, her not remembering is her mind coping. You just have to remember not to challenge her truth, as long as it will not hurt her."

Tears were streaming down Eden's face at the thought of what Rafe had lived through and the look of pain on Gabri's face as he spoke. She took the photos from him and examined each one. The middle photograph was a young Rafe sitting on a bed with a bandaged head looking blankly at the camera and Gabri holding a guitar blocking her left arm and looking at Rafe with a smile.

The photo on the left could only be described as— disturbing. Eden couldn't look at it long. It looked like a crime scene photo of a very young and unconscious child. It was Rafe in the hospital on a gurney and hooked to medical equipment. It was before she was cleaned up from all the blood and gore covering her from head to foot. Eden felt sick with horror at what she saw in the photo. Knowing it was Rafe laying there made it too painful to look at for long. Attached to it was a newspaper clipping Eden couldn't read because it was in Italian, but she guessed it was about what had happened.

Gabri watched Eden look at the photograph with horror and revulsion. "They had to take it," he said, "in case she died."

Shakily, Eden hid the photo under the others. "I had no idea," she choked out and wiped her tears away. The last picture was of Rafe sleeping at home with her arm in a cast and Gabri lying next to her reading a book.

"I went to her house every day after school and practiced my music," Gabri said and tried to smile, "then I helped her with homework until her father moved them away to Milano. Somedays, if she would get out of bed, she only stared at the page or drew in her sketchbook. Other days, she seemed happy and would devour the material and do the work easily," said Gabri who Eden could see was upset for Rafe.

"Her father sometimes would bring home gelato, and he would take us to the garden and discuss philosophy and great works. Rafaella's father wanted to keep her mind busy always, with things she had to concentrate on and ponder. He did this so she would stay with us and not fall into her trance. He knew Rafaella was intelligent from a young age because she always had to know everything and was good in school even when she didn't go. She was notorious with all her teachers for being truant but somehow getting outstanding marks."

He chuckled softly remembering the talks Rafe's mother had with her about skipping school. "So Ettore, he filled her life with books and information, puzzles and other mental challenges." He smiled at the memory. "She did all the other challenges on her own. Ettore took her to work with him to keep her safe when she was out of school, so she learned to read blueprints, use his calculator, and even mix cement. Everything he knew, he taught her. But you know all this because of her business." He paused to see Eden's reaction and was not surprised she looked stunned. "Did you know she named her business *Eroina*[8] because of Brettito?"

Eden couldn't hide her surprise. "No," she said softly, "I didn't know."

Gabri knew he couldn't hide the disappointment on his face at how little this woman knew about Rafaella. He wondered why Rafaella never told her even the story of the name she gave her company. "You will have to ask her about it someday," he said knowing it was not something he should

---

[8] Heroine

tell. He knew Rafe would want to be the one to tell it if she decided she wanted Eden to know.

Someday, if Rafaella told her, then he could tell her how ironic it seemed to him Brettito had called Rafaella *Eroina* when really it turned out Brettito was the hero in saving her life. "Rafaella's father showed his appreciation to me many times," he said changing the subject. "He paid for my education in music, and I would not be here in this home if not for him. He also paid for the education of Brettito's sister. He felt Brettito sacrificed himself and saved Rafaella, which he did, and he wanted to try and help his family because of what he had done for Rafaella."

Eden handed the photos back to Gabri. "She was lucky to have you both," she said softly.

"No," he said softly, "we are lucky to have her. Without her, we are nothing." Gabri pulled another photo out of the packet and handed it to Eden. "This one is the one I always see when I think of my Rafaella," he said proudly.

Eden took the photo and felt the sting of him calling her *his Rafaella*. Then, after looking at the picture, she looked up at Gabri in surprise. "What's she doing?"

Gabri laughed at Eden's expression. "She is flying," he said with a wink. "She jumped from her father's roof to the neighbor's, and I took the photo. It was the only way we could think of to have her surrounded by the sky and the sunlight."

Looking at the photo again, Eden shook her head. It was horrifying to her mothers' heart, but also beautiful. Rafe's body was stretched out in the air as if she were running and reaching for something in front of her as her hair flowed behind her. You could make out the smile she had on her face.

"She looks like she's happy," said Eden.

"Yes," Gabri agreed, "she loved adventures and challenges. I was very relieved she made it. I did not want to have to explain to her father if anything happened to her. This was a time after Brettito died when it was like she had no fear, and she was very reckless. I worked very hard to keep her safe for her father, and for myself."

Eden handed Gabri the photo back. "But why did her father, and now you, want to keep what happened to her a secret?"

Gabri nodded at her question as he took the photos back, glancing at them for a moment and then putting them back into the file. "She does not even remember wearing a cast on her arm," he revealed with a shrug. "We show her the pictures where you can't see the cast," Gabri paused to gather himself. "In America, it is no good to have these problems, and sometimes the same in Italy. Ettore wanted to protect her life. Also, the fewer people who know, the less likely Rafaella's memories will be challenged."

"Okay," said Eden, now having a new respect for Rafe's father. "But why was he so hard on Rafe? Letty said he was horrible to her and blamed her for her mother's death all the time. Even Julia and her father think he was a tyrant or something."

Frowning at what Eden was saying, Gabri sighed and nodded. "It's hard sometimes for Rafaella and for me to hear bad things said about her father," he said as he looked around the office at all he had because of him. "Here in

Italia, Ettore Salvaggio was a great man. But, in America, it seems everyone hated him. I think they didn't understand him or were jealous. He was a great businessman and never hesitated to act when he saw an opportunity. He tried to teach what he knew to me, and to Rafaella."

He paused for a moment, thinking back to when they were younger, and Rafe was sick. "Rafaella and I always say her father was a great man, but he was not a perfect man. Rafaella was a lot for him, even with help," he explained. "She was a lot for us all to handle, even before she was sick. She had this energy, and it seemed to keep her in motion all the time. Her mother, before she died, would call her a wild child and she always depended on Brettito and me to tell her if Rafaella was thinking about doing something dangerous. Like jumping off the house."

Gabri smiled for a moment remembering a conversation he had with Brettito about Rafe where they were trying to determine if when they called her *Eroina,* they meant heroine or heroin because of some of the crazy things Rafe found to do making it seem like she was on drugs at times. But they knew she just loved her adventures and always needed to be doing something.

"It got worse and much more dangerous after her mother and Brettito died. I sometimes wondered if she did those things to prove to herself she was still alive or if she needed to do them to feel something missing in her." Gabri rubbed his eyes and the bridge of his nose. "Ettore, he barely had time to grieve, and then he had to watch Rafe go through all those things, then deal with her skipping school and all her adventures and challenges she would do, so he became angry and took it out on her sometimes, and on others. But Rafe found a way to cope with his anger too. She loves her father very much."

"I know," said Eden softly remembering the promise she made to defend Rafe's father when people talked badly about him.

Gabri took a deep breath to clear his mind of the past. "Now you understand why you need to go back home and let Rafe get better," he said and took a sip of his drink. "Everything that happened when she was young, and the things she has gone through since her father got sick then died, has made it very hard for her."

Eden shook her head at his words. "I still have things I need to talk with Rafe about. I want her to come home with me."

"No," said Gabri firmly. "She's come too far. I don't know if you understand how hard it was to get her to where she is now. I told you, we had to challenge her memory about New York, and I want to be sure all her progress is not taken away."

"I want to help her too," said Eden. "I went to New York," she confessed. "I know she didn't have an affair. I'm not going to let her or anyone else think she did anymore."

"Good," said Gabri, glad she had found out the truth for herself. "Rafe will be glad you know the truth."

"I told her," she said instantly. "I told her I don't believe she had an affair."

"I'm glad you did," said Gabri. He pulled another photo from the file and handed it to Eden. "Do you recognize this?"

Eden looked at the photo and saw a very young Rafe standing in front of a fireplace. "It's Rafe," she said. "It looks like she's in her father's apartment in New York."

"That's right," he confirmed. "The doctor and I have a theory about how Rafe came to manifest the woman she believed she had an affair with when she visited New York."

"A theory?" repeated Eden.

"Yes, you see the real Lauren Street told me about Rafe burning a painting in that fireplace," he said, motioning to the photo. "We think the copper lipstick she describes came from the copper panels below the mantle. The white clothes are possibly from the white marble or the bust on the mantle."

Eden pulled the photo closer and saw the bust in question. It was of a man with ruffles running down from his collar. She wasn't sure what to say so she stayed silent.

"As far as the skin color of this mystery woman," Gabri continued, "we think it can be explained by the black smoke from the burning painting. It's all theory, but we think it makes sense."

Eden nodded her agreement. "It does make sense now," she conceded and handed Gabri the photo. "Does she know about your theory?"

"She does," said Gabri. "She is convinced of her innocence more and more, but there is more she needs to work through." He put the photo away then leaned his arms on the desk. He now needed to make sure Eden would not undermine all the progress Rafe had made. "I don't think Rafaella is ready to go back to America or to be pressured by you about your relationship."

"I need to hear it from Rafe," Eden said defiantly, working to hide her anxiety. She felt so overwhelmed by everything she had heard. Eden could never have imagined such horrifying things happening to Rafe, but she had seen the proof. She wished she knew all of this sooner. Maybe then she would have been better equipped to help her.

28

SCRUTINIZING THE STUBBORN woman in front of him, Gabri De Angelis shook his head and knew he would have to give her a clearer picture. This woman was still selfish and cruel not to leave Rafaella alone so she could get better.

"Do you remember when I asked you why Rafaella was calling herself the betrayer?"

"Yes," Eden answered hesitantly. Rafe had talked about betraying her in their conversation in the garden.

"She still thinks she betrayed you, and others," he revealed. "Do you remember what Chiara told you we were saying when I was talking with Rafe in her room?"

"Chiara said the two of you were talking about Dante, and she was calling herself the betrayer," Eden answered not sure where he was leading her. "I really didn't understand what you were talking about. Chiara said it was from your childhood." She clasped her hands together. "Rafe told me several times she knew she was the betrayer. She told me today she still thinks she betrayed me somehow, but I still don't know why she's saying it."

"Chiara was correct," said Gabri, "it is from Dante." Gabri tightened his jaw to control the emotions threatening to explode from him because Rafe was thinking those thoughts again. He lived for months with fear of losing her to those dark thoughts, watching her spiral in and out of days of manic activity. He remembered the hopelessness when she fell into days of almost no movement at all because she was in one of her trances. He sometimes thought he was going mad with her because of all the time they spent together. "You see, she aligned herself with the Traitor, the Betrayer in Dante's Ninth Circle of hell. You call him Cain.

"Cain?" Eden repeated.

"Yes, he is the first and the worse of all the Traitors."

"I thought Judas was the worse traitor," she said confused. "He betrayed Jesus."

Gabri gave a short laugh. "Judas?" He shook his head sadly. "Yes, I suppose *you* would think so." He saw Eden's face flush with either anger or embarrassment. Gabri did not know which because she did not know Judas was a very different kind of traitor than Cain. He continued without explaining the difference to her. "When we were young, we read Dante. Mostly because we liked the art in the book we found in her father's library. We were reading it and acting it out sometimes. We did very well when we had to study it in school," he said and took a sip of his drink.

He knew by the look on Eden's face he had to tell her more. "You understand Rafaella feels guilty for her mother's death." It was not a question. "When Rafe's mother died,

Rafaella showed me the part about *The Traditorè*. She thought she was the betrayer because she believed her actions led to the death of her mother. I thought she was just grieving and tried to tell her it wasn't true, and it was forgotten."

He took a breath and shook his head sadly. "Then Brettito died. We were all blood brothers you know, well, and sister. It was Rafe's idea for that too. For weeks, I had to hear about her being the betrayer to her mother and Brettito. She would dream about it and talk about it in her trance. She did and said so many manic things that she has no memory of," he said and frowned as he recalled how frightened he was for Rafe. "I had to read all Dante's poems to find things to prove her wrong. I was desperate to find something she would grasp and help her. The doctors worried about stopping her dreams and helping her stay out of her trances. I worried about staying part of her world even if she was in a trance or dreaming. It was foolish, I know now, but I think it did help her to know someone was with her. She would tell me things she wouldn't tell the doctors. I would tell them what she said and the things she was doing. She trusted me to do this." Gabri looked in the file on his desk and pulled out some sheaves of paper. "These are drawings she did when she was sick back then." He handed them to Eden and let her look at them.

At first, Eden was amazed at how detailed the drawings were then remembered Rafe had art lessons at a young age from her mother. As she looked closer, she could see there was a girl in the midst of an enormous cavern of ice. Hands were reaching out to the girl grabbing her feet and clothes to pull her under a lake of water in the center of the cavern. The others were of the same girl in different stages of being captured and pulled into ice or of the girl encased in ice. Eden looked up at Gabri questioningly.

"Are these self-portraits Rafe did?" she asked shakily.

"Yes," said Gabri and pulled more pages from the file, "but there are better drawings like these." He handed her drawings Rafe had done of herself walking on rays of sunlight toward a golden goddess. Another was of her glowing with light and surrounded by people in the shadows outside the light. "I talked to Rafaella one day about *Paradiso*, Paradise, and the rays sent down by Cyprian the Fair. She liked the thought of the goddess and her rays of frenzied love and began talking about it and making drawings. We decided we were her children and we would love many. I will always think, no matter how strange it sounds, finding the part in the poem about Cyprian and sharing it with Rafe helped her. I could be wrong. It could have been time or medicine, but still, I want to feel like I helped her."

Eden handed the drawings back to Gabri, uncertain of what to say. "I think you did," she said hesitantly. "She's very lucky to have you."

"I never wanted to hear her talk about being the Betrayer again," Gabri said unable to hide his anger. "And she never did until the day I came to see her and found her sick again. I was furious with you all and knew I had to take her away. When I got her here and settled, she told me more of what was happening to her, and about her dreams. I knew I made the right decision," he said sternly. "Now you have come, and she is saying it again. So, if you really want her to get better, you need to understand she needs to be here, and you should go home until she is ready."

"I do want her to get better," said Eden, fighting her anxiety. "I don't understand why you won't let me help h—"

Gabri slapped his hand on the desk interrupting her with a thundering boom making her jump in her seat. "First, she felt she betrayed *you* with an affair," he growled barely able to control his temper. "Then she felt she betrayed me because *you* took Bronte from her. Then she felt her betrayal of *you*, the affair *you* accused her of, led to *you* almost being killed and Bronte being taken by those people. At the time, in her mind, loving *you*, telling *you* she loved you, would lead to your death—like her mother and Brettito. She considered you family! Family she betrayed!" He fought to control himself. "Can't you see the pattern? You have brought all this back into her mind, and she wasn't ready!"

He watched as Eden just sat there silently wringing her hands and looking at the floor. He thought about what Nora would say and knew she would not like him interfering with their relationship. But when it hurt Rafaella medically, it was his responsibility to act.

He thought about how happy Rafe was about Bronte being here and knew she would want to spend more time with the baby. So he didn't want to risk Rafe becoming upset if Eden decided to keep Bronte away. He took a breath knowing what he had to do, though it was hard for him.

"I won't keep Rafe away from you and the baby while you are here," he said softly. Eden's head shot up, her eyes widened with surprise. "But if you cause her any more setbacks, I will ask you to leave. I know Rafe wants to spend time with the baby. And maybe she wants to spend time with you, I don't know. You say you love her and maybe it's true. Nora thinks love will help her. But I also know love can cause problems, too. Look at what Brettito was doing for love. He was running with the wrong people making the wrong decisions, and it got him killed!" He rubbed his eyes so no tears could escape. "I don't want to see Rafe hurting and living in torment again."

"I don't want to hurt her," said Eden finding her voice again.

"Then think about what you're doing, the words you say, and the consequences they may have," he said evenly. "Rafe is so much better than she was when she got here. She is laughing and happy and living again. Don't take her happiness away from her."

"I won't," she whispered. "I want her to be happy and have her family back. I do love her."

"Then this discussion of Rafaella's childhood is now over," said Gabri and put his hand on the file. "Remember, none of this is to be discussed, for Rafaella's sake, with anyone."

"Of course," said Eden, holding herself together.

Gabri stood up, taking the file, placing it back in the cabinet, and locking it. He walked toward the office door. "Let's go see what Nora and the baby are doing," he said and held the door open for her.

They made their way back downstairs and found Nora and Bronte in the music room. Nora was letting Bronte bang on the piano keys while she played some simple songs. She looked up at them and could see neither one was very happy. "I think she likes the piano," Nora said as she smiled at them. "Gabri, come and play for her."

"Gabri, Mommy, watch me!" Bronte called and banged on the piano keys some more. Gabri took Nora's place at the piano and began playing for Bronte.

Nora motioned for Eden. "Let's sit over here and listen," she said and sat down with her. "Tell me how you met Rafe," she said and put her hand on Eden comfortingly. "Was she irresistible or did you make her work for you?"

Eden couldn't help but smile when she remembered how they met. "She was irresistible."

29

MONDAY, THE VILLA was filled with activity since the early hours of the morning. Nora De Angelis was happy because, so far, everything had gone well. Gabri, Stefano, and Rafe had actually put the furniture back before people started showing up, as promised, and the place looked normal again. Lyka came back to work and had the kitchen running smoothly between what she was in charge of and what caterers were doing. Stefano had the schedule for everyone who reserved a studio time slot and was already helping a guest with a recording session.

Outside, the gardener had the lawn and the landscaping looking great. The driver and the extra help he found had picked up musicians at the airport and train station on time.

The tents were put up in the garden with lights for all the night time activity.

Nora stepped out onto the back patio, and as she looked around, she couldn't contain her excitement. Later tonight, they would go into town and listen to as many performers as they could and enjoy the festival. Later in the week, she and Gabri would have their own performances at the festival too.

She looked down the path and saw Gabri driving the golf cart toward the tent with the sound system he needed to set up, and he waved when he saw her. There would be music at the villa tonight until early morning. Performers would be pumped up after playing at the festival. They would want to continue playing and singing while others would want to practice. Still others would just like to relax and play together for pure enjoyment.

Nora caught sight of Rafe showing a guest to the pool and sending one of the many volunteer helpers for towels. Nora wondered if there was anything Rafe couldn't do. She looked like a general or maybe, more appropriately, a foreman directing a work crew who worshiped her. She somehow had recruited all kinds of volunteers who showed up this morning and jumped at her every command with a smile. They had never had this much help during festival week. Nora made a mental note to ask her how she did it or to make sure Rafe was here for the festival every year from now on.

Last night, Nora and Gabri talked with Eden and played with Bronte until after dark. They were hoping Rafe would come and join them, but she never came up. They invited Eden and her friend Julia out to listen to music at the festival and gave Eden tickets to a few special shows. They couldn't invite them to stay at the villa since they already booked all the available rooms. Nora told Eden they didn't know when they would be available the rest of the week because of the festival and all the guests they were expecting, and she seemed to understand. After Eden left Gabri walked back down to check on Rafe. Not long after she heard him come into their room and leave again. Nora knew he had taken Rafe a pill so she could sleep.

"Hey," said Rafe as she ran up to her with a smile and gave her a quick hug. "Gabri said I'm supposed to make sure you get some rest. So come on," she said and began pulling Nora inside, "let's go relax."

"Are you kidding me?" Nora laughed, glad taking the sleeping pill had helped Rafe. "There's still a ton of work to be done."

"It's under control," Rafe insisted as she put her hand on Nora's back and directed her inside with ease. "I've put Becky in charge of the volunteers, and she knows what to do."

"Who the hell is Becky?" Nora asked with a chuckle.

"She's a grad student who's here working on her thesis," Rafe informed her. "She's very organized and motivated. It'll be fine."

"Where did you find all those people," she asked as Rafe helped her up the stairs.

"Around," said Rafe and grinned.

They made it to Nora and Gabri's suite, and Rafe happily helped Nora get out of her shoes and into bed for a rest before the evening activities.

"Lay down with me, Rafe," Nora requested.

Rafe lay down on the bed facing her. "You've been up since before dawn, and Gabri said you're supposed to rest and try to sleep. You're not supposed to stay awake telling me all your plans and worries right now," said Rafe as she got comfortable.

"No," said Nora softly, "that's not why I want you here. I want to know how you're doing. I feel responsible for bringing Eden here and making things worse for you. Gabri wasn't very happy with me. I'm sorry."

The smile left Rafe's face and her body tensed. "I'm fine," she said evenly. "It's not your fault. You were just trying to help." She forced herself to relax her body. "Maybe you did help."

Nora smiled and rubbed Rafe's arm. "I talked to Eden for a long time. We waited to see if you would come and say goodnight to her and Bronte. She told me a lot about herself and how you two met. She talked about your relationship before you left too. She told me all the things you both went through." She watched as Rafe turned her face away. "She was angry at herself for upsetting you yesterday." Nora poked Rafe in the ribs, and Rafe flinched and groaned. "She told me you kissed her," she grinned. "Apparently, you make her lose her mind when you kiss her." She chuckled.

Rafe rolled her eyes and shook her head. "She didn't tell you that."

"So, you did kiss her." Nora laughed. "I knew it!"

Rafe groaned and rolled over onto her back. "I didn't kiss her."

"Oh, so you play hard to get," Nora teased. "Is that how you get women to fall in love with you and follow you halfway across the world?"

Rafe just gave her a quick smirk, not amused.

"Okay, she didn't tell me you kissed her," she relented and sighed. "Well, it's all very romantic, don't you think?" Nora asked thoughtfully. "A woman is so desperately in love, she follows the object of her desire across the ocean to declare her love in hopes of living happily ever after. It's a lot like one of Gabri's songs."

"Hmph," Rafe grunted. "Gabri never writes about the reasons they're so far apart. Probably because it wouldn't sell any CD's, unless he starts writing country and western songs," she quipped.

"Or epic ballads," Nora teased. "People love those if they're done right." Nora could see by her facial expression Rafe was thinking about yesterday. "Would you like to tell me about it?" she asked softly. "I'm a very good listener."

"I'm sure you are," said Rafe and gave her a tolerant smile. "She didn't declare her love," she said softly and looked away. "I thought you said you and Gabri weren't going to get involved in my relationship with Eden."

"No," said Nora, her heart breaking for Rafe as she saw the sadness in the way she held her entire body now. "I said we weren't making decisions about your relationship for you. There's a difference between inserting ourselves and making decisions for you and being a friend you can talk with." She put her hand on her arm to show her comfort.

"I don't even know where I would start if I wanted to talk to you about it," said Rafe and put her arm over her head breaking away from Nora's touch. "You need to get some rest."

"You don't have to tell me everything that happened," said Nora ignoring Rafe's words about sleep. "Eden already told us the stuff you both were going through."

Rafe looked over at her with a confused frown. "She told you everything?"

"Well, everything from her point of view," said Nora softly lifting herself onto her elbow. "Why do you think she really traveled all this way to see you?"

"What do you mean?" Rafe asked with a sigh.

"I mean there's got to be a reason she came and that she feels is important enough to need to see you in person," said Nora thoughtfully. "Do you think it's money?"

"What?" Rafe asked with a scowl.

"No, you're right. It couldn't be money," said Nora waving the reason away. "You gave instructions for Gabri to make sure she had anything she asked for, and you've probably already left all your money to Bronte, so if anything happened to you," she said coyly and shrugged. "You probably even made Eden executor or did something so she'd have access somehow." Rafe rolled her eyes, and Nora laughed. "You did, didn't you?"

Rafe took a deep breath and let it out slowly.

"I knew it!" Nora chuckled. "She told Gabri she loves you," she paused, "so maybe you were wrong about the whole closure thing, even if she didn't declare it to you," she pointed out, and Rafe didn't respond. "Why would she come and say she loves you? What could saying she loves you help her get?" Nora thought for a moment. "Maybe she's here to see how sick you are so she can sue you for full custody of the baby."

"She wouldn't take custody away," Rafe growled not liking what Nora was doing but trying not to show it. "She's probably just saying it for Bronte's sake."

"I'm sure you're right," said Nora seeing she had upset Rafe. "I'm sorry," she said softly. "She has your trust when it comes to the baby. I didn't mean to make you doubt her. I'm just trying to figure out why you let her leave yesterday."

"I let her leave because I'm sick," said Rafe and sat up. "I let her leave because I don't have anything to offer her, and she deserves to have some happiness. I let her leave because of everything that happened, and I don't know if I can trust her." She closed her eyes and leaned her head into her hands.

Nora sat up in bed and leaned against the headboard with a pillow behind her. "But you love her," she said softly. "I can see how this is so hard for you." She rubbed her hand over her belly as the baby moved inside her. "I think this kid is going to be an acrobat." She moaned. "It feels like he's constantly spinning in there just for fun."

Rafe sat up and turned to Nora with concern. "Are you okay? Do you need me to do anything for you?"

"No," said Nora as she held the side of her stomach. "I'm fine." She looked back at Rafe and patted the bed. "Come here," she said and waited for Rafe to decide if she would do it. Finally, Rafe climbed over, sat close to her, and ran her hand over Nora's stomach feeling the baby move. "You know that Gabri and I love you, right?"

"I know," Rafe said softly and leaned against the headboard.

"We want you to be happy and have love in your life," said Nora. "Soon, we'll be gone, traveling all over for Gabri's music, and you'll be here on your own. We worry about you a lot."

"I'll be fine," said Rafe as she studied the fresco on the ceiling. "I'll still be doing everything I do now, you just won't be here."

"I'm trying to understand why you think you have nothing to offer Eden," Nora said as she put her hand on Rafe's arm. "You're so full of spirit and love, and you're so caring. You really are the whole package. Any girl would be lucky to have you. But in all the time you've been here, you've never brought anyone home. Is it because it's hard to find gay women in Florence, or is it because you want Eden in your life again? If it's because you can't find any gay women here, maybe you should stay where you can find someone to love and not be so isolated."

Rafe shook her head and laughed softly. "There are plenty of gay women in Florence. Even ones who come to visit or to study." She grinned at Nora. "We are everywhere," she teased dramatically. "I'm just not interested in looking for anyone. I'm trying to get well. Plus, it wouldn't be fair to whoever I was with, or to me, to bring them into my life with so much history that I'm not ready to share," she said, realizing how much her words echoed her father's when deciding to tell a women she was dating about her problems. *He was right*, she thought. "That's why I'm not with anyone, including Eden."

Nora contemplated Rafe's words and didn't believe her. She was sure the reason Rafe was not with anyone was due to her feelings for Eden, and because of what happened in New York. Gabri told her Rafe, along with everyone else, thought she had an affair, but it turned out it wasn't true. She thought there were pretty good odds Rafe hadn't found anyone else because, when she left America, she had been trying to reconcile with Eden, and if she found someone else, it would be an affair and hurt Eden. There was a deeper reason she wasn't letting herself be with Eden, and she wanted to know what it was.

"Okay," she said softly. "So, you trust Eden with Bronte and with your money." She paused. "What is it you don't trust her with? Are you afraid she's not telling the truth about being in love with you?"

Rafe shifted in the bed looked up at the ceiling and sighed. "Something like that," she said reluctantly. She didn't want to be in a therapy session with Nora and talk about all this.

She looked over at the door and wanted to leave. If she did, Nora would probably get upset. Then Gabri would be upset at her for making Nora upset. It would not be a good situation with everything else going on, especially with all the people at the villa and the festival. Rafe felt a bit trapped.

Nora could see Rafe was uncomfortable, so she put her hand on her again to comfort her. "I know there's a lot I don't know and may never understand. I don't mean for this conversation to upset you. I care about you, and I can see you're hurting yourself. You said yourself you're sick."

Rafe frowned, not liking her own words used against her.

"I guess I would advise you to look at things from a different perspective," Nora continued. "You aren't married to Eden, but you did make certain promises to each other. You both made a lot of mistakes, but you love each other despite them. So maybe you should think about the promises you made and decide if they are ones you can keep."

"I don't know what you're talking about," said Rafe and sighed. "We broke up, so we can't be held to those promises anymore."

"But you broke up because of something you know now didn't happen. There was no affair," Nora said calmly. "So if you both want, you can hold yourselves to those promises again."

"But there was an affair," said Rafe trying to hold in her agitation.

"There was?"

"Yes, Eden had an affair with a man online, and she left me for Jake," she revealed. "So even if I didn't have an affair everything else that happened would have probably still torn us apart. Her leaving me for a man and all her feelings she can't help."

"Online," Nora repeated with a frown. "Oh, yeah, I remember her talking about that now." She thought about her visit with Eden again as she kept hold of Rafe's hand so she wouldn't leave. "Well, it looks to me like she's in control of her feelings now. She took a big risk and put herself in a very vulnerable position coming to see you here. People don't do those kinds of things unless they're sure about their feelings." She glanced over at Rafe who was leaning back and looking at the door. "I guess she's not worth the risk to you, though."

Rafe frowned her gray-blue eyes sparking. "Maybe you're right," she said hotly. "It doesn't matter anyway, because what she's sure of now is—she's with Julia. She's probably better off."

"Maybe," said Nora softly seeing she hit a sore spot. "Did she say she was?" She held her own against Rafe's angry eyes. Rafe looked away, and Nora knew Eden had not actually said she was with Julia. "If she was with Julia, she could have just sent a letter or done something easier than coming all the way here." She thought about the possibility for a moment. "I guess it's possible she's trying to make up her mind," she said softly. "If that's true, then there's still hope, and she does love you or she wouldn't uproot her life and create this opening for you."

Nora let her words settle in Rafe's mind.

"Let me tell you what I see. I see you working so hard to get better and making progress. I see you leaning heavily on Gabri and me to help you—which you should because we love you. Gabri worships you and would do anything for you." Nora could see the appreciation in Rafe's eyes. "But Gabri and I can never give you what you had with Eden. We can be a sort of family, but we'll just be an imperfect substitute for your real family with Eden and Bronte."

She paused and watched Rafe process her words.

"I see a woman who's reaching out to you desperately, even if she doesn't realize it or the cost. She might even be risking one possible love for another. She may lose them both if she's with Julia and coming here causes problems for them. Eden told Gabri she loves you and wants to help you get better. I see she's taking a huge risk for love despite the emotional toll it's taking on her with her anxiety problems. She's been through a different hell than you, but she's been through one all the same, and she wants to help pull you out of yours if she can."

She could see Rafe was taking her words seriously, so Nora felt emboldened enough to keep talking. "I can see all the problems between you won't be solved overnight, but you have a chance not many people get. If you don't take it, you may never truly get better."

She saw Rafe frown and didn't want her to be upset, but she needed to be clear.

"Oh, you may find someone and start a new family. But you'll always have to wonder 'what if' every time you see your child or see Eden. Who, by the way, might find someone else or actually stay with Julia like you believe. But she'll have the knowledge she tried. She took the risk, even if it didn't turn out the way she would have wanted."

"Nora," Rafe said in frustration, "there's just so much more to everything that you can't understand, and Eden can't understand, either. My life will never be," she hesitated, "it will never be free of demons and secrets and pain. I have betrayed every person in my life that's trusted me. I don't want to do that to her again and see her disappointment or horror or pity for me."

"No," said Nora. "You haven't betrayed Gabri or me."

Rafe's eyes glistened sadly. "You don't know," she said softly. She knew Nora would never understand the deep sodden courses of betrayal she was still trodding through endlessly every day of her life. There was no escaping any of it because she was who had carved every channel. Eden had proven it by bringing the school bag back to remind her it would never end.

"I know you and Gabri have a lot of secrets," Nora revealed and noticed Rafe's surprise. "Don't look so surprised. I'm a sensitive and jealous woman," she said dramatically then smiled at Rafe. "I can tell when something is going on and I'm not included. But I also understand it isn't done to hurt me. You both do it to protect yourselves. You both put your emotions into projects like his music or his job at the estates and your art or all the other things you seem to find time to do. The difference between you and Gabri is Gabri has found someone to share his secrets with— he has me." She saw the question in Rafe's face. "Oh, he hasn't shared them all yet. Sometimes he just confesses the fact he has them. I think he feels the need to share them with me sometimes, and he trusts I'll keep his secrets."

Nora leaned over close to Rafe. "I have secrets too," she whispered in her ear. "I'm positive one day I'll know all Gabri's secrets, and he'll know all mine." She sat back up and adjusted the pillow behind her back. "You, from what I understand, have never shared all your secrets with anyone. You share most of them with Gabri, and your father knew them, but if anyone else knows about them, you weren't the one who told, so you still hold them inside."

"I've told Eden secrets," she said softly, wondering if her regret could be heard.

"Has she kept them?"

"I don't know. I think so."

"Well then, there's another thing you can trust her with," she said thoughtfully. "Did you ever think maybe holding in all those secrets over the years was part of why you got sick? It is a lot of work to hide so much for so long."

"Maybe," said Rafe softly. According to her father, Rafe had to keep everything secret.

"If you never open yourself up and let someone who truly cares about you in, you'll shortchange yourself in life."

"I let her in," said Rafe evenly. "I let her in and look what happened." *Punishment.*

"You didn't really let her in," Nora argued gently. "You never shared your secrets or let her know who you really are. I think you thought you let her in enough and, because she didn't know certain things, you got hurt. Is that her fault?" Nora saw Rafe frown but pressed on. "I'm not saying everything was your fault." Mostly Nora blamed Rafe's father, but she knew she could never say anything negative about him to Rafe or Gabri. "I'm just saying the only way she can really know you is if you tell her who you are. She says she loves you, and you're right, her feelings may change after you tell her things, but you may be wrong too. Don't you want to be sure? Don't you want to stop having all those worries and dark thoughts keeping you awake at night? At least the ones where Eden is concerned? I've seen your notebooks full of drawings of Eden. Gabri told me you burned some of the pages. Are you giving up before you try?"

Nora could tell Rafe wasn't happy with her. "Okay," she said softly. "She's leaving soon and who knows if she'll be able to come back between taking care of Bronte and having to work, and other things in life that just happen. Remember this—right now, Eden is standing in front of you, reaching her hand out to help you, and she just might be offering you love and a family. If you don't let the people who love you help you, especially when you're sick and hurting, you're making another mistake." She patted Rafe on the leg. "I'll let you go now," she said and slid down to get comfortable in bed. "You and Gabri wear me out."

As Nora got comfortable, Rafe got out of the bed. She leaned over and kissed Nora on the forehead. "Thank you for caring. Sweet dreams."

"I really do care," she whispered. "I love you, even though you're more hard headed than Gabri."

Rafe smiled. "I always beat him," she said and closed the door as she left.

Nora chuckled to herself then sighed and closed her eyes to sleep.

30

JULIA HAWTHORN WAS going a bit stir-crazy and had to get out of the hotel. Eden was back in the room having lunch with Bronte. They would probably take a turn around the square but wouldn't be out of the room too long. They waited all day yesterday and most of the morning to see if Gabri or Rafe would contact them again. So far, there had been no word. Julia tried to convince Eden to get out today without success. Eden had been on edge and afraid to miss their call. Julia assured her, if they rang, they would leave a message, and she would be able to ring them back. But Eden still insisted on being there, or at least not gone far or long.

With the excuse she would scout a good place for dinner and suss out where the event Gabri had given them tickets for tonight was at, Julia crossed the city on foot. It was not a big city, so it didn't take long to find the music venue and a place for dinner. She walked around the area surrounding the venue, looking in the shop windows and taking in the hustle of the vendors and tourists crowding the street.

Foremost in Julia's thoughts was the fact this trip wasn't going the way Eden had hoped. However, it was going exactly how Julia thought it would. She had known Rafe since she was fourteen and knew Rafe had a history of dropping off the planet then turning up whenever she felt like it later. It was just one of the arguments she had in her arsenal to help convince Eden to move on when they left without Rafe. It was also a good contrast against her own history of consistency and stability she felt Eden needed right now.

It may take time, but Julia truly thought she and Eden could be happy together. She could get Eden out of Rafe's house and out from under the cohabitation agreement by letting her move into her condo. She thought it would help Eden move on even more. She also knew they would still have to see Rafe because of Bronte, but after a while, she thought Rafe would respect her and Eden's relationship. Rafe was the one who left Eden in the first place, after all.

Julia felt a conflict within herself. She had wanted to date Rafe since their school days. She always hoped someday Rafe would change her mind since telling her they should just be friends, but she never did. They had a passing awkward kiss in high school after which Rafe laughed and declared their future would only hold friendship. For Julia, it was heartbreaking because the kiss was something she had wanted for a long time. She wanted it as soon as she saw Rafe kiss another girl, reasoned out she was gay herself and wanted her.

No matter how hard it was, Julia couldn't stay away from Rafe. She kept being her friend not only because of their adventures but also with the hope of more in the future. She had dated other women, even ones Rafe had dated. She realized, after a time, she was doing it to be closer to Rafe. She didn't really understand why because she had never had sex with Rafe. For years, Julia had held the women she had dated up against Rafe, and none of them ever compared—until Andrea. But even their relationship didn't work out the way Julia planned, leaving her heartbroken again.

When Eden left Rafe for Jake, she thought maybe it was finally the right time for Julia and Rafe. But it seemed like Rafe was still far away even when she had moved in with her. Then Greer came into the picture, and Julia could barely bring herself to be around them. She finally accepted Greer, but then she left, and Rafe was suddenly getting back with Eden. It took a lot for Julia to get back to being a friend, but she did it. She decided to show her friendship and help Rafe by helping Eden. At first, helping Eden was frustrating and painful. She knew the help she gave was lined with bitterness toward Eden. But after a while, something changed.

It was hard to put her finger on exactly what changed until her talk with her father and the crazy dream she had while in New York. Then she knew she was falling in love with Eden. After Rafe left, Julia's feelings for Eden seemed to get stronger. Her therapist said it was just transference again, but she knew it was something more.

The more time she spent with Eden, the more she was sure her feelings were real for her and not just transference. They had been spending a lot of time together since Rafe left so suddenly. She had been helping Eden with everything. She made sure dinner was on the table, would be there when Eden was feeling low or just needed to talk to someone. She made sure they got out of the house and enjoyed pushing Bronte in her pram around the park and through the shops. She liked the feeling she got when people thought they were a family. Bronte was a wonderful, precocious child, and Eden was a very good mother.

Sometimes, Julia thought she could be just as much a mother to Bronte as Rafe. Neither Rafe nor herself shared DNA with Bronte but, unlike Rafe, at least Julia was there helping Eden. She genuinely felt she could make Eden happy and give her the consistent stability she and Bronte needed.

She was also sure she was seeing Eden differently for the first time. She wasn't seeing her as Rafe's wife, girlfriend, or partner.

She wasn't seeing her as Salvaggio's Paradise anymore.

She was seeing her as Eden Kingsley. A woman who was full of love for her daughter, who had a positive outlook on life, and who was in need of someone who could be there for her and give her security and stability. She also had begun to see her as a desirable woman who she wanted to show affection and offer to share her life with when Eden was ready. Julia's dreams were filled with emotion and images of

Eden. It was difficult waiting to be able to express the desires she could only dream about and hiding her sexual angst.

Julia also felt she could help be a buffer if Rafe started causing problems in the future with Bronte or their friends. She really didn't think anything would happen, but it wouldn't hurt to be prepared.

Julia was looking through a selection of silk shawls, hoping to find something that might cheer Eden up, when her thoughts and her shopping were interrupted by a commotion not far away. She looked over at the obstreperous group of people making their way through the vendor stalls. Julia could pick up the gist of what they were saying as they were laughing and talking loudly in Italian. They were surrounding someone who according to the words used must be female. Julia thought it must be one of the musicians or some famous person being mobbed by mostly men and a lot of children. Then she heard a familiar name and perked up to look closer at the mob.

"Rafaella!" a little boy cried out, and a man shoved him back before he could say more.

Julia watched as Rafe talked to some of the people for a few minutes, including the little boy who had handed her something that she put in her jacket pocket. Then she shook their hands, and they all disbursed, some of them running and others just walking away. Rafe began walking down the street again, and Julia noticed she was wearing the hat she wore when she drove her father's car. She tossed the scarf she was holding down and headed directly toward her.

Julia couldn't believe Rafe was so close to the hotel and out doing who knows what while Eden was waiting in her room for a call. She caught up with Rafe and snatched at her arm.

"Rafe," she said forcefully, "what the bloody hell are you doing?"

Rafe turned in surprise toward the person assaulting her. She saw it was Julia and frowned. "I'm helping Gabri with his festival," she said and yanked her arm away.

Julia stared at her a moment not sure what to say. She wanted to show her anger and berate her for not calling Eden. On the other hand, she didn't want to encourage her either because of her own developing feelings. As those thoughts made it to her head, she felt guilt rush over her because she had promised to help Eden bring Rafe home. She could do nothing but scoff at the whole situation. "Well," she said trying to save herself from embarrassment, "are you ever going to talk with me again?"

Rafe recognized the expression of guilt on Julia's face. She sighed and looked around but realized there really was no escape. This conversation would have to happen sometime so she might as well get it over with. "Sure," she said with a shrug, "I'll talk with you. Let's go over to the café."

Rafe led Julia to the café and waved to the owner as she walked inside and went to the counter to order. Once they had their coffee, they sat at one of the patio tables. Rafe took a sip of her drink then leaned back and studied Julia. "So, do you love her?"

Choking on her coffee, Julia coughed at the unexpected question. When she was able to breathe again, she felt frozen by the question because she hadn't realized she was so transparent. Finally, she brought her eyes up and met Rafe's expectant gaze.

"I really think I do," Julia said softly and watched as Rafe gave a barely perceptible nod. "I've been spending a lot of time with her," she went on in a rush. "At first, I just thought it was fondness, because of our friendship. But she just became more lovely and dear to me as time passed. We've become closer and... it," she hesitated, "just happened." She moistened her mouth and swallowed as Rafe just glared and said nothing though her jaw moved like she might at any moment. "I didn't plan to fall for her," she said earnestly.

"No," said Rafe evenly. She had not missed Julia's subtle hint about having sex with Eden. "I'm sure you didn't."

"I promise, I'll always take care of her, Rafe."

"I'm sure," said Rafe flatly.

It was all Rafe could do to hold back her anger at Julia and the realization she would actually take advantage of this situation. Rafe knew she said things to push them together but, as Nora said, she was sick. She remembered accusing Julia of grooming Eden to be her lover. She wondered if she had guessed right, and Julia had already been going after Eden back then. Right now, she felt like her heart was being stabbed at the same time she was being stabbed in the back. She took a deep breath and wiped her hand over her face to release some internal tension.

Rafe didn't know why she was feeling so angry and hurt. She had been sure this was why they were here, and now she knew she was right. She had also been telling herself it was for the best because Eden deserved to be happy. Maybe Julia was who made Eden happy now. Still, she couldn't help the anger flaring in her at the thought, and she fought to push it down. *It's for the best,* she reminded herself. *I betrayed her. I'm still betraying her.*

"Does she love you?" Rafe asked softly.

Julie bit her lip and shook her head. "I honestly don't know. I think she could."

"Is it the reason you're here? To see if she could."

Looking down at her coffee, Julia hated herself for wanting to say yes, because it was why *she* was here. But she knew it wasn't why Eden was here.

"No," she said finally. "Eden still cares about you. She wants to know how you are, and she wants you to see Bronte and be in their lives. You can't just leave like you did and expect her to be okay," she said letting her anger ease into her words.

"She has you," said Rafe holding in her emotions, "so she must be fine."

"She's not fine," she retorted in exasperation. "You know she's not."

Rafe glowered at Julia as a rush of thoughts about Eden and everything else that had happened flooded through her mind. All the times Eden left her, all the pain and heartbreak she felt waiting for her to come home, only to find one day she left again. All the time she wasted waiting for her to leave Jake. She knew now the affair hadn't happened, but knowing did not erase the things that had happened because of believing it was real, and the pain caused to both of them.

It had been just over six months, and Eden apparently must be feeling perfectly fine. She must be fine to be having feelings for someone else already, or she wouldn't be having sex with Julia. Rafe felt herself getting hot, so she took the cap off her head and wiped her forehead. She twisted the cap angrily in her lap because it seemed so unfair. She didn't understand how it was so easy for Eden to get over her so fast again. Especially when, before she left, Eden kept saying she had never stopped loving her when they were apart.

She had to stop thinking this way. This was the betrayer taking and wanting and not thinking of what was best for Eden. All she had to do was make them leave. Make them want to leave.

She looked up at Julia and tried to keep control of the emotions storming inside of her. "I guess I can understand Eden coming here to figure things out," she said softly. "What I can't understand is why you want to hurt me like this when you know how I feel."

Julia scoffed at Rafe with disbelief. "Know how you feel? Rafe, no one knows how you feel. You let *that man* take you away like he did, and we haven't heard from you in months," she shot out, trying to control her volume. "You don't answer calls or emails. You don't make any attempt at all to communicate with anyone, and you think we know how you feel?" She frowned as Rafe just stared back coolly.

"I guess you're right," said Rafe her voice strained as she fought to control herself. "I have no excuse for my actions at all. It's not like I was sick or anything." She got up and pushed her chair in. "Just a little friendly advice," she said evenly. "When she starts having feelings for someone else she just can't help, don't waste your time waiting for her to come back to you." She started to walk away but stopped and turned back, "Oh, and fuck off, because you're not my friend anymore."

"Rafe," Julia shouted after her, "I am still your friend!" She watched as Rafe put her cap back on, but she did not look back. "Goddamn you, Rafe," she growled as anger and guilt tore through her. "You're the one who fucked things up, sick or not," she mumbled to herself. "Other people in the world deserve happiness too." She got up and made her way back to the hotel.

31

TWO DAYS HAD passed since Eden Kingsley's visit to the villa, and she had heard nothing from Rafe, or from Nora and Gabri. She and Julia went to the music festival on Monday and Tuesday hoping to find Rafe in the crowd or get a glimpse of Nora and Gabri on stage, but neither had happened. Eden was getting worried because she would have to leave in a few days. Julia offered to pay so they could stay longer, but Eden was worried about how it would affect her job and being able to stay in Rafe's house.

They had a late night so, while Eden was feeding Bronte, Julia was still asleep in her room next door. Everyone in the hotel had been so good to Bronte, and she was making out like a little princess. They brought her lots of sweets and treats. The au pairs competed to take care of her and take her to the carousel. When they finally decided to get out of the hotel for a while, the manager had recommended a lot of special places to take Bronte that were a lot of fun. The only thing they were missing was Rafe.

Eden wished she could share everything Gabri had told her with Julia or someone. It seemed like her life was being chained up with secrets. Secrets she had to keep and trusts she dare not break for fear of the consequences that always seemed to be as terrifying as the secrets themselves. Now on top of not being able to talk about the secrets Rafe had told her, she had to keep secrets from Rafe of all the information Gabri had told her.

Thinking about the photographs she saw of Rafe and the drawings she made when she was young unbalanced her. Eden knew Rafe had a lot of things happen to her in her past, but the level of trauma and the reality of what she lived through were overwhelming. Now Gabri said she couldn't talk to Rafe about what he had told her, and she couldn't look at Rafe with pity. She didn't know how she could look at her with anything else at the moment.

Eden put a dab of Nutella on a breakfast roll and gave it to Bronte who decided to lick the chocolate off before eating the bread, getting it all over her face. As Eden laughed at Bronte and tried to wipe her face, there was a knock at the door.

"I wonder if Zia Julia is up," she said as she put the napkin down and went to answer the door. "Good morning," she said as she swung open the door with a smile.

"*Buongiorno*," said the hotel bellboy with a smile. "For you," he said and handed her a small envelope.

"Thank you," said Eden as she took the envelope, curiosity burning in her. The boy smiled again then scurried away. Eden closed the door then opened the envelope and pulled out the crisp folded paper from inside. Her eyes widened in surprise as she read the note and recognized the handwriting. She rushed up and snatched Bronte from her chair then went out the door and knocked on the one next door. "Julia! Julia, wake up!" she called as she pounded on the door.

"What the hell?" said Julia as she jerked open the door and saw Eden holding on to Bronte. "What's wrong?"

"I need your help," Eden said excitedly and shoved the note into Julia's hand.

Julia took the note as Eden walked into the room. Her eyebrows rose as Eden grinned excitedly. "Another note demanding something," she mumbled and read the note.

Eden– Please, come with me today. Meet me on the left side of the Hotel toward the plaza. Get Julia to watch Bronte. She owes me. Bring a jacket. –Rafe

"It's not a demand if she said please," Eden pointed out happily. She knew Julia had been unhappy about having to wait around for Rafe or Gabri to call, but now she could stop being so gloomy about everything. Things were starting to look better, and she wasn't going to let Julia's mood bring her down.

"And why is it exactly I 'owe' her?" Julia asked with annoyance as she waved the note around.

"Will you come over and have breakfast and watch Bronte like she asked?" Eden grinned. "I need to hurry and get dressed."

Seeing Eden's excitement, Julia sighed. She wondered what Rafe was up to and if it was going to take away the light showing in Eden's eyes right now. She had not told Eden about her conversation with Rafe or the fact she had seen her yesterday. She didn't think it would help either of them. She also had a feeling Rafe's comment about 'owing her' was probably because of their conversation.

"Fine, I guess this is why we're here," Julia relented and put her robe on. She followed Eden back to her room, not knowing which path of guilt to follow so she settled on staying at the crossroad balance at the edge of them all.

Inside the room, Eden put Bronte back into her seat at the table and hurried into the bedroom. Julia sat down at the table and poured a cup of tea. She read the note again. "She says to bring a jacket," she called back to Eden then spoke to Bronte. "Your mama thinks everyone should jump when she shouts."

"Mama lives in a garden," said Bronte as she ate her fruit happily.

Julia sighed. "Brilliant."

"Okay," said Eden breathlessly as she came out of the bedroom. "How do I look?" she asked expectantly.

Julia rolled her eyes and shook her head thinking she looked very good in her jeans and form-fitting cap-sleeved blouse. She knew when Eden lifted her arms or moved in a certain way, the shirt would raise, and the skin of her trim waist would show.

"You look fine," she said, cutting off her train of thought. Eden rushed into the bathroom to comb her hair and brush her teeth, and Julia looked over at Bronte again. "I hope your mommy isn't getting her hopes up just to have them dashed," she said and gave her a piece of pastry.

Bronte handed the pastry back to Julia, "I don't like this one. I want the chocolate."

Julia surveyed Bronte's chocolate covered mouth. "I think you're seeping chocolate out your openings."

Eden came out of the bathroom and kissed Bronte. "Be good for Zia Julia."

"I need chocolate," insisted Bronte.

Eden quickly spread Nutella on a piece of bread for her then and kissed her chocolatey face again. She turned to Julia excitedly. "I have no idea when I'll be back. Will you be okay?"

"Of course," she said, though she was apprehensive about Eden's excitement.

"Everything will be fine," Eden assured Julia, looking into her worried eyes. "She's here, she's waiting for me." Eden felt joy and excitement she hadn't felt for a long time. "I know she loves me." She saw Julia's concerned look and smiled. "It's a good start," she said and grabbed her ID and some cash from her purse and put it in her front pocket. She turned back and hugged Julia. "Thank you,"

"No problem," said Julia knowing she was holding Eden longer than she should. She was hoping Eden was right but at the same time not wanting her to go. "You'd better hurry before she changes her mind," she said sarcastically to hide her jealousy of Eden's excitement and then released her. Julia couldn't help noticing the scent of the perfume in the air that had not surrounded Eden since Rafe had left.

Eden smiled happily at Julia then grabbed her jacket and headed out the door of her hotel room.

Julia looked over at Bronte who was licking the chocolate from her bread. "Your mommy indulges you with chocolate. You'll be needing a good washing up, I suppose."

Bronte laughed and held out her bread. "'Dulge me."

Julia rolled her eyes at Bronte's chocolate covered face then took the bread to add more Nutella. "Precocious yet impertinent. Not unlike someone else I know," she mumbled.

32

SKIPPING THE PAINFULLY slow lift, Eden Kingsley took the stairs down to the lobby and walked out the door onto the busy sidewalk in front of the hotel. The note told her to meet on the left side of the hotel, so she turned and walked down the sidewalk as directed. She searched the faces of the people walking along the sidewalk but didn't see Rafe anywhere. She wondered if Julia was right when she said she had taken too long, and Rafe had changed her mind. Her anxiety threatened to rise up in her, but she pushed it down.

She was in Italy on a mission. She was here to get Rafe back and take her home, and now she had another chance to make it happen. She had been working hard on her own with Dr. Cathcart on all the things that had come out in the therapy sessions with Rafe. She was prepared to work even harder on anything else Rafe needed her to work on.

When she finally came out of the fog of her anxiety and fear after Rafe was ripped from her life, it was clear to her, now more than ever, she needed Rafe in her life, and she was in love with her. Rafe was her soulmate, and her life wasn't complete without her. She would do anything to get her back in her life and back to California. She hoped, by spending time with Rafe, she could show her they still had a connection. Then convince her to come home and continue therapy where they could be together.

When Eden walked almost halfway down the street, a person dressed all in black leather and sitting on a motorcycle held a helmet out in front of her. Eden looked from the helmet to the person sitting on the motorcycle. Through the visor opening of the rider's helmet, she looked straight into the eyes of Rafe. Her heart leaped, and she felt it thud hard in her chest just before those eyes looked away. That involuntary reaction had only ever happened for one person.

She swiftly put on the jacket she brought and shakily took the helmet, clumsily putting it on as Rafe waited. When she had the helmet on and secured, Rafe moved forward on the bike and motioned for her to climb on behind her. Eden held on to Rafe to steady herself as she swung her leg over the bike. Then she sat in the seat and slid her arms around Rafe's waist. Rafe started the engine and maneuvered them away from the sidewalk and out onto the road. Eden's mind reeled at the knowledge she was sitting so close and holding on so tight to Rafe's body again.

33

FINESSING HER WAY through the chaotic Italian traffic, Rafe Salvaggio felt Eden holding on tight. At times, Eden held on a little too tight, and Rafe could tell she was scared as they passed large and small vehicles and crossed from lane to lane into openings in the traffic that would move them forward. She would have used one of the cars at the villa, but Gabri and his guests were using them all.

Soon, Rafe had maneuvered them outside the city walls, and they were on the interstate. Eden was holding on tight again. Rafe knew it was the combination of speed and the traffic making her hold on so tight, but this was the most direct route to where they were going. One of the benefits of riding a motorcycle, in Rafe's mind, was the silence. Each of them was wearing helmets that kept their thoughts to themselves while they traveled, and they didn't have to make small talk or worry if there was any awkwardness.

After her conversation with Julia yesterday, Rafe was angry with both of them. She did what she had to do to make Julia want to leave, but it didn't stop her anger. She wanted to tell Gabri to handle everything. She wanted to tell him to send them away and start selling everything in California. She felt like there was nothing to go back to, so why keep the house or the property there. She had even thought about just giving Letty and Ephraim the house and the building the Kiki Bistro was in. Then she wouldn't have to worry about waiting around for it all to sell. Eden could move in with Julia because she was sure it was where Eden was headed anyway.

The rest of her things she could get Katheryn to help arrange for shipping to Italy or selling. Then life in America would be finished except for the occasional trip to New York to take care of things she inherited from her father's estate holdings. It was what she wanted to do. But she knew if she did, Gabri would have questions she didn't want to answer. So she had to handle everything herself and try to do it with order and control.

She would begin taking back control of everything today—first Eden then the school bag and its contents. After today, she could go back to her routine, and bide her time Gabri and Nora were ready to leave on tour. Then she could start over somehow. Maybe she could find a new therapist. One Gabri doesn't talk to. She could talk to them about how to do it—start over. She loved it in Italy, but she thought she would have to go somewhere else, somewhere new. Maybe Barcelona, Spain, or some island somewhere. There would be time to figure it out.

34

EXITING THE INTERSTATE, Rafe Salvaggio turned the motorcycle onto a road with less traffic. After a few miles, she turned onto a dirt road and followed it for a few miles until she pulled up to a small estate. She stopped in front of one of the smaller buildings then turned off the bike. She pushed out the kickstand and let the bike gently lean as she turned the handlebars to park. As she unstrapped her helmet and took it off a woman came out of the building and let out a shout of joy when she recognized Rafe.

"*Rafaella! Sei tu! Cosa ti porta oggi? È così bella vederti,*"[9] said the smiling woman as she looked past Rafe curiously at the woman behind her.

"*Sono venuto a dare un tour privato,*"[10] Rafe shouted back and gave her a wink as Eden climbed off the motorcycle and took off her helmet.

"*Capisco! Beh, vi lascio ad esso quindi,*" the woman laughed. "*Fammi sapere se hai bisogno di me.*"[11] The woman waved and went back inside the building.

"Where are we?" asked Eden as Rafe got off the bike and hung the helmets on the handle bars.

"The land of wine and honey," said Rafe with a smile and a quick wink. It was warm, so she took off her gloves and jacket. She laid them across the bike, and Eden did the same with her jacket. "Come on," she said and started toward the building where the woman had gone.

Eden followed Rafe closely, and as soon as they entered the building, she was hit with a cool pleasant smelling air. She took in everything inside and realized it was a small store selling wine and honey products along with a few other things that went along with the theme. The smell in the air was beeswax from all the candles on the shelves and hanging from rods suspended from the ceiling. There were shelves with honey and all kinds of other products made with honey, from bath products to lip balms to candy. There were also shelves of wine and different things to go with it like cheeses

---

[9] Rafaella! It is you! What brings you today? It is so good to see you!
[10] I came to give a private tour.
[11] I understand! Well, I leave you to it then. Let me know if you need me.

and jams infused with wine and breads to go with them. She followed Rafe around the store as she took a few things from the shelves and loaded them into a basket.

Rafe put the basket on the counter and flashed a smile at Eden. "Just a little breakfast. Let's find Carisa."

Rafe led Eden through a large set of double doors then made her way through the back room. There were large vats of liquid wax and water in one section of the room and tables with tools for carving candles in another. Standing over one of the wax vats was the young woman who had greeted them. She was dipping wicks into the wax and the water alternately.

"Carisa, I'm pilfering your stock," said Rafe in English as she walked up to the woman.

"Are we speaking English today?" the woman asked with a melodic laugh.

"Yes," said Rafe and motioned to Eden. "This is Eden from America. I'm going to show her around."

Carisa hung her candles and held out her hand to Eden. "Hello, it's nice to meet you."

"*Ciao*," said Eden shyly. "*Bellissimo negozio.*"[12]

"Thank you," said Carisa proudly. "Are we changing to Italian?"

"No," said Eden, blushing as Rafe looked at her with surprise. "I only know enough to hopefully make myself understood." She couldn't bring herself to explain that the reason she had been determined to learn some Italian was so she could find Rafe.

---

[12] Beautiful shop.

"Well, you're lucky to have Rafe around," said Carisa. "You should give her private lessons," she said to Rafe with a wink.

As Rafe chuckled, Eden forced herself out of her shyness to speak again. "You're very creative." Eden looked at the candles to hide her nervousness and avoid eye contact.

"Gabri took a big chance on me, and it's worked out well for us both," said Carisa.

"Gabri?" Eden repeated.

"Gabri rents her the space," explained Rafe. "Carisa has beehives in the vineyard, and she sells the honey and makes the candles and other things in the store. She also consigns the wine and other local products."

"Oh, that's really smart," said Eden impressed.

"Yes, Gabri learned to diversify from my father," said Rafe with a grin. "Now, with tenants like Carisa, the estates practically run themselves."

Carisa laughed and put her hand on Rafe's shoulder. "You've been a big help too, though. I've got a big candle order for a wedding, and I'll be recruiting help as soon as the festival is over. Let me know if you want to help out again," she said and ran her hand down Rafe's arm as she headed around her. "Let me write down what you're taking."

Eden had watched Carisa run her hand down Rafe and felt a jolt of jealousy shoot through her. She wondered how close they were but pushed the thought away as she followed Rafe back to the front of the store.

Rafe watched as Carisa wrote down everything in the basket on the counter. "My daughter is here," said Rafe with a smile.

Carisa looked up in surprise. "Really?" she asked as Rafe nodded happily. "You should bring her, and I can show her the bees and how to make a candle."

Rafe turned to Eden. "Would you like to bring her?"

"Oh, sure," said Eden caught off guard by the question. "She'd love it."

"Oh, my god. You're the baby's mother?" asked Carisa and Eden nodded shyly. "Rafe, why didn't you say something," she chastised her. She went around the counter and gave Eden a hug, oblivious to Eden's discomfort. "Welcome," she said. "You should come anytime. We have fun things to do for kids and adults all the time," she said as she released her. "We're just slow out here this week because of the festival in the city. But you can visit our street stand. We give the children honey sticks while they last."

"Thank you," said Eden. "We'll look for you." She was surprised by the hug and felt the discomfort she always felt when a stranger touched her. She looked to Rafe for reassurance, but there was none. Rafe only smiled at Carisa as though she were amusing in some secret way.

Rafe picked up the basket. "I'll put the basket back before we leave. Make sure you go see Gabri play," she said as she headed for the door. "Come on, Eden."

Eden waved to Carisa and rushed to follow Rafe out the door. Outside, Eden caught up with Rafe. "So, have you spent a lot of time with her?"

"Not a lot," said Rafe with a shrug as she walked over to a small park area. "I just helped her and her husband out a few times for something to do."

"Oh." Eden breathed out relief. "She seems nice."

"She is," said Rafe as she sat down on one of the benches with the basket. "Have a seat." She dug into the basket, pulled out some bread, and tore it apart then handed some to Eden. Then she broke off some cheese, opened a small jar of honey, and dipped the cheese in it and put it on the bread. "I know it seems weird, but it's good," she said at Eden's doubtful look then took a big bite. "Try it," she said with her mouth full. She dug out the large bottle of water and opened it as Eden tried the honey and cheese concoction. "Good, right?"

"It's different," said Eden not sure if she would describe it as good or not. She was sure Bronte would probably like it, though. "Bronte will love it." She took the bottle of water offered and washed down the food.

Rafe laughed and brushed the crumbs off her shirt and hands. "Then she needs to have it." She tore off more bread and put honey on it then put the basket on the ground. She handed some of the bread to Eden. After they ate the bread and honey, she took the water bottle from Eden and took another drink. She leaned back on the bench and looked out over the vineyard. "It's beautiful every season here," she said softly.

Eden licked the honey from her fingers as she drank in the vision of Rafe. To her, no other beauty really mattered. It felt like a miracle that she could see her beautiful face again with her long lashes, smooth skin, and full lips. She wore her dark hair pulled back and bound at the nape of her neck, but pieces at the front had come loose and curled around her face. Seeing her again was like a balm, even though she knew they had things to talk about and they weren't going to be easy.

"I come out here and run sometimes," said Rafe, breaking their silence.

Eden took her eyes off Rafe to look at the vineyard. "It seems peaceful."

Rafe hitched her shoulders and took a sip of water. "I guess a lot of people think so. There are a lot of regulars who come early to run the paths."

"Thank you for spending time with me," said Eden softly.

Rafe gave Eden a slight smile but looked away quickly. "I'm sorry about the last time you saw me."

"No," said Eden. "I'm sorry. I never meant to upset you. I didn't know you wouldn't want the school bag here. I was just doing anything I could think of to make Gabri let me see you."

"You only had to ask," said Rafe quietly and fidgeted with the water bottle.

Eden wasn't sure if Rafe knew or not that she asked many times and got nowhere.

"Anyway," said Rafe before Eden could speak. "Before I left, you were talking about finding happiness and wanting to talk to me about things." She decided to just get it over with like she did with Julia. "I hope you've found some happiness because you really do deserve to be happy."

She hoped Eden understood she was okay with her being with Julia.

That was a lie, though.

She wasn't okay with it. She was angry. But she knew it was probably for the best. It would be hard, but someday, maybe, she would be able to face Julia and Eden together again. She knew this might be the last day she ever spent with Eden alone. "1 just hope you don't regret the time you were with me."

Eden snapped her head up at Rafe's words. She would never regret her time with Rafe, and she came here to get their happiness back. She didn't need to go find what she felt she had with her. She realized Rafe must think she came here to end things.

"Rafe," she said softly. "Rafe, look at me."

Rafe forced herself to look at Eden.

Seeing Rafe's intense gray-blue eyes filled with uncertainty, Eden couldn't stop herself as she leaned in and kissed her. She saw the surprise on Rafe's face and kissed her again.

Recovering from her surprise, Rafe dropped the water bottle then pulled Eden closer and kissed her deeply. She could feel the dopamine rushing through her brain and causing the familiar dizzy sensation that always happened when she kissed Eden. She missed the feel of her under her hands and the taste of her lips. She missed having Eden close and feeling her touch as she ran her hands through her hair and down her arms and over her back. The sensation of Eden's soft lips against hers and the feel of her breath and her tongue in her mouth as she kissed her made her heart beat hard and everything except Eden seemed to fade away.

As her senses slowly came back to her, Rafe wondered why this was happening. Was Eden doing this to check her feelings or to say goodbye? She pulled away and put her head against Eden's.

"What are you doing?" she asked heavily feeling Eden's breath against her face.

"I'm kissing you," Eden said softly as she smiled.

"No, I know. I mean, why are you doing this?"

"I'm doing it because I love you," she said and kissed her again. She had been dreaming about this for months and couldn't believe it was finally happening. It was much better than any dream. She felt alive again.

"What about Julia?" Rafe breathed as Eden kissed her.

"Julia?" she repeated softly.

"Yeah," Rafe said between kisses. "What about her?" She pulled away. "Are you just checking your feelings to make sure you're in love with her?"

Eden grimaced in confusion. "In love with her? No," she said and could feel herself getting flustered and turning red. "Why would you think I was?"

"You came here with her," she answered, "and you looked happy together." She shrugged not sure what to make of Eden's flustered look.

"I only love you, Rafe," Eden said softly and kissed her, stopping her from talking. "I don't want to love anyone else." She kissed Rafe again. She held Rafe close and spoke softly into her ear. "She helped me come here to find you. That's all. I haven't heard from you for so long except for what you sent Bronte. I was worried you had forgotten about me, worried you found someone else. I had to come because I wanted to tell you in person that I'm still here, and I'll always be here for you because I'm so in love with you."

Rafe pulled away and shook her head wondering now what Julia had been talking about yesterday. Based on what

Julia said, it sounded like they were together. She looked away from Eden's pleading eyes. It didn't matter because she had already made up her mind about what she was going to do. She knew no matter what Nora said, she would always be the betrayer.

"Oh, Eden," she whispered and pulled away. "I'm not sure you should wait for me. I don't know how long it'll take me to get better. You deserve to live your life and be happy. You shouldn't wait on me."

"But I," Eden stammered, "I love you. Don't you love me anymore?"

"Of course. Of course, I love you," said Rafe sadly and touched Eden's face gently, knowing she would probably never love anyone again like she had loved her.

Eden trembled a bit as her mind took in the fact Rafe had just told her she loved her. It had been so long since Rafe had said those words, and Eden had been so worried. Eden could literally feel every cell in her body celebrating and sending signals of warmth and tingling in waves through her. It felt like she was going to be lifted off the earth and float to heaven. Eden tried to look into her eyes again, but Rafe looked away.

"I love you and Bronte very much," said Rafe as she looked away. "But I don't know if we can go back to how things were. I told you, I'm just now getting into a good place where I'm able to see things more clearly." She smiled sadly. "I thought I'd have more time to figure out what to say to you. I haven't even thought about you, no, I've thought about you. I've thought about you a lot. I haven't thought about us and our relationship. I don't know if it's fair to you."

"Fair?" Eden asked as the feeling of euphoria came crashing down around her as she realized what Rafe was saying. She was unable to hide her hurt at the reality Rafe may still be pushing her away. "All I've been doing since you left is thinking about you, and us, our relationship." She took Rafe's face in her hands and kissed her again. "I'll think about us. You think about getting better. I want to help you. I'll do whatever you or Gabri tell me to do. I love you."

Rafe shook her head and looked down remembering the words of her father about the possibility of this exact situation. He was right. It wasn't fair to saddle her problems on an innocent person. She should have ended her relationship with Eden long ago, just as she did all the others. She would be alone, but she wouldn't be causing anyone pain. The argument over telling or breaking up was an old one. The last time Rafe and her father argued about telling Eden everything Rafe had accused her father of wanting her to be alone forever. Now she knew he was protecting her from this very situation.

"What if Gabri tells you to leave?" asked Rafe. "What if I tell you to go find someone else? I can't make you wait for something that might never happen."

"Why are you doing this?" she asked shakily. "Don't push me away. Please, I just got here. You can't tell me to go without even trying. Please, just give us more time together."

Rafe leaned over and put her head in her hands. "I just don't want to hurt you again," she said wishing that doing this didn't hurt so much.

"I don't want to hurt you either," said Eden and lifted Rafe up gently so she could see her face. Rafe turned her gray-blue eyes away as Eden pushed back the strand of dark hair that had fallen into Rafe's face. "I love you, and you just said you love me. That should give us both a lot of happiness. I know it's given a lot to me." She leaned in and gave Rafe another small kiss. "We should take this chance to try and to spend time together. It could be good for both of us." She pulled Rafe close and kissed her again. When Rafe didn't resist, Eden took the kiss deeper and wrapped her arms around her, feeling the crazed need for her that was hard to restrain. She never wanted this to stop. She wanted it to go further. She felt Rafe pull her closer and move her kisses to her jaw and neck. She couldn't help the moan leaving her and had to kiss Rafe's honey-coated lips again.

Rafe broke away breathing heavily. She had no idea what she was doing. She didn't know if it was right or wrong. She just knew it felt good to have her, claim her, possess her again. She leaned her head against Eden's and didn't know whether to laugh or cry. Julia was in love with Eden and was promising to take care of her. Nora was telling her Eden was reaching out desperately for her. Eden was saying she was still in love with her. Everything that had happened before she left home was still unresolved. Her father's words kept haunting her. Threaded through everything was pain and confusion and lies mixed with truth. Then the weight of the secrets and the betrayals she was hiding from everyone felt so crushing that she wished she could just close her eyes and not wake up sometimes.

"Rafe," Eden called her softly out of her thoughts, "tell me what you're thinking right now."

"I don't know."

"What don't you know, babe?"

"I don't know anything. I don't know what to do or what to think. Too much is happening." She looked up at Eden. "I'm out of control, Eden. You don't want to be with me if I'm not in control."

"What aren't you in control of?"

Rafe avoided looking into her eyes, remembering when all she ever had to worry about was getting lost in them. She chuckled softly at the thought.

"What?" asked Eden as she smiled.

That smile. God, she missed it. "You smell just like I remember," said Rafe softly changing the subject to something safe.

"I know," said Eden in her sultry voice and ran her hand over Rafe's face. "I brought the perfume you like, and I'm wearing it just for you."

"Do you think it's why Julia's in love with you?"

"What?" Eden laughed and slapped her arm playfully. "Why do you keep saying those things? Besides," she said huffily, "this is the first time I've worn it since—" She stopped and looked down at her hands angry at herself for bringing up anything negative today. "I only wear it for you."

"Oh," said Rafe with an arched brow. "What do you wear for her? Maybe I'd like it, too."

Eden frowned. "I don't wear anything for her."

Rafe laughed softly. "See, I'd like you wearing nothing."

"That's not what I meant!" Eden pushed her back gently.

"Well, what do you mean then," Rafe challenged intently.

Eden grabbed Rafe's shirt and pulled her close. "I mean, what I wear, or don't wear, is for you and no one else," she said and kissed her soundly. "Got it?"

"If you say so." Rafe chuckled as she broke away and stood up. "Let's go." She picked up the water bottle and the basket, and they headed back up to the little store.

35

SMILING AND FEELING like she had won a huge victory, Eden Kingsley followed Rafe back to the honey and wine shop. She had already accomplished part of her mission. Rafe had told her she loved her, and she got to say the same words to Rafe. No matter what else happened, she would consider this a good day just because they both said that one fantastic thing.

She knew Rafe was having a hard time and wasn't saying what was really on her mind, but at least she was still spending time with her, and they were getting along so far. She didn't want to upset her by talking about going home yet. It was clear Rafe wasn't ready to talk about the subject. She hoped the more time they spent together that Rafe would see they loved each other and the easier it would be for Rafe to open up. Maybe then she could convince Rafe to come home with her and Bronte and get the help she needed there.

Inside the sweet-smelling shop, Rafe picked up some bottles of wine and sat them on the counter. "Carisa! I'm back," she called out. She looked over at Eden. "Do you see anything you want?"

"Oh, I don't know," said Eden looking around trying to take everything in again. "I really haven't looked."

"Well, look around," said Rafe. "I'll be right back. I'm going to see if I can find Carisa." She went through the double doors leaving Eden on her own. When Rafe made it to the workroom, she found Carisa setting a newly carved candle on a shelf. "There you are," said Rafe.

"Hey," said Carisa as she turned with a smile to greet Rafe. "Sorry, I just can't stop in the middle of one of those." She thumbed over her shoulder at the candle. "I knew you'd understand." Rafe looked a little pale. "Are you okay?"

"I'm fine," she said abruptly. "Eden is picking some things out. Can you show her the teaching beehive? I need to use the restroom," she said and quickly headed off.

"Sure," said Carisa confused by Rafe's abruptness. She shrugged it off and went to do as Rafe had asked.

Rafe made it into what she was sure was the world's smallest bathroom and leaned against the miniature sink. She looked up into the tiny mirror and could see the uncertainty in her own eyes. The weakness she saw made her sick. She had already made the decision about what she was going to do about Eden, and now she wasn't sure if it was the right thing or not.

In the back of her mind, the conversation she had with Nora kept nagging at her. Maybe Eden really was doing what Nora said and reaching out. If it was the reason she was here, then Nora was right, and she was wrong about Eden and Julia being together.

Julia's confession of love for Eden pushed itself forward. Rafe just couldn't understand why Julia told her they were together and that she loved Eden. Why would Julia say it if it weren't true? She didn't understand why either one of them would lie. *Eden has lied before,* she thought, *but so has Julia. Lies, lies, lies and more lies. They seemed to never end.* Rafe squeezed her eyes shut to block the voice in her head. It was even more confusing if they were both telling the truth. Maybe they were together, but Eden didn't really love Julia. Maybe it was the reason Julia didn't know if Eden loved her or not. Maybe Eden felt tricked again, or maybe trapped or just confused. Eden had promised if she was having a hard time with her feelings that she would talk to someone. Maybe it was why she was here. To figure out if her feelings were still there, or if they had changed and were now there for Julia. From what Eden had just said it seemed like she had made up her mind and didn't have feelings for Julia. Rafe looked in the tiny mirror again.

This is good, right?

"I don't know," Rafe whispered.

Her mind flashed to the other thing Nora had talked to her about. Secrets. Nora had asked if Eden had kept her secrets. Rafe hoped she had, but didn't know for sure. Then Nora had pointed out keeping secrets could be causing a lot of her own problems. Rafe talked to her doctor about the possibility, and the doctor agreed with Nora. Secrets could cause problems. Memories from when she was at her home in California and having bad dreams joined the confusion in her mind. After she told Eden about one of her secrets, it seemed to help her fight the darkness. Maybe it was a sign. Maybe she should tell Eden another secret.

Rafe turned on the sink and cupped some water in her hands then splashed it over her face. She grabbed a paper towel and dried her face then looked into the tiny mirror again. "Maybe," she said softly.

Walking through the double doors back into the store, Rafe saw Eden and Carisa standing at the counter going through an assortment of goods. Carisa was making a list, and Eden was listening to her talk about the items. They both looked up as she entered.

"There you are," said Carisa happily. "Is there anything else you want me to add?"

"Hey," said Eden as she slipped her arm around Rafe, "we found a lot of things Bronte will like and some beautiful candles."

"Good," said Rafe softly then spoke to Carisa. "I think that's all."

"Okay, I'll have Frankie deliver all this to Eden's hotel after lunch. I don't think some of this will hold up well in a saddle bag," she said with humor in her voice.

"Is it a lot of trouble?" asked Eden shyly. "I don't want to be any trouble."

"Oh, no!" Carisa assured her. "He'll be here to pick up re-stock for the booth if he needs it and his lunch anyway."

"Okay," said Eden, smiling at Carisa's friendliness. "How much do I owe?" She reached into her pocket for Euros.

Carisa furrowed her brow at Rafe. "Rafe?"

Rafe smiled and put her hand on Eden's arm. "Don't worry about it," she said. "Carisa has it all written down, and it'll be taken care of later."

"Oh," stammered Eden, "Okay."

"I almost forgot," said Rafe as she reached into her pocket for the bracelet given to her by a little boy the last time she was in town. "Rowena's little brother gave this to me the other day. She wants to sell them in your store."

Carisa took the bracelet. "She does a good job. Very creative. I'll talk to her."

"Great! Ciao, Carisa." Rafe waved and headed for the door.

"Bye," said Eden and followed Rafe.

Outside, Rafe stood beside the motorcycle and took the helmets from the handlebars. "Are you ready for another ride?"

Eden took a deep breath and smiled bravely. "Sure."

Rafe gave her a small smile because she could see she was nervous about getting back on the bike. "I'll be careful."

"I know."

As Rafe watched Eden put her jacket on, she reflected on the conversation with Nora about secrets. She looked over at the saddlebag on the motorcycle and contemplated the secret she was planning to take care of today. She took the helmet she was holding and handed it to Eden then stepped closer to her. Her stomach turned as she looked into her eyes. "Do you trust me?"

"Yes," she said softly.

Nodding, Rafe posed an even harder question to ask. "Am I really who you love?"

Eden looked up into her searching gray-blue eyes and could see how important the question was to her. "Yes, Rafe. You're the only one I love."

"Have you kept my secrets?"

Surprised by the question Eden nodded. "Yes, yes, I've kept them."

"I," she hesitated, "I have another one." They both stood silent for a while. "Do you want to know it?"

Eden put her hand on Rafe's arm and wasn't sure how to answer. She now knew how hard it was to hold on to secrets and how they tied your hands if they came with severe conditions. She also knew Rafe would not offer without reason.

"Do you want me to know?"

"I don't know," said Rafe and could feel water in her eyes, but she blinked it away. "I could just take you back to the hotel."

"Okay," said Eden seeing this could be Rafe reaching out to her. She didn't want to lose a chance to help her, and she definitely wanted to spend more time together. She rubbed her arm and pulled her into a hug. "Okay, I want to know."

"Good," said Rafe, "that's good." She took Eden's chin in her hands and lifted it to bring her lips into her kiss. "*Mi ami, Ede*?"[13] asked Rafe her low voice revealing her wariness. Rafe was not sure if she could ask anything of Eden anymore, especially to keep another secret. After all, she was still betraying Eden.

"I do," Eden breathed into the kiss. "I do love you, Rafe."

---

[13] You love me, Ede?

36

MANEUVERING THE MOTORCYCLE through the Italian traffic with ease, Rafe Salvaggio made her way back toward Florence as Eden held on tight. Traffic was lighter, but it only meant the speeds were faster on the Italian interstate. Pulling off the interstate, Rafe smiled to herself as she felt Eden relax slightly. It had felt at times like Eden would squeeze the air out of her.

The place they were going was not too far outside the city, and soon, they were going down very narrow roads that were walled on each side. Rafe slowed, pulled over into a narrow parking lane, then stopped and turned off the bike. After parking the motorcycle, she pulled off her gloves then unstrapped her helmet and took it off.

"This is our next stop," she told Eden and waited for her to get off the back of the bike.

"Where are we?" asked Eden as she held her helmet she had already taken off. She looked around and only saw high walls on both sides of them.

Rafe took Eden's helmet and locked it in the saddle bag with hers. She opened the saddlebag on the other side of the bike and took out a canvas bag. Taking Eden's jacket, she put it inside the saddle bag along with her own.

"This way," she said without answering Eden's question and walked through an opening in the wall.

Eden found a sign at the entry and was surprised to see they were at a cemetery. "Why are we here?" she asked nervously, but Rafe kept walking, so she followed.

It didn't take Rafe long to find the place she wanted to go. She had been in the cemetery about five months ago, so it was easy to find. She looked up at the marble structure then over at Eden who wasn't far behind her.

"This is the Salvaggio family mausoleum," said Rafe as she opened the wrought iron gate and stepped inside the cool stone room. "I think my father will be the last Salvaggio to be placed in here," she said as she ran her hand over the plaques with her ancestors' names on the walls. She touched each one wondering what it would have been like to know them, to know any of them. The only ones she knew where her mother and father. She only knew her mother as a child and her father she only knew when he allowed it. "I think my father paid for another ninety-nine-year lease on it when my mother died. So, unless something changes, they have about seventy-six years or so to be buried next to each other before the lease is up and all the bones and ashes in here go to the ossuary, and some other family takes it over."

While Eden looked around uneasily, Rafe sat on the small bench and leaned back against the cold stone. "I don't think I want to be buried here," Rafe said softly. "I'm the only one left, so I don't really see the point. I think it's cremation for me, and I think I'll direct my ashes be turned into the biggest diamond possible. Then I want it pressed into the cement of some great building, maybe between two random bricks. I haven't figured out which building yet. Maybe one that my father and I worked on."

Eden didn't like Rafe talking and thinking about her death. She also didn't like being in a cemetery inside a mausoleum. She sat down next to Rafe. "Why are we here?" she asked nervously watching Rafe.

Rafe put her fingertips against her temples to rub away the pain starting to form. Memories of her conversation with Nora filtered into her mind again. Nora and the doctor agreed about secrets. It was probably why those conversations kept coming back into her mind so much. It seemed strange for anyone other than Gabri and her father to even know she had secrets. But now Nora knew, the therapist knew, and Eden knew. She really didn't know if anyone else knew. Maybe everyone back in California knew. It was terrifying to think they might guess or try to find out what the secrets were because then her life would be ruined. Her father had warned her over and over again no one could know but family.

She looked over at the canvas bag beside her and the secret it contained. No one else alive knew the secret it held. She looked over at Eden. She was supposed to be family, but Rafe didn't let her father tell Eden anything. Eden left, so maybe she never really was family. Eden came back though, so it was all very confusing. But Rafe had an overpowering feeling that she needed to tell someone.

"Did you tell Cathcart the secrets I told you?"

"No," Eden said firmly, wondering why she was asking again. "I told you, I haven't told anyone, I swear."

"I've been told keeping secrets hasn't been good for me," she said softly. "I talked to my therapist, and she agreed."

"Oh," Eden said softly. She understood Rafe had just trusted her with something from her therapy. This had never happened before, and Eden felt good they were taking this step forward. "I can see how it might be true," she said trying to be positive for her.

"My problem is... I'm sure if I tell my secret, I'll lose someone." Rafe sighed and rubbed her head. "I can't take losing anyone else right now."

"You won't lose me," Eden assured her, "no matter what the secrets are about. You can tell me anything." She wondered if there was more to what happened to Rafe than what Gabri had told her.

Rafe looked away from Eden and bit the inside of her cheek, fighting the urge to remind Eden they had already lost each other. "I do need someone I can tell this secret," Rafe said softly, "but I don't want to tell a therapist or someone I don't know. I want to tell someone who cares about me. Someone I can trust." Rafe wondered if Eden was doing the right thing by trusting her again. "Can I trust you, no matter what happens between us? I'm worried if things don't go well between us, you might use my secrets and hurt me again."

Those words and the look of fear on Rafe's face cut through Eden painfully. She knew she had done things and hurt Rafe, and she knew Jake had used the things she said in confidence to hurt Rafe too. She had spent months talking and speculating about just how much she had hurt Rafe and how to talk to her about it if she ever had the chance. All that time, she had also kept her word and hadn't told anyone the secrets Rafe had told her.

"I think I've proven I wouldn't do anything like that to you," she said and put her hand on Rafe again. "I won't ever tell anyone the things you've told me unless you say it's okay. I'll never use your secrets to hurt you, no matter what happens between us. I promise." She looked up into Rafe's gray-blue eyes and saw her looking back at her, searching. "Do you need me to swear like I did before?"

"No," said Rafe and looked away, "you don't need to swear on your life. If you break your promise, it's my life that'll be affected, and it's me who'll be hurt. So, if you care about me at all, you'll keep the secret. If not," she shrugged, "nothing will matter anymore, will it?" She looked back into Eden's shining golden brown eyes but couldn't hold the gaze for long. "It'll be my fault for trusting you. But I think I need to trust you," she said hesitantly.

"Rafe, you don't have to tell me if you don't think you can trust me," said Eden, worried about Rafe's haunted look. "You can tell Gabri or his wife."

Rafe shook her head "No, no, I can't tell them."

"You can tell Julia. You've known her for a long time. She'd like to see you. She misses you too."

Rafe let out a sharp bitter laugh. "I don't think so," she said with a frown. She was not sure what she was going to do about Julia, but she certainly wasn't going to tell her any secrets. She was sure Julia was already demonizing her in Eden's eyes by telling her all kinds of things she didn't want her to know while making love to her.

She couldn't think about Julia right now. She knew if she thought about her and Eden together, she would just get angry, and she needed to get through this today. She shook her head to clear it of those thoughts.

"No," Rafe said firmly. "I don't want to tell her anything." Eden watched her with questioning eyes. "I think I need to tell you my secrets. I've already told you some, and you're right, you've proven you're trustworthy. It's just hard," she said and rubbed her eyes.

It was difficult for Eden to see Rafe so vulnerable. It was part of herself she kept hidden, along with all her secrets. Remembering Rafe saying she was out of control and seeing her in distress now suddenly made Eden doubt herself. She wondered if Gabri had been right, and she should have waited to come. Doctor Cathcart said no one could be expected to be in control all the time. He said everyone needed help sometimes. Everyone kept telling her to grow up and help, including Julia, and she desperately wanted to help Rafe if she could. She thought now she was in a place where maybe she could help Rafe. She could help with this secret and then prove, even if it was just to herself, that she could take Rafe home and take care of her. She moved closer to her and held on to her arm. "I'm sorry things are hard for you right now," she said then leaned close and kissed her softly. "I love you very much."

"Okay," said Rafe and pulled away gently as she looked up at the gate. "We have to be careful here. We can't do things like this in a Catholic cemetery. Italy isn't like home."

"Oh," Eden said looking out the gate of the mausoleum. No one was there that she could see. She wondered, if no one was around, why Rafe was worried about being careful here, but not at the vineyard. She turned her attention back to

Rafe and didn't argue. "I'm sorry. I understand." She gave her a reassuring smile. "It's like going back to my hometown. There are just certain places that are safer than others."

"Right," said Rafe returning her small smile. She would let Eden think what she wanted. Right now, though, she just couldn't have her so close and saying those things. She picked up the canvas bag and put it on her lap. "Do you remember this?"

"Yes," said Eden nervously. "I'm sorry I brought it. I didn't know it would upset you."

"I know," she said as she opened it and pulled out the drawing pad from inside. She opened the pad and pulled out what looked like a flier. "This was for my mother," she said softly. "I didn't have any made for Papa."

Eden already knew what the paper was that Rafe held. It was the death announcement for Rafe's mother. "She was beautiful," she said nodding to the photo on the page.

Rafe just nodded and folded the paper again then put it in the canvas bag. "Do you remember when I told you about my first kiss?"

"With Maria under the bridge." Eden smiled and nodded. "How could I forget? It was very romantic."

Rafe tried to smile back but couldn't hide the pain in her eyes. "This is my school bag she took."

"What?" Eden said in surprise. "How did you get it back?"

"My mother got it back," she said and fought the tear threatening to break away from her eye. "Remember I told you my first kiss led to her and Brettito's death? Well," she hesitated as her mouth went dry and she worked to get the moisture back, "that's the secret I need to tell you about."

37

HER HEART ACHED at the pain she saw on the face of the woman she loved. Eden Kingsley could see Rafe was upset by the memory of whatever happened when she was young. What she didn't understand, based on what Gabri had told her, was why Rafe thought a kiss led to an auto accident and a shooting outside a jewelry store.

Mindful Rafe was worried someone would see their affection, Eden carefully put her hand on Rafe again. "You can tell me," she said softly, forcing calmness into her voice like she did for Bronte. "I won't tell your secret. What happened?"

Rafe put her hand over Eden's finding comfort in the warmth of her touch. She took a breath and managed to moisten her dry mouth. She cleared her throat and tried to swallow, but it took a couple of tries before she could find her voice.

"I could never forget her kiss," Rafe said softly as the image of the dark-haired, dark-skinned and dark-eyed Maria filled her mind. She could see her and the way her body moved, her smile and the way every color looked so vibrant against her skin. "I had to see her again. So I made up a game for me, Gabri, and Brettito. We would spy on the *zingari* and try to learn their magical ways. I told them I just had to know how things worked like crystal balls and tarot cards, whatever I could think of to make them want to play the game." Rafe closed her eyes and forced her emotions down. Finally, she found the strength to look up into Eden's soft eyes. "I wanted to be with Maria, but I couldn't tell anyone." She looked away, took a deep breath, and then continued. "While Gabri and Brettito were playing the game, I was spending time with Maria and making excuses for me not to be with them." Inside, she churned with a mix of frustration and guilt. "I was supposed to like boys. I was supposed to love and marry someone like Gabri or Brettito. I did love them," she choked out sadly, "but I knew, after kissing Maria, it would never happen. I also knew I couldn't tell anyone back then."

She glanced at Eden who she could tell didn't yet understand the depth of her betrayal. "For months, we played the game, and I made excuses to separate myself or skip school and go be with Maria," she said as she stared at her mother's tomb.

"After my mother died, I sought out and found Maria again," she continued her confession. "She missed me and was so happy to have me again. She helped me and took me in. Her whole family was happy to see me whenever I came to see them. They knew my mother had died because Maria had told them, and they let me be part of their family whenever I was there. I knew people didn't like the *zingari* or transient people—or whoever they were—but they were just like everyone else. They love and feel and have pride. I think I was lucky to have known them. They were my secret comfort for over a year."

Rafe hesitated in revealing how deeply she felt about Maria. She had never talked with anyone before Eden about her first love and all the emotions accompanying that life experience. It was a pivotal moment in her life, and it put her on the path to who she would eventually become. It was a path she couldn't regret taking. But it was also one occupied by the ghosts of everyone she had caused pain. Ghosts who would not stop following her.

"I was spending time with Maria and her family, and I told Gabri and Brettito that I was there to find their secrets. I would tell the boy's stories about what happened and about all the magical things I saw to keep them interested in the game."

Rafe looked over at Eden again who stayed quiet as the words she spoke soaked into the veined white marble of the tomb that was almost as cold as the ice it resembled. *This was very close to where all Traditorès belonged*, she thought.

"I imagined I would run away with Maria," she finally revealed, knowing it was nowhere close to revealing her true *aeipathy*[14] for Maria. "We both knew her family would never accept her being with me if they knew about our love. I didn't think mine would either. So we made the plan of a thirteen and a fifteen-year-old to always be together. Then Brettito died," she said shakily. "It was very hard for me."

Eden could see just how hard it still was for Rafe in her haunted face. She remembered everything Gabri told her about Brettito. The image of the photograph Gabri showed her was burned into her mind. She saw Rafe, so young, lying

---

[14] An enduring and consuming passion.

on the hospital bed covered in blood and gore, unconscious. She could feel herself sicken and tremble at the thought of Rafe going through such intense trauma. Her heart went out to her and in her empathy could feel what she knew was probably only a small fraction of the pain Rafe had felt. She wanted to touch her and hold her to give her comfort but stopped herself as Rafe started to speak again.

"I was sick, and Gabri would come over to spend time with me," said Rafe softly. "I ran away once, looking for Maria, but I couldn't find her. Then my father made sure I couldn't leave the house."

The anguish on Rafe's face told the story of how much it hurt not to be able to find Maria. Eden wondered if Maria and her family were with the people Gabri mentioned who were driven out of town because of the shooting. They may have been afraid of being blamed further, or of the possible retribution the injured or the families of the dead might seek. She remembered how a big part of their last therapy session was talking about how Rafe had felt abandoned. She wondered if she felt abandoned by Maria, too.

Rafe rubbed her temples and fought the ache spreading from the center of her forehead to the base of her neck whenever she thought about everything that happened when she was young. She pushed through the pain to finish what she had started. "Gabri went to Brettito's house and got the notebook Brettito's mother said proved his death was my fault."

"Wait," Eden interrupted, unable to help herself. "His mother blamed you for his death?" She watched Rafe nod in confirmation, but Eden couldn't fathom how anyone could blame a child for a shooting over a jewelry robbery gone wrong.

"Yes," Rafe said as she nodded then took a shuddering breath. "I knew she was right, but she was wrong about the reason." She knew the guilt was showing on her face, and she tried to hide it and ease the pain in her head by wiping her hands over her face. "Brettito was trying to find out more *zingari* secrets for me, and I was spending time with Maria." She fought back a tear from the pain and the memory. "He thought he would do it all for me, and I would love him and marry him. He died for nothing," she spat, angry with herself. "I would never have married him," she said sharply then took a calming breath. "After finding out about the things in the notebook, I don't think I could have run away even if I wanted to." The memory of her and Gabri burning the notebook, the evidence of her guilt, flashed through her mind. "Lucky for me, my father took me far away, and I worked on being a good daughter so he would keep me with him. Now he's gone too," she said wishing she could crawl inside the tomb with him.

Eden remembered Gabri saying Rafe ran away a lot and wondered if she was looking for Maria all those times or if she was running from her guilt over her friend's death. She waited for Rafe to continue, but she just looked lost and far away. "How did your mother get the school bag?" she asked softly to bring Rafe out of her thoughts.

Rafe sniffed and wiped her eyes so no tears would fall. Tears were a weakness. She had to maintain control. She was sitting in front of her father, and he would expect control from her, especially when she talked about her mother.

"For a long time," she started, making sure her voice was clear, strong, and unwavering. "I thought my mother died because I had been skipping school a lot, and she was always trying to get me to go. Remember, I told you I planned to skip that day, but she insisted on going with me. I found out later Brettito's little sister heard us talking about it and told on us." She saw Eden nod and knew she remembered what she was told. "Years later, I found out skipping school wasn't the only thing my mother knew about." Rafe hesitated, seeing Eden's misery, but ignoring it. "She knew about Maria," she whispered because she had never said it out loud before, and it felt wrong. She watched Eden for her reaction, but by the slight widening of her eyes and the tight frown of her mouth, Rafe knew she still didn't truly understand. Rafe opened the drawing pad and flipped through the pages then handed it to Eden. "Read this," she said softly. "When my father sent me his car, the first thing I did was clean it and have it detailed. That's when I found the bag in the trunk. This old drawing pad was in the bag, and I found the letter as I flipped through it. I think she wrote it just days before she died."

Eden took the pad nervously. It had taken everything in her not to read it when she found it and now she wasn't sure she wanted to. She took a breath and then looked down at the pad and read.

Rafaella,

My beautiful wild child. I'm writing to you because I don't want you to feel you're in trouble. I'm writing in English so you're not embarrassed if one of your friends finds this when you don't want to share it.

Last week, I found a lovely girl who was selling your book bag near where I was painting. I asked her about the bag because I knew you needed a new one to replace the one you lost. She told me it was a magical bag, and it had the power to bring love to the owner. When I looked in the bag I laughed because I knew from the nametag inside it was the bag you had lost a few weeks ago. I bought the bag from her. She was a very beautiful girl and hard to forget.

I saw the girl head for the grotto so I followed her to ask her if she would sit for me to paint. As I looked for her, I saw you. I was very surprised to see you out of school again. I saw the girl take your hand with a smile. Then you kissed sweetly before walking away together.

Yes, I was shocked and confused because you were kissing a girl. I admit I went through a whole catalog of emotions as you walked away with her. I was even tempted to march up to you and drag you straight home, but only for a moment. The reason I stopped was that I asked myself if I trusted you, and I knew I did. I also reminded myself the world is full of all kinds of love, and it's all so very beautiful. What concerned me most was the possibility she was taking advantage of you, and I was worried because I could tell she was older than you.

So, I confess, I followed you for a short distance. I saw you seemed to be quite in control of the situation. She was showering you with gifts, and you refused them all. She tried to kiss you, but you refused until you were ready. She stole from a vendor, and you paid him. I was amazed at you and how you handled yourself because you're only twelve, but you showed me you're very mature and my trust was justified.

It's true now I can see you will love women. I can see you are naturally drawn because we have never talked about love, and you're doing what feels natural to you. I don't know if you'll always have a love for women or if you will love both women and men in your lifetime. I know your father thinks you'll be with Gabri or Brettito when you grow up because you're all so close. I have talked to your father about what I saw, and he too understands he must let you love who you will love. That being said, we also agree you must stop skipping school to see her. You already know all the arguments about why you should not be skipping school, and they all apply to this situation too.

We do hope you will bring her home and introduce us to her when you're ready. We'd like to know her name and all about her. I would love to talk to you about how you met her, and how you feel, and all the other things mothers and daughters talk about involving love. I admit I may not know everything you'll want to know, but I'm sure all the basics of love are the same for every soul.

When you go through life, my wild child, most importantly what we want you to know is—we love you. We know whoever you love and give your heart to will be very lucky. We know you will love them in your special way and be thoughtful with their hearts, and we hope you will always be thoughtful of your own heart too. Let your heart lead you but allow your head to hold the reins.

Someday, when you grow up, all your adventures may suddenly not be enough anymore to make you happy. You'll want to have a stable life full of love and joy and family. When the time comes, I hope you find a love like the one your father and I have together.

Find someone, the person of your choice, who thinks about you as much as you think about them. Someone who shares a love for the same things you do and for the things you feel are important in life. Though I know you will be as beautiful as your father, I hope you won't judge others by their looks or other superficial things like money or class status. I hope you find your equal in passion and in intellect and they share your goals for your future. Look for a good heart, a happy soul, a tender and caring disposition, yet do not be afraid of one who challenges you and pushes you to grow positively.

You'll know when you find the right person, just as your father and I knew. There's not a moment that goes by where we don't feel the love we have for each other. Our world is better because we're friends who have respect for each other as well as lovers who share a passion for living and the small things making up our lives every day. When I met your father, my heart settled into a warm place even before we knew each other's names. That feeling has never left me, and I know it will be with me all my life. If we came together from two very different continents and overcame challenges like language and traditions and income and the differences in our ages, I know you can overcome any challenges life may put in front of you when it comes to finding love.

I love you, my beautiful wild child. Be who you are, always, and know you were brought into the world as a result of deep and true love. This means you are blessed as many are not, and this gives you an advantage in life because some people never see love at all. I know love will not be easy, it isn't easy for anyone all the time, but I know when the time comes, you will be up to the challenge, and the adventure love will bring you.

Love who you will, love them well, and allow them to love you equally. It will be your greatest adventure, and you will prevail, my loving wild child.

Mamma

Scribbled at the bottom in Rafe's clear, neat handwriting:

I found her, and my heart is settled into a warm space. I like the way she sees me. Her name is Eden, and she is golden like the rays of love from Cyprian the Fair. I wonder if she is the one who takes me to walk on those rays. I'm in love with her. I think you would love her too. I'm the happiest I have ever been and can't wait to begin our adventure!

38

LOOKING UP AFTER reading the last lines on the page, Eden Kingsley saw Rafe had been watching her. The letter was beautiful, and Eden couldn't hide the emotions it brought out in her. "It must have been amazing to read this," Eden said looking down at the page. "Your mother loved you very much."

"She did," Rafe agreed. "But don't you see?" she asked, upset that Eden was missing the point of why they were sitting in a cemetery. "She didn't die just because I was skipping school. She knew everything. She was even talking to her and painting her. The day she died, she was making sure I didn't skip school to be with Maria. She and Brettito both died because I was sneaking around to spend time with Maria," she said in a low grumbling tone, "because I wanted to be with her all the time."

Rafe snatched the drawing pad from Eden. "I couldn't tell them. I couldn't tell anyone. I had to keep the kiss with Maria a secret, and it led to their deaths!" she explained in frustration as she pointed to herself, her feelings of guilt and sorrow welling up inside. "I couldn't tell anyone." She stared at Eden intensely. "You can't tell anyone!"

"I won't," said Eden shakily, shocked at Rafe's reaction.

Rafe took a shuddering breath. "If Gabri ever knew, he would hate me," she said in distress. "No one can know what I did. He helped me, and he loves me. I don't think I could live if I lost him from my life," she said feverishly. "He's the only one left who was with me and really knows everything.

He went through everything with me and has always been the one I could talk to about everything," she paused, "everything except Maria. He thinks that going to America made me gay." She chuckled miserably. "He was very upset when I told him we would never marry, but loved me enough to remain my friend. If he knew Brettito was wasting his time back then, trying to impress me by getting involved with the *zingari* boys, and I was the reason he was shot in the street..." Rafe's eyes were filled with desperation. "I don't know what he would do. He would hate me! He would never want to have anything to do with me!"

"I don't think he would hate you," said Eden quietly. "You were all just kids trying to find your way."

Rafe was in disbelief at how wrong Eden was. "He would hate me!" she said forcefully. "Then, on top of that," Rafe gave a manic laugh, "my father told me I couldn't talk to anyone about either my mother or Brettito. We had to keep my being sick a secret and not cause damage to his career and my future."

Eden tentatively put her arm around Rafe. "I'm sorry you had to keep so many secrets," she said softly. She wondered why Rafe hadn't mentioned any anger at the fact her father had known about Maria and had never said a word to her about it all her life. He just left the painting out for her to find triggering an emotional breakdown and now causing her so many problems.

Rafe pulled away and looked down at the sketchpad with the precise handwriting her mother left behind. After she found the notebook, she wondered a thousand times what her life would have been like if she would have found it sooner.

"I decided, after Brettito died, I wouldn't keep the fact I was gay a secret. I told my father. I told my teachers. Eventually, when I worked up the courage, I even told Gabri. I told everyone. I couldn't live with myself if something else happened because I kept it a secret." She tore the page out of the sketchpad then dug into the canvas bag and pulled out a lighter. "We have to burn this so no one will know what I did. So it never shows up unexpected again."

Eden and put her hand over Rafe's. "Wait," she demanded. "Rafe, this is a beautiful letter from your mother. You can't burn it," she insisted.

"I have to," she said shakily and pulled a small hammer and a chisel from the bag. "We'll burn it, and we'll put the ashes in the tomb with my father. I put the painting with him," she revealed while looking at his tomb. She ran her hand over the plaque and the cement around it. "I think I can chip off the cement and work out a brick. I can put it back then tell them it was vandalized. They can fix it, and I'll pay for the repairs."

Eden couldn't believe Rafe was planning to break open her father's tomb to add a page of ashes. No. She could not believe Rafe was planning to break open his tomb–period.

"Wait, I don't think you should do that," said Eden trying to think of a way to stop what was happening. "Can't you put the ashes in one of these smaller places, or in one of the urns? What am I saying..." she mumbled as she ran her hands through her hair nervously. "You can't burn the letter. Don't you want to keep it? I'd love to have something so loving from my mother and have it to show my daughter someday."

Rafe could not hide the expression revealing she found Eden's words insane. "No. I don't want to keep it. I'll remember what she wrote. I can't keep this," she waved the page in front of Eden. "It's a reminder of what I did, and it will hurt Gabri if he ever finds out. It'll destroy my life if anyone else knows! You have to help me get rid of it, and no one can ever know that my mother knew about Maria. No one else can ever know about Maria. It's why we're here! You promised!" She sat on the floor of the mausoleum and pulled the canvas bag to her. She reached inside, pulled out a metal bowl, and sat it in front of her. She rolled the letter up and pulled the lighter out of the bag to start burning it.

"Wait!" Eden called, and Rafe looked up at her. "Here," she said, "let me see it." She took the letter from Rafe's hand and unrolled it. She folded it part way down and creased it. "Look, if I tear it here, you can keep the bottom part. This way you burn the part talking about Maria and about being gay, but you can keep the rest of what your mother wrote to you. What do you think?"

Rafe considered her words for a moment as she examined where Eden folded the letter. "Okay," she said softly, "Okay." She nodded in agreement.

Eden carefully tore off the lower section of the letter then looked down at Rafe. "This is mine now," she said as Rafe watched her fold the page and put it in her back pocket. "I want this to stay in the world. This is good advice from your mother, and the part below it is what you wrote about me and how you feel about me." Eden met Rafe's eyes again and saw she was looking at her with a frown. "I don't want this burned or left in a mausoleum in Italy, and I don't want you to get rid of it someday. This is not a secret we have to keep," Eden said assertively. "No one has to know there was more to this letter. If you really think you need to, you can burn this," she said as she handed Rafe the top half of the letter. "But now I don't think there will be enough ashes to justify opening your father's tomb. Let's just," she stammered, "just put it in the back of one of these smaller openings. No one will even need them for over seventy years, right? I think that'll be good enough. Don't you?"

Rafe thought about it and examined the ossuary vaults Eden was talking about and then back to the section of the letter. "Okay," she agreed softly. "Sit down and block the air in case there's a breeze."

She waited for Eden to sit down in front of her then began burning the small section of the letter. She let the paper burn catching the ashes in the small metal bowl. When the paper was consumed and was nothing more than ash, she took the bowl to the mausoleums empty ossuary vault where Eden suggested they put the ashes. She then slid the entire bowl back as far as she could by climbing inside. "There," she said as she pulled herself out of the small square hole. "It's pretty far back. It may never get noticed unless the vault gets used by the next family who pays for the mausoleum." She brushed the dust off her clothes and picked up her canvas bag shoving the drawing pad and the tools inside. "Come on," she said, and they walked out of the mausoleum.

39

WALKING THROUGH THE cemetery, Rafe Salvaggio led Eden closer to the ossuary building, finally stopping in front of a grave. "This is where Brettito used to be," she told Eden. "But now he's somewhere in the building over there." She pointed to a building that looked like a small church. "It's the ossuary for the in-ground graves. They moved him a couple of years ago. He's been dead for over twenty years, but sometimes, it still seems like it was yesterday to me."

"Why did they move him?" Eden asked, surprised they would move a body from a grave.

Rafe shrugged. "To make room," she explained. "My father paid for twenty years. His family thought it was enough. Now he's in a very small box piled on top of other small boxes full of bones. I never like the thought of all those bone boxes. I would take them all to America, but they belong here." She shifted her eyes toward Eden. "But I don't belong here," she said firmly. "I don't want to come back here again." She turned and started walking to the cemetery gate.

Eden followed with feelings of confusion and concern. She didn't understand why Rafe was being so insistent about not belonging in the cemetery. The memory of their therapy session and Rafe's outburst about death needing a choice ran through her mind. Gabri said she was doing better. Eden worried Rafe was thinking about or planning her death. It scared her. She caught up to Rafe and touched her arm. "Rafe," she said taking her arm to stop her. "Rafe, wait."

"What?" Rafe turned to Eden with a frown. She wanted to leave this place.

"Why are you saying those things?"

"What things?"

"The things about not belonging here and being turned into a diamond," she said. She felt a small trickle of sweat run down her back. "It scares me," she confessed. "I don't want anything to happen to you. I don't know what it means when you say those things. Do you think about death? Are you thinking about hurting yourself? Please," she said shakily, "please don't—" She was stopped from saying more by the anxiety thrumming through her.

Rafe scowled down at Eden. "I'm not that sick," she retorted. She wondered if she should feel insulted because Eden thought she was so weak or pride because Eden thought she was brave enough to end herself. She could never quite figure out if suicide was a product of weakness or strength. She knew that sometimes she wished she would just not wake up, but she didn't think it was the same as self-harm. "I only wanted you to know that, when I die, I don't want to be here. It doesn't mean anything. It probably won't matter anyway because Gabri knows. We're here, and I was telling you other things, so I just told you that too," she said with a shrug.

Eden wondered if Rafe was telling the truth or covering her tracks. "Okay," she said softly. "Good. Bronte and I need you."

"If you say so," said Rafe, doubtful Eden really needed her anymore for anything. "Let's go." She turned once again to make her way out of the cemetery with Eden following close behind.

40

HOLDING ON TIGHT as she rode on the back of the motorcycle, Eden Kingsley thought about how, so far, the day had not gone the way she thought it might. Spending time in a cemetery, burning secrets, and talking about death made her wonder exactly what kind of help Gabri was getting for Rafe. She thought that maybe Rafe would be better off going home to get better help.

Eden was glad she convinced Rafe not to burn the entire letter her mother wrote. She was telling the truth about wishing her own mother loved her as Rafe's mother had loved her. It was interesting to know Mary talked to Ettore about the possibility of Rafe being gay. *Maybe it's why he was so nice to me*, she thought. *Maybe he knew Rafe would find the letter.*

She thought about the possibility, remembering what happened to Rafe when she saw the painting done of Maria by her mother. Eden wondered if Ettore let Rafe find the letter to see if she would get sick and planned to do the same with the painting before he died. She could not think of a reason Rafe's father would want to hurt her and put her through such turmoil again, but the whole thing pricked at her mind.

Eden remembered Abby saying Rafe changed soon after she got the car from her father. Then, after seeing the painting while she was grieving for her father, Rafe had an emotional blackout. She wondered if Rafe was right, and Ettore was still punishing her even after his death. A surge of anger at Ettore rushed through Eden, and then a wave of protectiveness for Rafe followed. Eden would always hope she was wrong because if she weren't, it would be very hard to defend Ettore the way Rafe wanted.

Lifting her head to see if she could tell where Rafe was taking them, Eden saw they were back in the city. She hoped Rafe wasn't taking her back to her hotel. She wanted to spend more time with her. Her heart sank as she saw they were, in fact, heading to the hotel. Rafe stopped and parked the motorcycle. Eden held on to her a little longer than she needed to, then she sighed and got off the bike.

Taking off her helmet, Eden turned to Rafe. "Do you want to come up and see Bronte?" she asked hopefully, trying anything to keep her longer. "Julia might be there too unless she got an au pair to stay with the baby for a while."

"Oh, you want to go up?" asked Rafe as she stowed the helmets and unzipped her jacket. "I thought you might want to walk around."

Eden could not help grinning. "Yeah, I'd like to walk with you."

"We can get Bronte if you want," Rafe offered with a shrug as she fixed her hair tie. Remembering how hard it was for Eden to be away from Bronte, she thought maybe Eden was worried about the baby.

"No, I think we can spend more time alone together," said Eden. She couldn't help noticing how beautiful Rafe was with her hair pulled back and in her sexy leather outfit. "I'd like some more one-on-one time." She smiled, trying not to show too much excitement.

"Okay." Rafe gave a weak smile back. She grabbed the key to the bike, locked the saddlebags, and then walked with Eden down the street.

"We went to the music festival," Eden said as she walked happily next to Rafe. "We didn't see Gabri or Nora, but there was a lot of good music. Nora gave us tickets to a couple of the bigger shows."

"They play tonight," said Rafe. "Gabri will be revealing his new music and promoting his CD. They'll go on tour after the baby is born and Nora can travel."

"Maybe we can go see them tonight. Together," Eden suggested, trying to be nonchalant.

Rafe smiled but made no promises. It was well past noon, and the familiar restaurant they were passing didn't look too busy.

"Are you hungry?"

"Sure."

"Great, let's go in here," Rafe suggested then led Eden into the restaurant. "I'll buy."

They walked inside, and the owner, who obviously knew Rafe, immediately accosted them. Eden noticed he called her Rafaella and was very happy to see her. He gave them a private table and yelled at the waiter who promptly brought them their dishes and cutlery. Rafe talked to the owner for a moment then he left looking very pleased.

"Do you come here often," she asked with a smile as the waiter brought wine and poured it for them.

"As a matter of fact, I came here almost every day for about a month." She nodded toward the wall.

Eden examined the wall covered with an aging mural then smiled with confusion at Rafe. "What am I supposed to be looking at?" Rafe leaned over putting her hand on the wall. Eden arched her brow when she saw Rafe's name painted there. "Did you paint the mural? It looks old."

Rafe chuckled. "That's the point," she said. "The owner had a problem with the wall bowing because of a structural problem. I helped him find the right people to fix it then so it wouldn't look like a new wall, I aged the brick and painted the mural. He paid for all the supplies, and I provided the labor."

"What's that devil face in the corner?" she asked.

"Oh, it's just a logo for the company I got the paint from. Cifarelli Restoration Pigments. I met *Maestro* Cifarelli's niece, Tait, and she was kind enough to help me get a great deal. They're very expensive and hard to get."

It took more than a handshake to get the expensive and exclusive paint. It took being vetted, signing usage agreements, and help from Tait Cifarelli. The paint formula was so precise that, if not for the Cifarelli logos included within the work, the mural could be mistaken for a historical piece. But no one was ever interested in the preparation process, just the result.

Eden nodded as she studied the mural in wonder, once again impressed with Rafe's talent. "You never cease to amaze me," she said with a wink.

Rafe laughed and took a sip of her wine. "What made it fun for me were all the customers coming in to watch me paint," said Rafe. "Once word got out his wall was fixed, and someone was painting a mural, people came to watch the progress and brought a lot of friends. The owner was so happy that I now eat free whenever I come in," she said with a cocky smile.

Eden laughed. "Oh! Now I know why you offered to buy."

"Yep." Rafe grinned as the waiter placed their lunch on the table.

Eden watched Rafe as she ate and was glad she seemed to be doing better. She loved seeing Rafe sitting across from her again. "Do you remember when we vacationed here and stayed in the apartment overlooking the river?"

"Yes." Rafe nodded and sipped her wine.

"It was perfect, wasn't it?" asked Eden, recalling the trip they took years ago before they moved in together. "Maybe we can stay there again some time."

Rafe shrugged. "My father sold it," she said then took a bite of food.

"It was your fathers?"

"Yes," said Rafe with a short laugh. "You don't think I would come to Italy and stay in a hotel or rent someplace when he owned so much real estate here, do you?"

"I guess I never really thought about it," Eden admitted as she ate.

"Yeah, you were just thinking about sex," Rafe teased her.

"Rafe!" Eden hissed as she looked around. "I thought you wanted to be careful."

"They don't speak English—much, anyway." She laughed at Eden's shocked expression. "Plus, we aren't in a cemetery now."

Eden looked thoughtfully across at Rafe again. She loved seeing the mischievous spark in her eyes again. "Well, you might be right," she conceded. Her heart beat hard for Rafe at the reminder of the times they made love on that trip. "But I can guarantee, you weren't thinking about real estate, either."

"Definitely not." Rafe winked then sipped her wine.

After finishing lunch, Rafe gave a long goodbye to the owner. Then she and Eden stepped outside to walk around Florence for a while taking in the sights. Rafe led Eden along directing her just like she used to do. Eden loved it when Rafe put her hand on her lower back, or took her arm to get her attention, or just stood close when they were looking at some piece of sculpture. It reminded her of when they were on vacation, and things were good between them. Sometimes, it even took her back to when Rafe was painting her portrait. Rafe would only touch her when necessary. Eden didn't understand why at the time, but it drove her mad. Now she knew it was because it was making her want Rafe to touch her and be close.

Soon they came to the famous *Ponte Vecchio.* The famous bridge lined with shops selling jewelry, art, and souvenirs. They walked along slowly enjoying the sights and shops with all the beautiful jewelry and art.

"This is the shop where I bought your birthday present," said Rafe as they looked in the jewelry store window.

"My birthday present?" asked Eden not knowing what she was talking about. Her birthday was months ago, and she hadn't received anything from her.

"Yeah," confirmed Rafe as she smiled. "Did you like it?"

Eden didn't know what to say. She wondered for a moment if Rafe was joking around, then she remembered the packages Gabri gave her. They were still in Bronte's backpack unopened. "Uhm," she stammered, "actually, I just got all the things you sent me from Gabri when I saw him the other day. I haven't opened any of them."

Rafe stopped and a frowned. "What? You didn't get the things I sent you?" She shook her head and wondered why Gabri wouldn't send the things she asked him to send.

Eden could see Rafe's mood turning dark, and she didn't want anything to put a damper on the day. "I think Gabri was worried if I got the gifts, I'd try to come to see you sooner. He was probably right. But I have them now. He wasn't keeping them from me forever. Maybe I can open them when I'm with you. Then you can watch me see the gifts for the first time," she offered as she rested her hand on Rafe's arm. "I know I'd rather open them with you and have you close to thank in person."

"We'll see," she said turning away from the store window and walking down the bridge again. She thought Eden was probably right about why Gabri hadn't sent the gifts, but he should have told her. She knew he didn't do it to hurt her, but she had spent all this time thinking Eden received the things she wanted her to have. Now she wondered if she made a mistake sending her those gifts, and it was the reason Gabri kept them. Looking over, she saw Eden was still walking beside her. "I'm sorry you didn't get your present on your birthday. But I don't think getting my present would have made much of a difference in when you came. You might have been here a week or so sooner, maybe. He should have sent it."

"Don't be angry with him," said Eden. "He's in love with you, remember? He probably just wanted you all to himself. I just feel sorry for Nora."

Rafe laughed, happy to be brought out of her worried thoughts. "Oh, really? You don't feel sorry for yourself?"

"No," Eden said, dragging out the word then looked over at her seriously. "You've never told him you were in love with him, and I have it in writing you're in love with me," she reminded her patting her back pocket.

"I wrote those words a long time ago," she replied uneasily. "It may mean nothing now."

"There's no date on the letter, and I just read it today, so I say it means something now," declared Eden then smiled and walked to the next shop.

Rafe laughed and followed her. "I remember you now," she teased and bent close to her. "Bossy Eden," she whispered and laughed softly.

Eden's eyes sparkled. "That's right. You should do what I say."

"What do you want, Bossy Eden?" asked Rafe, enjoying the game. "Would you like jewels or sweets? Or maybe I can give you a surprise."

Eden could tell Rafe was enjoying herself, so she continued to play. "I apparently have jewels waiting for me," she said, raising her eyebrow. "I'm not really hungry, so I think I would like the surprise."

"Okay," said Rafe with a grin. "Come on," she encouraged, taking Eden by the arm. She led her swiftly from the bridge and turned them left through the vendors until they came to an alley. She turned left again and led her down the narrow street. "Here we are," said Rafe breathlessly leading Eden under the bridge.

Eden looked around, and it was not an impressive place. It was dirty, there was a lot of trash, and it smelled a bit. "Why are we here?" she asked with uncertainty.

"This is where it happened," Rafe announced with a smile. She turned in place with her arms out offering Eden a view as if it were a gift. "The kiss with Maria you think was so romantic." Looking around, Rafe noticed how different the place looked from when she was twelve. "I don't think it looked like this back then. More tourists litter now, I guess." She shrugged off her disappointment with the new reality of the place that held such an important memory.

"No, it's nice," said Eden hesitantly, not wanting to bring down the mood. "I can see how a kid would want to make out down here."

Rafe smiled at Eden's attempt to see something good about being under a bridge where it was trashy and smelly. "Well, it wasn't exactly making out, and I don't remember much other than my interaction with Maria and the kiss," she confessed as she kicked a plastic bottle aside. "I guess it just shows how good the kiss was." She pointed toward the end wall of the bridge. "I was backed up to the wall about there," she said and walked over. "I don't think I'd lean against it now. It kind of smells like pee," she said scrunching her nose then chuckled. "Okay, I guess some things are better left to memory. Let's get out of here." Taking Eden by the arm, Rafe led her back up to the alley.

"It's hard going back to places from your childhood," said Eden as they walked. "I'll bet if I went back to the old church where I had my first kiss, it wouldn't be the same either."

Rafe laughed at the absurdity of the thought. "I think the only thing changed about your old church would be some poison ivy maybe, or a lot of weeds. I don't think thousands of people tramped through your churchyard, used it as a trash can, and peed all over the side of the church." She turned them down another small street where they came upon an open plaza. "We can go look at the garden and the grotto if you want. They've been taken care of much better. I've been to them a lot."

"Are you disappointed," Eden asked sympathetically. "I'm sorry if going back there wasn't what you expected." Rafe shrugged dismissively. "Thank you for taking me. I like seeing places important to you, even if they've changed. I like knowing things about you. Really, I just like being with you. I've missed this."

As Rafe was about to answer, a chorus of voices called her name. Turning, she saw a group of school-aged kids heading for her. "Rafaella, Rafaella!" called one. "*Rafaella, siete venuti a dipingere?*"[15] called another "*Dove sono i vostri colori?*"[16] one asked. "*Hai portato carta per noi?*"[17]

---

[15] Rafaella, you have come to paint?
[16] Where are your colors?
[17] Did you bring paper for us?

asked another. "*Ho il mio libro di disegno,*"[18] called another. "*Noi comprare gelato oggi?*"[19] asked another boldly.

Rafe laughed as they gathered around asking questions and telling her things. "*Non sto dipingendo oggi,*"[20] she told them and saw they were disappointed. "*Sto mostrando un amico la nostra città. Si tratta di Eden.*"[21]

They all gawked at Eden judgingly, as children sometimes do. "*Ciao, Eden,*" they all said over each other pronouncing her name like Rafe did with the e's sounding like hard a's.

One of the small boys turned to Rafe "*Noi comprare gelato oggi?*" he asked again.

"*Dovremmo chiede Eden. Lei nostro ospite,*"[22] she told him then turned to Eden. "He wants to know if we're buying gelato today. What do you think?"

Eden took a long look at all the children who were waiting for her answer, then looked back at Rafe. "If we don't, I'm the bad guy, right?" Rafe just smiled and raised her eyebrows. "I say *si* to gelato!" she said to the kids lifting her arms into the air. They understood 'yes' and 'gelato' and jumped up and down cheering.

With the children, Rafe and Eden made their way toward the next bridge and to *Gelateria Santa Trinità* for gelato. "Am I to understand this is a regular occurrence?" Eden asked as they walked.

---

[18] I have my drawing book.
[19] We buy ice cream today?
[20] I'm not painting today,
[21] I am showing a friend our city. This is Eden.
[22] We should ask Eden. She's our guest

"Usually we paint or draw first, but today, you're our guest, so we have to be polite and have gelato," Rafe informed her with a grin. "Now I wish we had Bronte here."

"She would love this," Eden agreed. "Maybe we can do it again before we have to go home."

"Sure," said Rafe but lost her smile at the thought of them going home.

They made it to the gelato shop, and Rafe paid and gave each child a receipt they could take and get some ice cream. "What flavor do you want?" Rafe asked Eden.

"Chocolate," said Eden with a smile, thinking about how Bronte would probably ask for the same.

"Do you trust me?" Rafe asked with an arched brow.

"Sure," she said, aware this was not the first time Rafe had asked. She knew there was more to the question than ice cream flavors.

"Good, go find a table," Rafe instructed. "I'll get the gelato."

Eden found a table outside the little shop and watched all the people pass by as she waited for Rafe.

"Here you go," said Rafe with a smile. "This will keep you awake all night," she promised with a mischievous grin. "It is mocha gelato, and this is a double shot of espresso. You just pour the espresso in with the gelato like this," she said, pouring the coffee into the gelato cup. "It's a heavenly energy buzz." She scooped out a bite and ate it. "Oh, man, so good! Here, you try it." She scooped out a bite for Eden. "*Godete.*[23]"

"Oh, my god!" said Eden savoring the gelato. "This is great!" She proceeded to pour her espresso in with her gelato

---

[23] Enjoy.

and scoop out bites of the treat. "Why have I never had this before?"

Rafe laughed as she watched her eat. "I have no idea," she said and ate more gelato.

As they ate, the children all talked with Rafe and Eden. Eden did her best to use what little Italian she had learned. The children asked Rafe a lot of questions about Eden, but finally, they all left to go play.

"They're happy you came and decided to get gelato," said Rafe. "They also think you're very beautiful. One boy has offered himself for marriage when he's older."

Eden laughed and blushed. "I hope you let him down easy."

"I did my best," she assured her and grinned. "It's too late to go to the grotto now. We should walk back to your hotel." Rafe was relieved they wouldn't go to the grotto today. It was a place hard for her to visit alone sometimes. She needed more time to be able to take Eden.

"Okay," agreed Eden, not sure why it was too late and disappointed the day with Rafe was ending.

"Maybe I could stay for a while and spend time with Bronte," Rafe suggested as they walked back to the hotel.

"She would love it." Eden smiled and put her hand tentatively on Rafe's arm. "We both would love it."

41

AS SHE WALKED into the hotel, Eden Kingsley felt hopeful and happy because Rafe was beside her. Their stroll back had been calm and sweet. It felt good just being beside Rafe, even if they were silent at times as they walked. It almost seemed at times like she had *her Rafe* back. Rafe seemed so happy and full of life, joking around like Eden remembered. Sometimes it was hard to comprehend the truth Rafe was still sick and dealing with problems from her childhood and the troubles from back home. But then strange and scary things happened, like the situation in the cemetery, or the way Rafe talked about being out of control.

After climbing the stairs to her floor, with Rafe following, Eden unlocked the door to her room. They entered, finding Julia sitting on the couch with an e-reader.

"How'd it go?" Julia asked as she set aside her e-reader. She looked up to see Eden with a huge smile on her face and Rafe standing next to her. "Well, hello," she said as she stood in surprise.

"Hi," Eden greeted her happily and looked around the room. "Where's Bronte?"

"She's in the bedroom sleeping. She just went down for her nap," she said watching Rafe head into the bedroom without a word to her. Julia frowned at Eden. "What's wrong? I don't even deserve a greeting?" she asked hurt, but knew it was probably because of their conversation yesterday. "Is she still mad at me?" she asked, hoping Eden would think she was talking about the things that happened back home.

"We've had a really good day," said Eden quietly. "Just give her time." She looked toward the bedroom. "I'm going to see what she's doing." Eden walked quietly into the bedroom and saw Rafe sitting in the chair next to the bed looking at Bronte as she slept. "Hey," she said quietly.

"Hi," said Rafe not taking her eyes from Bronte. "I missed her," she whispered. "She's grown so much, and she's such a talker now. I'm sorry I've not been there for her."

"You've been there the best you could," said Eden and put her hand on her shoulder. "She loves the videos you sent and asks to see them all the time."

"It's not the same," said Rafe sadly. "I'm missing her grow up, too." Looking down, Rafe fought to control the tears of sorrow welling in her eyes. She wiped them away before they could fall, and then she took a shuddering breath. "Thank you for letting me spend time with her. I was so happy she remembered me."

"I would never let her forget you," said Eden as she ran her hand over Rafe's back. "You're her mother, and she loves you." She wanted to wrap her arms around Rafe and comfort her but wasn't sure if she should. "Julia's still out there. Don't you want to talk to her? She helped me get here, and she's been worried about you."

"Really, you think she's worried about me?" Rafe asked with a frown. "I don't think she wants to talk to me."

"I think she's worried," said Eden trying not to show her amusement at the fact Julia had just asked if Rafe was still mad. They still acted like school children sometimes, but they had been friends for a long time. Eden knew they would work things out. "She was a bit hurt you didn't even say hello to her." Eden took Rafe's hand. "Come on," she encouraged her, "let's go talk to her."

Rafe allowed herself to be pulled up from her chair and led out of the bedroom by Eden. She really didn't want to deal with Julia. She did not like finding Julia rooted in the room like she had every right to be there. But if Julia was with Eden, then she did have the right.

Rafe was still angry with Julia about their conversation yesterday. She didn't like Julia saying she was in love with Eden and saying things like 'it just happened' between them. Rafe knew she may have to accept it, but she didn't have to like it. She didn't like it because it made her feel like she was losing Eden all over again, and it hurt.

The other thing Rafe didn't like was Eden professing her love today, knowing Eden was sleeping with Julia, or at least had been, Rafe wasn't sure. Rafe particularly didn't like the fact there was nothing she could do about it, and she had probably caused it to happen because she was sick. Most of all, Rafe did not like having no idea when she would be better and knowing she would have to live with the pain. She was uncertain if she could ever just accept Julia and Eden being together.

They found Julia sitting in the armchair beside the couch like a turgid sentinel waiting for them expectantly.

Eden sat on the couch and pulled Rafe down, so she sat next to her. "We took a ride on Rafe's motorcycle," said Eden happily, putting her hand on Rafe's leg as if to hold her in place. She loved having her so close that she could touch her again. "It was a bit scary, but closing my eyes helped." She smiled at Rafe then looked over at Julia. "I don't think I could drive here. It seems like no one stays on their side of the line."

"Those lines are just suggestions," said Rafe with a shrug, smiling for Eden when she laughed. "I'm sorry there wasn't a car available. Gabri is using them all for his guests."

Julia bristled, holding in her thoughts that wanted to burst out about sending cars with huge Italian men to take children from their mothers. It was something Rafe's father would probably have approved of doing. What didn't surprise her was Eden letting Rafe get away with what she had done.

"It's okay," Eden assured her as she rubbed Rafe's leg. "I thought it was fun. I wouldn't mind riding with you again sometime."

Rafe turned and saw Julia's chafed look. "So," said Rafe lifting her chin with an aggressive dark look to let her know she was still angry with her, "how have you been?" She stared menacingly.

"Brilliant," said Julia, shifting uncomfortably. She got the message. Rafe was still angry, but she obviously hadn't told Eden about their meeting yesterday. "It looks like you're doing well."

"Better than I was," she said evenly, not letting the threat in her eyes make it into her voice.

Julia held Rafe's stare, determined not to be the first to break eye contact, but she finally looked away. Still, she wouldn't apologize for her feelings nor would she allow Rafe to intimidate her. She knew the path of destruction Rafe was capable of leaving behind, and she would be there for Eden.

"Everyone at home misses you," said Eden happily, missing their silent exchange.

Rafe turned her attention back to Eden. "How is everyone else?"

"Abby was a wreck for a while without someone to complain about, but she's good now," said Julia with a smirk.

"She's actually trying to do a screenplay," said Eden excited to share the news. "I've been giving her tips and helping her."

Julia rolled her eyes at what she thought was a waste of time, but at least Eden got paid. "Flynn's working on a new phone app, and it's equally ludicrous. It is an add-on to the GPS app that does things like cuss you out when you make a wrong turn or talks dirty when you do things right. He has several options."

"It sounds fun," said Eden, trying not to show her annoyance at Julia for not being supportive of their friends. "I think it'll do well." Eden watched Rafe who was still sitting on the edge of her seat looking at Julia with a frown. "Jude's doing well," Eden said and rubbed Rafe's leg again, hoping she would relax. "She wanted me to thank you for still helping her with supplies for her art classes. She's got a girlfriend," Eden revealed with a smile. "It's Susy from her massage business. She's very sweet. I've taken your advice and gone for some massages."

"Good for you," said Rafe breaking her gaze from Julia. "I'm glad things are going well for Jude." She was happy to hear her friends were okay. Rafe looked around the room to avoid looking at Eden. Sitting between them in their room made Julia's words about her and Eden being together seem even more real.

"Stacey moved out," continued Eden. "She got a job in New York about three months ago, I think." She looked to Julia for reassurance because she had not been around the girls much lately. She had been working a lot to save for the trip. "Is that right?"

"Sounds right," said Julia, glad Rafe was not staring at her anymore. "Abby was happy to see the back end of her. They never got along."

"Letty asked me to tell you to call her," said Eden. "She really misses you. She and Ephraim are looking into opening a second location."

Rafe frowned down at her hands. She felt bad about not contacting Letty, but she knew if she did, everyone would expect Letty to be the messenger. Rafe didn't want to put her in the middle. "I'll try," she said but made no commitment. "Tell her to send the information about the new location to Katheryn if she wants my help. I'll tell Gabri to look for it." She still needed time before she started talking to everyone again, but she wanted to help Letty if they needed it.

"Everyone at home has been thinking about you," said Julia, seeing her chance to try to get some helpful information out of her. "They're all wondering when, or if, you'll come home."

Rafe glanced at Eden then down at her hands again. "I don't know when I'll be back," she said softly.

Julia nodded and observed Eden's expression of disappointment. Rafe might be angry with her, but she obviously wasn't going to do anything Eden hoped she would do. "Can you tell us anything at all?"

Rafe glared at her with a spark of anger in her eyes. She knew Julia was provoking her and it pissed her off. "Not at the moment."

It was clear to Julia it wasn't going to be easy to get things out of Rafe, which had always been par for the course. She decided to change the subject for Eden's sake because she looked like she was about to cry. "When Bronte and I went out for a walk, I found out your friend will be performing tonight. I think the flier called him the *Angelo di Firenze*. So I guess he's the Angel of Florence."

"Yes," said Rafe and her mouth twitched for a second with a slight smile, "that's Gabri. He's very good. I hope you get to hear him." Rafe was happy the subject was not about her or what happened or when she was going home. She wasn't sure what she was going to do about the Eden and Julia situation—if anything. She did know she couldn't go home right now. "His wife, Nora, will be performing too. She has her own set then she'll do a couple of songs with Gabri. They sound beautiful together. They're recording an English version of Gabri's CD and hope to tour in America."

"I can't wait to hear them," said Eden. She was happy things were going well, but not with the way Julia was pushing Rafe. "Maybe we can all go together," she suggested, hoping to spend more time with Rafe and let her see Bronte again.

"Maybe." Rafe avoided eye contact with her and stood. "Well, I need to go. I need to change clothes and see what Gabri needs me to help with tonight."

"Oh." Eden was surprised the visit was ending so soon. "Well, when can we see you again? Will you be at the festival?" she asked as she stood and followed Rafe to the door.

"I don't really know," said Rafe honestly. "It depends on what's going on at the villa."

"I'll bring Bronte," said Eden, hoping it would motivate her to meet them. "She loves the music and the excitement."

"I'm glad she likes the music." Rafe smiled seeing through Eden's ploy. "Gabri will be happy about it too." Rafe turned her attention to Julia. "See you around, I guess," she said gruffly knowing it would be a long time coming before she saw her again if she had anything to say about it.

"You too," said Julia noting Rafe's non-committal to Eden.

"Well," said Rafe hesitantly. She gave Eden a light chaste kiss on her cheek. "Goodbye," she said and walked out the door.

Eden followed her out and took her arm as the door to the room closed behind her. She looked around momentarily. Seeing the hallway was empty, she pulled Rafe close and lifted herself up on her toes, kissing her on the lips. "Bye," she said softly.

"Bye," said Rafe sadly. "You should probably get back to Julia," she said, then turned and made her way down the stairs.

42

MISSING HER AGAIN with every step carrying her away, Eden Kingsley watched Rafe Salvaggio until she was out of sight, and then she went back inside the room. Eden had been worried after her first visit with Rafe that she wouldn't see her again, and today, she felt was a wonderful gift. What gave Eden the most hope, though, was the way Rafe kissed her and told her she loved her. She had been dreaming and thinking about being that close, and closer, to Rafe for a long time. Since before Rafe left for Italy. Today was a start to getting their life together back.

"That was awkward," said Julia when Eden finally came back inside. "She barely made eye contact with you."

"She's trying," said Eden, feeling great about everything. "We really did have a good day."

"I'm glad things went well, but I think we need to talk," said Julia firmly. She needed to take control and get Eden to open her eyes. "Come and sit down."

Eden wasn't sure why Julia was so unenthusiastic about today. She was able to spend time with Rafe. She got to be close to her and kiss her. She had a note in her pocket she couldn't wait to read again saying Rafe was in love with her. She definitely wanted more, but at this point, she would take what she could get.

"What's wrong?" Eden asked, fighting to stay positive as she promised herself and Dr. Cathcart she would do.

"What's wrong?" Julia asked and tried not to scoff. She put her hand on Eden's shoulder with sympathy. "She just told us she wasn't coming home, and she didn't know when she would be. I don't think we have enough time to convince her to go home or to convince her friend Gabri to let her go. Are you prepared to go back home without her?"

"But she said she still loves me, and she misses Bronte so much," said Eden pulling away and not wanting to believe what Julia was saying until she was sure. "How could Gabri keep her away from us? If he does, he'll be the one being cruel."

"I don't think he'll see it the way you do," mumbled Julia but knew Eden understood her. "We have to talk to him again. The problem is he's busy with this festival. If I'd remembered it was going on, I would have suggested we come at a different time, but here we are," she said and threw her hands up.

The truth was, she did know about the festival. Rafe talked about it many times over the years. Julia suggested coming at this time because she knew everyone would be busy. She thought it would either be a good buffer or a distraction from dealing with Rafe. "There just isn't enough time now. You may need to call your job and say Bronte got sick or something, and you can't fly back yet." There was no risk with this suggestion, and it was the only reason Julia offered it. "I can always take more time off. If we can't extend here, I'll find a different hotel."

Eden shook her head in dismay. "I can't take more time," she said upset. "I can't take the chance I'll lose my job. You know if I don't have a job, I can't stay in Rafe's house. I really pushed them with all the time I took off when Rafe and I were going through everything last year. If I start taking time off, I'll be a liability again."

"Well, maybe my father can give you a job," Julia suggested. "Even temporarily." If Eden worked for her father, it would mean they could be closer. Then they would have even more in common to keep them together once she left Rafe. "You know, we are thinking of investing in film production and need a board of advisors." She thought Eden would be perfect for the job on the board. Eden knew potential clients in the film industry and had a great head for what would be successful therefore investable. Plus, it didn't hurt that they knew each other so Julia would have a board member in her pocket if she needed one. "Maybe you can help us."

"I don't know anything about the financial world," said Eden in frustration. "I read scripts and do a million little things to help get them through to the production people in hopes they will be made into a movie. Plus, I really love what I do. I love seeing something I touched make it through the process. I have no idea how I could be any help to your company," she said feeling a little frantic.

"Calm down," said Julia at Eden's overreaction. She was glad she hadn't brought up the other suggestion she was going to make, about Eden moving into her condo. "I'm not saying you have to make a career with us," she said calmly, though she hoped once Eden was ensconced she would stay, especially if it were a successful financial scheme. "You can get another job, maybe even a better one, after we get Rafe home. If we get her home."

Julia knew she was walking a fine line. She wanted to be supportive of Eden's efforts, but she didn't want to build her hopes to the point Eden would be crushed again when Rafe refused to go back with them. Julia also wanted Eden to see she truly cared about her so when they got home and allowed time to pass after this trip, then she could talk to her about a possible relationship. "Your only other option is going home and waiting for Rafe to decide to come home or for Gabri to let her go. Maybe you can visit her again sometime. Can you live with a plan to revisit her?"

"Why are you doing this now?" Eden complained tears seeping from her eyes. "I was having such a good day."

"Because we only have four days remaining—three really, since our flight is on the fourth day. I'm afraid you're running out of time," she said firmly. "I'm afraid your hopes will be dashed, and I'm worried of what it will do to you." She watched as Eden wiped away tears. "Don't cry, Eden. I'm sorry," she said softly. "I care about you," she paused, "and Rafe," she added cursorily. "But Rafe has people taking care of her. She has money, and she's free to do whatever she wants. You have all of us at home, though, and we're worried about you," she revealed. "No matter what Rafe does, we'll all be by your side."

Julia wanted to convince Eden the others at home felt the same about Rafe's behavior. Julia hoped, if Eden saw the others felt she should move on, then maybe, finally, Rafe would become an occasional penumbra in Eden and everyone else's life. "You won't ask Rafe for more money, and we can tell you're just getting by. You're practically allowing yourself to be held hostage to your job and to Rafe."

Julia hesitated again because she had to be careful and not be too negative about Rafe. She had to push Eden gently until she realized for herself that Rafe wasn't coming back. Only then could Julia step in to offer more than friendship.

"You could move out of Rafe's house. Then you wouldn't feel so trapped and would have more money," Julia said, once again purposely leaving out the mention of moving into her condo right now. "What's it going to take for you to do what's right for you and Bronte?" she asked, knowing Eden wouldn't be able to answer. She waited for a moment anyway. "I'm afraid Rafe isn't going to be there for you when you need her. It may not even be her fault. I know she may still be sick and may need time to get better, but you can't just stop living and wait for her forever."

"You don't know what you're talking about," said Eden with frustration. "I could call Katheryn and get all the money I want just by asking. But it's not why I want to be with Rafe. I know things aren't perfect, but she told me she loves me too. I'm going to hold on to hope," she said trying to calm herself. "I want, no, I need to be there when and if she comes home. So I'll make due with less and stay in our house. Do you know why I don't mind living with the cohabitation agreement?"

Eden watched Julia shake her head and wait for her reasons. "Because Rafe gave me something that day. She gave me Eden Kingsley again. When I was going through everything with my anxiety and fears, I was so caught up with thoughts of what being Salvaggio's Paradise meant and with feelings making me think I was losing myself. I thought I was just... disappearing. I don't think Rafe even knows what she did for me. She made us equal, and I am determined to hold up my side of everything financially and emotionally. If it means waiting and taking care of her until she's better, then that's exactly what I'll do! She took care of me for years through everything with my parents to how horribly I treated her when I was going through my anxiety problems. Then there are all the things I did when I was with Jake and all the things he said and did to her. I owe her. I owe her time. I owe her patience. I'm not trapped! I love her!"

"You're not beholden to her," said Julia worried Eden believed she owed Rafe something. "She made choices causing herself problems. And yes, maybe most of them was because she was sick. But you can't owe her for what she did to herself or what she did because she was sick. Do you really think if she wasn't sick that she would have done some of the things she did, including going and challenging Jake? She wasn't in her rational mind. If she were, most of these things wouldn't have happened."

"You're missing the point, Julia," said Eden, ready to end the conversation. "Sick or well, everything she did was based on the fact that she loved me. You're the one who kept telling me I had to grow up! Well, I've had almost six months to go through every detail of the things that happened, on my own and with my therapist. I see very clearly the motivation for her choices—even if they were wrong choices. I, on the other hand, made my mistakes because I was looking inward at myself. Rafe was right—I stopped seeing her."

Eden thought about the note in her pocket and knew now why Rafe kept telling her she didn't see her anymore. "I think we all stopped seeing her. If we hadn't, we might have seen she was sick sooner." She gave Julia a determined look. "I'm not going to let you or anyone else tell me to give up on her. I will do anything, *anything*, to keep myself in a position where I can stay in her life because I do owe her. I owe her as much love as she has shown me and more, and I intend to love her for the rest of our lives."

Julia could see the determination in Eden and knew she wouldn't budge tonight. Since Rafe departed, Eden had changed and become much stronger. She had a handle on her anxiety and fought harder to get her way when she thought it was needed. Julia sighed, deciding not to push anymore tonight. There was still time to convince Eden to see things her way.

"Well, I hope you're prepared to spend a lot of time alone," she said coolly, seeing her job was going to be harder than she thought. Her only hope was to see if she could show Eden how futile their efforts were when Rafe stayed in Italy like she was sure would happen. "I suggest we figure out how we can convince Rafe to come home and get Gabri to agree," she said, positive Gabri would never agree, and it was fine with her. "Time's running out, and who knows when you'll get to come back."

If ever, she thought to herself.

*To be continued in Book Ten,
the Salvaggio's Light conclusion— Frenzied Love...*

Salvaggio's Light

Book Ten
FRENZIED LOVE

C.L. Cattano

NOTES

Cyprian (chē-prian) the Fair – Another name for Venus used by Donte in his poem *Divine Comedy* in the third *cantica Paradiso* (Paradise) in describing the third sphere of heaven he called Venus: The Lovers.

"The world, when still in peril, thought that, wheeling, in the third epicycle, Cyprian the Fair sent down her rays of frenzied love, ...and gave the name of her with whom I have begun this canto, to the planet that is courted by the sun, at times behind her and at times in front." -*Paradiso*, Canto VIII, lines 1–3, 9–12, Mandelbaum translation. Wikipedia 3/23/2016
https://en.wikipedia.org/wiki/Paradiso_(Dante)

Translations: For translations of Italian, French and Spanish use: www.Babblefish.com

The chapters in this book were arranged with the intent of saving paper. This chapter style saved 30 pages. Original Total Book Pages 351 — Final Pages 321.

♫♪♫

Music mentioned in this book.

No financial incentive was given for the mention of the following artists in this work. The author is a fan and felt mentioning them worked in the story. For the use of their name, credit is given, and links to their work are below.

Enjoy!

Julia Weldon

Website: http://juliaweldon.com/
Facebook: https://www.facebook.com/julia.weldon
iTunes: https://itunes.apple.com/us/album/lig...
Twitter: https://twitter.com/juliaweldon
YouTube: https://www.youtube.com/user/juliaweldondotcom

Marshall, Edward, Writer – Venus by Frankie Avalon. Publisher: Sony/ATV Music Publishing LLC

ABOUT THE AUTHOR

C.L. CATTANO LIVES in the Midwestern U.S. with her partner and their dog somewhere between the city and the forest. With a joy for traveling, she and her partner have visited many countries and have a love for meeting people and learning about the places they visit. When possible, she likes to include references in her work about the things she has learned, the places she has been and people she has met while on her travels and in her everyday life.

Cattano has a variety of creative interests including, but not limited to, creating fine art, writing, photography, and supporting women in the arts. She considers herself a 'Jack of All Trades' dabbling in what she terms the 'whimsies of her soul' that pull her toward happiness and fulfillment.

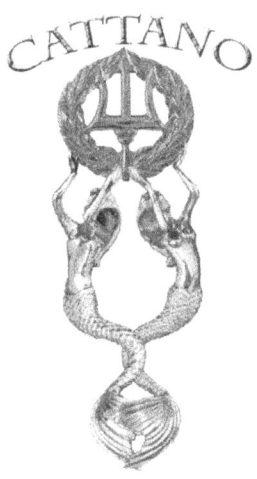

OTHER BOOKS
By C. L. Cattano

Cursed Hearts is a love story transcending time and gender. Two souls, separated by a gift from a bored demon on All Hallows Eve, have been searching through time for each other and have been incarnated as both men and women.

Over time, the gift became a curse and a game for the demons. Connected by the power of love, the two souls have finally met again, and now they must fight for a life together.

Will love prevail? Will they finally be able to live together again for a lifetime? They have one night to figure out the riddle and get it right to break the curse.

NOTE: 18+ Lesbian Romance. Some light erotic moments.
Available in Paperback and E-book

Salvaggio's Light Series

It takes true love to survive secrets, lies, and betrayals from within and without.

Get ready to settle into this epic contemporary drama-filled romance entwined comedy, lust, danger, thrills, regret, tragedy, suspense, and love.

Now Available in Paperback and E-book
Shattered Paradise – Book One
Blue Inferno – Book Two
Secrets & Rivalry – Book Three
Wildling's Claim – Book Four
Sowers of Discord – Book Five
Fire of Wrath – Book Six
Confronting Darkness – Book Seven
Traditoré – Book Eight

Check out the Salvaggio's Light Facebook page to join in the discussions and fun! www.facebook.com/pg/SalvaggiosLight

Join the CL Cattano Mailing List www.clcattano.com

I love getting fan mail, and you can contact me at clc@clcattano.com

REQUEST FOR REVIEW

Thank you for reading **Salvaggio's Light** — *An Epic Contemporary Romance Serial.*

I hope you enjoyed book nine, **Cyprian the Fair**, and will consider leaving an honest review. It only takes a few minutes, so I encourage you to go now and leave a review!

Need help writing a review?
Try the Random Review Generator by A. E. Radley!
It's Free!

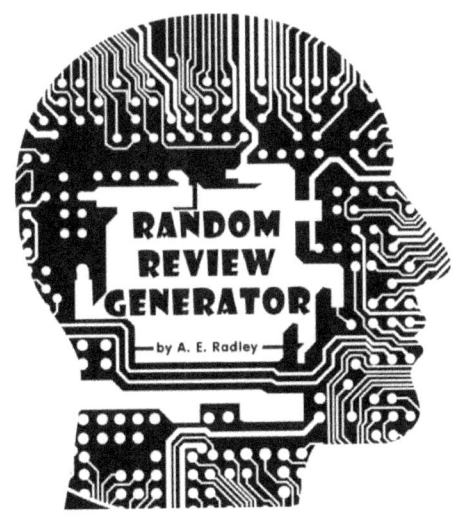

Find it here!
http://aeradley.com/review-generator/